MALIMAR THE FINAL CHALLENGE

A Brody O'Shea Book

Written By

JARED McVAY

Creative Texts Publishers products are available at special discounts for bulk purchase for sale promotions, premiums, fund-raising, and educational needs. For details, write Creative Texts Publishers, PO Box 50, Barto, PA 19504, or visit www.creativetexts.com

BRODY O'SHEA: BOOK 3: MALIMAR: THE FINAL CHALLENGE

Published by Creative Texts Publishers
PO Box 50
Barto, PA 19504
www.creativetexts.com

ISBN: 978-1-64738-033-5

Acknowledgements

Again, I want to thank my publisher, Dan Edwards of Creative Texts Publishers, for believing in me and suggesting I write this trilogy, which turned out to be fun.

I also want to thank my right arm, Jerri Burr. Without your help with all my mistakes, I would be lost.

And last, but by far, not the least, I want to thank all of you who read my books and leave such wonderful reviews.

SAILOR SUPERSTITIONS

- Mermaids cause ships to sink
- Dolphins means good sailing
- Cutting your hair cause the wrath of King Neptune
- Leaving port on a Friday is unlucky
- Except for figureheads on the bow of a ship, women on board brings bad luck
- People with red hair are unlucky
- Whistling encourages high winds and storms
- Red sky at night – sailors delight – good weather
- Red sky in the morning, sailor take warning – storm coming
- Sharks following a ship means someone is going to die
- Changing the name of a ship brings bad luck
- Person suspected of bringing bad luck is called, a Jonah
- Having bananas on board have negative effect on catching fish

MEANINGS

Fortnight – two weeks

Port – left side of the ship

Starboard – right side of the ship

Cat-o-nine tails – whip used for punishment

Jolly Roger – flag flown by pirates – skull and crossbones

Daft – means a person is thought to be crazy

Quill – sharpened feather used for writing

Ship's hold – lower area where cargo is stored

Tiller – arm used to steer the ship

Wheel – also used to steer the ship – replaces tiller

Hull – outside wall of the ship

Bulkhead – interior wall of a ship

Galley – Kitchen

Bristol – pristine condition

Doldrums – calm sea – no wind

Broach – ship leaning over on its side due to storm conditions

Old Salt – sailor with many years of experience

Bosun's Mate – Crew Chief – responsible for deck crew and equipment

Gimbal – pivoted support to keep equipment steady during pitch and roll of ship

Sculling – to move the ship sideways using only the wheel or tiller

Keel – weight at the bottom of the ship to keep it upright

Yardarm – long, tapered wooden pole at the bottom of square-rigged sail

Bridge – raised part of the deck at the rear of the ship where tiller or wheel is located

Deck – floor of the floor of the ship

Cyclone – severe tropical storm

Quotes from Brody O'Shea

"Life is like the ocean...It can be calm or wild with storms. But in the end, always, beautiful and beckoning."

"Every time I sail out onto the ocean, it's like going home..."

Table of Contents

PROLOGUE

During the fifteenth century, it seemed, no one could sail the oceans without the chance of being overtaken by a pirate and having all of your possessions stolen and you yourself being sold into slavery. Several of the most powerful wizards preferred playing at being pirates, using their powers to overcome their prey rather than doing good with their magical powers.

During this time, there was one name they feared most of all - MALIMAR.

Malimar was the second most powerful wizard in the world. The only power greater than him, was his older brother, King Neptune. And as I have been told by King Neptune himself, Malimar has no love for his older brother and would more than likely hang him from the yardarm of a ship if he thought he could find a way to do so, which would leave him alone as the most powerful wizard in the world.

Because King Neptune had been chosen to rule everything beneath the water by their father, the former King Neptune, Malimar was seized with anger and ran away to the surface where he could rule the waters above. In a short time, he became the supreme ruler of all the other wizards and pirates who sailed the seven seas.

For years, King Neptune has been waiting for me, his only nephew, to come to an age where I can be useful to him. By the time I turned thirteen years old, King Neptune could wait no longer and his only recourse was to recruit me, Brody O'Shea, and turn me into a young wizard in training. After bringing several wizards and pirates to justice, I was asked to capture and bring down the powerful rogue wizard, Malimar, who, as it turned out, happens to be my and my twin sister's blood father… which is where we get our powers.

No one asked, but in my opinion, sending me after Malimar is like sending a small dog into a fight with a huge, ferocious lion who hasn't eaten in six weeks.

Just so I don't confuse you, while I tell you this story, I will address my adopted father, the one who raised me from birth, as father - and my blood father, whom I know very little about, I shall address as Malimar.

For some time now, Malimar had heard rumors about some young wizard who was making his name known and causing the words "pirate" and "wizard", to be a laughing stock throughout the oceans.

Other than a name he'd heard, which meant nothing to him, he didn't know who this young wizard was and where I'd come from. But something inside his brain told him his older brother, King Neptune, had his hand in all of this. It was the only thing that made sense. But how did he know about a new young wizard being born, and he had not?

What Malimar doesn't know; and probably would have deny, is the fact that I and my twin sister, Cory Anne, are his blood children. Apparently, he knew nothing about our being born or our existence. Our mother was nothing to him and she had passed away shortly after our birth. Fortunately for us, her good friend left us on the O'Shea's doorstep and again, fortunately for us, the O'Sheas took us in and raised us as their own.

Knowledge of Malimar came to me only recently because my uncle, King Neptune, told me about him. And, since I now know who he is and how powerful he is, it makes this assignment the hardest one I'll ever have to face. How can I even consider facing my own blood father and possibly sending him to the gallows?

Like it or not, this is where my tale begins.

CHAPTER ONE

"Brody! Wake up! Brody, are you in there? Why don't you answer me? Brody, say something! Brody! You had better not be ignoring me!"

My twin sister, Cory Anne O'Shea, was yelling from the hallway outside my bedroom door, and as always, was trying to push my patience to the limits, but not today. Wake up, indeed! I've been up for the better part of an hour, washed, dressed and ready to go...

Since the very first words Cory Anne ever uttered, she could never just ask a simple question or make a request. She had to make statements and ask several questions all mixed together in rapid fire - like she was doing now. I knew I was driving her crazy by not answering her.

I stood in front of the full-length mirror to make sure I looked presentable, while all the time, chuckling to myself and allowing her to ramble on and on. I finally decided I looked fine and with that, I adjusted my hat to one side, giving myself a bit of a roguish look, then tiptoed over and climbed out of my second story bedroom window and scurried down the trellis and onto the ground. Through the window, I could still hear Cory Anne's rapid-fire rantings and ravings.

Still laughing, I strode around the house like a young swell and entered the kitchen by the back door. I could hardly contain myself for the prank I'd pulled on Cory Anne - leaving her standing there in the hallway, talking to no one. She would be fit to be tied when she gave up and came down and saw me sitting in the kitchen, drinking tea and having breakfast.

I had just stuffed the last piece of scone into my mouth when Cory Anne came racing into the kitchen, shouting to our mother, "He won't answer me, mot…"

When she saw me sitting there, smiling at her, she stopped in mid-sentence and turned on me. "What…? What… are you doing down here? You're supposed to be up in your room! When did you come down and why didn't I see you? You could have at least let me know you were awake and that you'd come down instead of letting me stand outside your bedroom door, talking to an empty room like some blithering idiot. Why don't you answer me?"

"Because, as usual, I can never get a word in crossways," I told her as I reached for another scone and two more sausages. Like I said, I had been up for an hour when she came banging on my door, and was as excited as she was about today, but I definitely was not about to tell her that.

I swallowed a piece of sausage and scone then grinned at her. "I think you need to worry about yourself, and leave me to take care of myself. And by the way, you look a mess. No boy is going to want to look at you dressed the way you are," I said, which was a lie. She looked gorgeous in her new three shades of blue dress, which offset her red hair and sparkling blue eyes.

"Oh! Someday, little brother, someday!" she said, stomping her foot on the floor before storming out of the house.

"Little brother, indeed! You're only a few minutes older than me!" I called out to the slamming of the kitchen door.

"Brody," my mother scolded in her soft way. "You shouldn't aggravate your sister so… You know you can get under her skin faster than anyone and you also know she only does what she does because she cares so much for you."

"Yes, mother. I know. But sometimes she can be a bit overwhelming," I said as she walked over and motioned for me to stand up.

With a mouth full of scone and sausage, I stood up as she ran her fingers through my hair and placed my hat on my head. "There. Now you're ready."

By that, she meant I was ready for the big horserace, today. I would be helping my father and our jockey, Conner McNealy, get father's and my horse ready for the race.

Today was not just any race. Today was the race of the year. People from all over were coming to challenge our two horses. And not to just race around a track – oh no, not by a long shot. This race would cover a little over five miles, racing across hill and dale, where there are no roads or tracks. The riders will have to swim their horse across two rivers, jump three rock-wall fences and conquer five good size hills that have several deep gulleys, before reaching the top, and several more on the way down. Then there was a three quarters of a mile race to the finish. No, this would not be just any race.

Another reason for my excitement was because I would be riding *Hurricane* and Conner would be riding *Beauty* – two horses other than our normal racetrack horses. *Black Lightning* and *Whirlwind* were great on an oval-shaped one and an eighth mile track, but not for this kind of race.

Beauty was one of the horses that father had brought over from Ireland and Hurricane was the gray, my sister had given me for my birthday. I had given him the name, Hurricane, because he seemed to have no limits. He had the power of a hurricane and could run all day long and jump fences much higher than I would have believed. But the best part was that he seemed to love having me on his back - and when a horse loves you, he or she will do anything to please you.

Of course, around Boston, the odds were on Beauty because she too, was a great long-distance runner and also because her jockey, Conner, was much smaller and lighter than me. But I wasn't worried because Hurricane was used to my weight and we worked well together. Even though I was only fifteen years old, I was a couple of inches taller and a few pounds heavier than my father, so, to offset my extra weight versus of that of a regular jockey, I left my saddle in the barn and rode him bareback.

Most of the towns people thought I was daft in the head when I announced I would be the one riding Hurricane – which gave them another reason to choose Beauty as the favorite to win against some very well-known racehorses.

During the week leading up to today, we had seen forty horses arrive and quite a few of them looked to be strong contenders. *Looked* to be, being the operative words. Thirty-two of them were brought over from Ireland and England. The others came from down in New York and as far away as Georgetown.

We were boarding fourteen of our competitors – all from Ireland, while the others were boarded throughout the surrounding area. The people were not only excited about the race, but more than welcomed the extra money that was spent before, during and after the race.

Horse racing was not a sport taken lightly in this part of the world, since many of the people living here came from either England or Ireland where horse racing was considered the sport of kings. Even the lowest of the low showed up to bet what little they might have at the horse races, hoping to go home with a fortune.

The race was to start and end here in one of our pastures. Ironically, the first fence to be jumped was on the boundary of our property. It was a stacked rock wall four feet high and three feet wide, that would prove to be the most difficult jump of the three fences. I was confident that, shortly after the start of the race, I would see my prediction come to pass. The fences were going to be far too hard for several of the horses, which of course meant the number of contenders in the race would be eliminated at the first obstacle – leaving the field shortened by at least a third.

Both Hurricane and Beauty were filled with nervous energy. They seemed to know the race was about to start and what was expected of them. They pranced around, eager to get started. Conner and I had practiced running the course so many times the horses could have run it with their eyes closed, but of course, that wouldn't be allowed.

Ropes had been staked out for the area where the horses would start the race to keep people from getting too close and hampering the start. Plus, keeping the crowd behind the ropes would keep them from being stepped on by a nervous horse, or trampled when the race started.

Father, Conner, and I, built a roofed platform at the start line, where the person who would start the race and the dignitaries from town could stand and be seen. My mother stood, smiling at all the turmoil while overlooking the start line. The Mayor of Boston was there, standing next to my sister and several other dignitaries, just behind mother - eagerly awaiting the start of the race.

Mother stood slightly to the front because, at father's insistence, she would be the one firing the pistol in the air to start the race. Mother had never fired a firearm before and didn't even like it that father had several guns. But, when he assured her there wouldn't be a bullet in the pistol, then and only then, had she agreed.

Excitement blistered the air like static… The sounds of horses stamping around and nickering, along with the sounds of their riders speaking to them, trying to keep them from bolting, filled the air.

Along with all that, there were hundreds of conversations going on all at the same time, making it hard to understand a person two feet away from you.

It was only a couple of minutes until the start of the race and the tension was mounting with both the racers and the crowd.

I looked up at the sky and tested the breeze blowing across the pasture. The sky was clear and the sun was shining brightly – the perfect day for a horserace.

A crowd of more than three hundred people had come to watch the race and were standing on both sides of the start line. Several them were in loud discussions over the final outcome of the race.

Out beyond the start line, between them and our barn and house, were ten good-sized tents where food and drinks could be purchased, along with a tent crowded with men hurrying to place their last-minute bets.

I was surprised to find out that neither Hurricane or Beauty were the overall favorite to win. In fact, because of all the outsiders, and the predictions that were being thrown around, our horses were listed as number eight and nine, which made it all the sweeter if we should win. With the odds against us, the winnings would be much larger than if we had been the favorites. So, with that in mind, I had bet heavily on both of our two horses to come in first and second. And I know my father had secretly bet a good sum on them, also.

What we didn't realize was, my mother and sister had also bet on our horses – and to the best of my knowledge, this was their first time to bet on anything.

Father was as nervous as a man about to be shot. "Now boys, don't be nervous," he told us. "I'm telling you this because your horse can sense it… and, as for the race, itself, stay just a little behind for the biggest part of the race and save your horse's strength. When you get to the last half a mile, turn them loose! Let them have their heads! They'll win the race for you. Ride fair and true, for you know there are men stationed all along the course to penalize or eliminate any rider who doesn't follow the rules - and O'Shea Stables doesn't need any bad publicity, nor do we want anything to hamper our chances of winning. Any questions?"

We smiled at him and shook our heads, knowing it was his adrenaline talking. We had covered this same ground several times before now and we were ready.

He stepped back and looked at us - then sighed, trying to calm his nervousness. It was obvious he was far more nervous than me or Conner. Both of us were looking forward to the race. Favorites or not, we believed we could win the race, first and second place. Which one of us would be in first place at the end was yet to be determined, but secretly I believed it would be Hurricane.

When neither of us had a question, he fussed with Beauty's bridle and saddle, making small adjustments. He even instructed us, again, to start a few rows back, not wanting anyone to say we had taken advantage of the fact that this race had been sponsored by us and the route had been laid out by us.

With a megaphone, the mayor called for the horses to line up, which in my mind was funny because there were no actual lines, just forty-two horses all grouped together, waiting to hear the pistol shot that would start the race.

Father gave each of us a leg up and when we were sitting astride our horses, Conner and I looked at each other and nodded our heads.

Conner and most of the jockeys wore the riding togs of whatever stable they were riding for but not me. Technically, I was not a jockey. I was far too large, and riding my own horse. Rather than stable togs, I was wearing easy fitting pants and boots, and a loose-fitting shirt with my name stitched on the back of it – which, of course, was Cory Anne's doing.

We eased our horses up to where we were only eight or ten horses behind the front line while all of the other horses were vying to take the lead right at the beginning of the race. They were packed as tight as sardines in a can. Horses were crowding against one another and it was all I could do to keep Hurricane from kicking his heels up to keep them away from him.

Mother stepped to the front of the podium and looked at the horses who were finally assembled and chewing at the bit to get started. Mother turned and looked at father, waiting for his nod.

Father looked around, and when he was satisfied, he nodded his head, slightly. Mother smiled, raised her hand in the air, called out in a clear voice, "Ready," and then fired her pistol. I knew she'd put pieces of cloth in her ears because she hated the sound of gunfire, but the rest of us heard it loud and clear.

CHAPTER TWO

With a mighty rush of hooves, the horses charged across the imaginary start line, with each one of the horses ahead of us, fighting for the lead. Knowing this was going to be a long, grueling race, I kept Hurricane just behind Beauty, who was eight horses behind the lead horse who led off at a breakneck pace.

The lead horse was a big roan with a white mane and tail and stood a good sixteen and a half hands at the withers. He had a long stride and I knew he would be good on a racetrack, but I wasn't convinced he would last in this kind of race, especially at the fast pace he was setting. For this, you needed a horse with a lot of stamina – one who could withstand the hardships of running across uneven ground, swimming rivers and jumping walled type fences, and either leaping across or going down into and back up out of the many gulleys in our path. Not all racehorses were built for this kind of endurance. Certainly not a racetrack horse, which is why neither Black Lightning or Whirlwind had been chosen for this race. They were racetrack horses, not cross-country runners.

Of course, neither Hurricane nor Beauty were one track horses. They were smaller and had been trained for just this sort of race. Beauty stood just fourteen and a half hands, and Hurricane, fifteen hands. Compared to all the other horses, they were the two smallest animals in the race. But being tall was no guarantee you would win, or even place, for that matter. Nor was being shorter, either. Stamina and agility were what was needed to win a race like this one. This race was all about stamina, surefootedness and desire on the part of the horse.

From what I could tell, all the other horses were thoroughbreds and well suited for what they'd been bred to do, racing around a track, but none of the owners seemed to know the difference between a racehorse and a cross country, long-distance runner, although they should have since steeplechase races were the rage of Europe. According to my father, Hurricane and Beauty had a huge advantage over all but a few of the horses in the race.

Riding bareback was no problem for me since that's how I rode Hurricane most of the time, anyway. The pace the lead horse was setting was going to eliminate a lot of the horses very soon because they weren't used to running long distances. With a great deal of pride, I knew Hurricane could run all day and still not be breathing hard. Of course, the race had just begun, so my prediction was still to be decided.

When we approached the first obstacle, the rock wall fence at the border of our property, which was four feet high and close to three feet wide, I could see three horses already down with their riders standing next to them looking confused.

I was surprised that there were only three of them down so far, knowing more would be eliminated as the race continued. Surprisingly, the lead horse and seven others, along with Beauty, had cleared the fence and were racing across the next pasture.

Hurricane sailed over the fence with ease, as he had done many times before and in a short time, he'd inched his way up to run side by side with Beauty.

"The fence took out a few of 'em," Conner yelled. "And will take even more."

I just nodded my head up and down. Even though we still had a long way to go and many obstacles to overcome, I wasn't in the mood for talking. I was giving the race my full attention.

I could feel Hurricane's eagerness to run. He hated to have another horse in front of him and I was having a bit of a time holding him back, but that was the plan - at least for the next three miles or so. By now we were into the race about a mile and a half, and I knew the other horses couldn't keep up this grueling pace much longer.

The crowded bunch of horses had now thinned out to a long line of riders and the number of horses still in the race was no more than twenty. Like I said earlier, this kind of racing isn't for short distance track runners.

We were circling the bottom edge of a stand of trees and I was just a little in front of Conner when I heard a rifle shot and felt the sting of a bullet crease my back, shoulder high. I leaned forward and put my heels against Hurricane's ribs and felt him surge forward just as a second shot rang out. Someone was shooting at me! Why, did someone want to shoot me? Of course, being shot at during a race doesn't give a person time or an inkling to stop and inquire.

We still had about two and a half miles to go, but when I kicked Hurricane in the ribs, he passed several of the horses in front of us like they were walking instead of running, with Conner following close behind, for he too, had heard the gunshots and could see the tear in the back of my shirt. Plus, we'd agreed to stay together.

Being just behind me, Conner could see the line of blood that stained my shirt and he pulled alongside of me and yelled, "Are you all right?"

I had felt the bullet scrape the skin on my back but I didn't think it had gone any deeper. "I think so," I yelled back. "I'm guessing it's no more than a flesh wound. A scratch."

Conner had a puzzled look on his face. "Who would want to shoot you?" he yelled.

Since there had been two shots, I came to the conclusion that maybe whoever it was, was trying to shoot both of us and had missed Conner completely because of our quick reactions.

"I think someone was shooting at both of us," I answered.

Our horses were running like they were being chased by wolves and Conner yelled, "What? Why would anyone want to shoot us?" His eyes were as big as saucers and it was hard to hear him because of the wind rushing past my ears and the pounding of the horse's hooves. But I could guess what he was saying by the look on his face.

His answer didn't take much thought and I yelled back, "Because whoever it is knows they can't win against us and they want us out of the race, would be my guess."

Just then, I felt Hurricane leap into the air and looked forward in time to see the rock fence we were sailing over, and adjusted myself for the landing on the other side, then Hurricane's surge forward. I looked over my shoulder and saw Conner and Beauty had also cleared the fence.

Knowing we had no more obstacles in front of us for at least another half a mile, I turned and looked back at the other horses to see where they were.

We were a good eighth of a mile in front of the closest horse. I counted and was amazed that the race had now been thinned down to nine horses.

Turning back, I yelled to Conner, who by now was almost alongside of me, again. "I think we should slow down a little and give the horses a breather!"

Conner glanced over his shoulder, then back at me and yelled, "I agree."

We certainly didn't slow down to a walk, but our horses were no longer running all out, either. The finish line was still some distance away and we still had a few more obstacles to conquer, plus three horses to beat.

Except for the stinging on my back, the rest of the race went smoothly. Swimming the two rivers was good for our horses because it cooled them down some. At the bottom of the last hill in the race, we knew the finish line was only about three quarters of a mile further on. I could see the top of our house and barn in the far distance.

Both of us looked over our shoulders and saw six riders flogging their tired horses, trying desperately to catch up, and at our slow pace, they were gaining on us.

Still, not pushing our horses, yet, we waited until we were no more than a quarter of a mile from the finish line, with the other horses now only a few feet behind us and still three horses in front of us. The horses in front and back of us were lathered and I knew they were running on nothing more than a desire to finish the race and go to the barn where they could rest. I grinned at Conner and yelled, "Now!"

And with that, we gave our horses their heads and let them run, and run they did! In short order, we passed the three exhausted horses in front of us. Both Hurricane and Beauty were excited at being able to race each other and stretched their legs as they flew across the pasture.

When we crossed the finish line, Hurricane won the race by no more than a head's length in front of Beauty. I think he could have done better than that if I had pushed him, but I was content with the win, no matter how close it was, especially since it was Beauty who came in second. The bookmakers would be groaning and shaking their heads.

We had already ridden off to the side, slowing our horses to a walk, giving them a breather, when what was left of the worn-down racehorses straggled across the finish line; their riders and owners sorely disappointed. But that's horseracing.

During the race, I had used my magic to will the flesh wound on my back to heal, so mother wouldn't get upset if she happened to see it. Cory Anne of course would have gone into a rampage, wanting to hunt down and punish the culprit.

After all of the cheering and the award ceremony was over, my father took me aside and asked about the tear in my shirt. When I finished my story, he nodded his head and said, He'd seen Big John Denton come riding across the pasture with a rifle across his lap and when he got off his horse, he had a sour look on his face. "He had a horse in the race that he'd promised several people would win, and I think they bet heavily on him," father told me.

"But would he go so far to keep us from winning, by trying to shoot us?" I asked, not wanting to believe it.

It was well known that Big John Denton had no liking for my father. He'd never won a horserace against him and I guess the thought of us winning this race did something to him. It was the only conclusion I could come up with.

"After things quiet down, we'll go out and see what we can find," my father said. "Now get up to the house and get your shirt changed before your mother sees it. And make some rips in other places so the shirt will have to be thrown away. And make up some excuse as to how it happened."

My father had never been one to lie, but as I look back, I could see a time or two when it might have been necessary to keep mother from feeling bad. Fortunately, I was able to dispose of the shirt and nothing was ever said about it.

Half an hour later, I met my father in the barn. He had two fresh horses saddled and we rode out to the area where I remembered being shot at.

As we rode away from the barn, I looked over my shoulder and saw the huge crowd of people who were setting down at tables for the food and drink that had been laid out by the venders.

Sure enough, after scouting around some, we found where both a man and a horse had been standing. My father kneeled down and examined the hoof tracks, then stood up. "Let's go see Big John," he said with a determined look on his face.

I wasn't sure what my father had in mind, but I was sure that if it had been Mister Denton who had done the shooting, he was in big trouble.

Father rode at a fast pace, with me next to him and neither of us speaking.

I had never seen my father so upset before. He had a look of determination on his face that sent chills down my spine. This was not the man I had grown up with. This was a man possessed by anger.

I could almost feel sorry for Mister Denton, if it turned out he was the one who shot at me.

My father and I rode up to the front of Mister Denton's barn and stepped down, ground hitching our horses, knowing they wouldn't stray, then entered the barn. We found Big John Denton cleaning a stall and when he saw us, he came storming out of the stall and stopped in front of us. He had his fists on his hips and a scowl on his face. "What're you doing here, O'Shea? You come ta gloat did ya? Well, if you did, you and your whelp can turn around and remove yourselves from my property."

Father ignored him and stepped around him and walked over to where a rifle stood, leaned against the wall. He picked it up and smelled the barrel, then stood it back against the wall. "It's been recently fired," my father stated.

"So?" Big John asked.

"My son, Brody, was shot at during the race and by luck all he got was a torn shirt and a slight scratch across his back. You wouldn't happen to know anything about that, would you, Denton?"

Mister Denton's face turned tulip red and his eyes were staring daggers at my father. "You accusing me of trying ta shoot your boy?" Big John asked, with a snarl on his lips.

"I'm not accusing you of anything; just hunting for some answers. You have a rifle that has recently been fired and Brody has a bullet torn shirt," my father told him.

"That don't prove a thing," Big John retorted.

"No, but maybe this will," my father said as he walked into the stall and lifted the horses' hoof and began to inspect it before Big John could stop him.

If you know anything about horses and horseshoes, you know that you can look at the shoe and tell if it's the same one that made a track on the ground. It's a footprint, plain and simple. And it will stand up in court, if it comes to that.

Big John must have known he'd been caught because he rushed into the stall and swung his right fist at father's head.

Father saw what was coming and dropped the horse's leg and slipped under Big John's swing and drove his fist into the big man's stomach, then followed with an uppercut to his jaw, which drove Mister Denton back out into the walkway between the stalls.

My first inclination was to send a bolt of lightning into Big John's body, but a look and shake of his head from my father told me not to interfere. Father motioned for Big John Denton to get to his feet. "You've been asking for this for a long, long time, and now you're going to get what's coming to you. Get on your feet, Denton!"

Now if this was an actual prizefight, these two men wouldn't be in the same weight class and for sure never put in the ring against each other. Mister Denton outweighed father by at least fifty or sixty pounds and stood close to a foot taller. I know father wanted to do this on his own, but I wasn't so sure he was able. So, I stood by, ready to help if he needed it. I had never seen my father in a fight, nor had I seen him as angry as he was right then, so I wasn't sure what to expect.

Big John climbed to his feet and spit into the palms of his hands and then doubled them up. They looked as big as hams and I shuddered to think what would happen if one of them connected with my father's jaw.

Not only was I surprised, but I was proud of the way my father took Mister Denton down, one punch at a time. He danced around and slipped under Mister Denton's swings, then delivered blows of his own – mainly to the big man's kidneys and stomach. And each time Mister Denton bent over, father pounded his face with lightning-fast jabs. I was in awe at my father's speed and agility. I had no idea he knew how to box. But, thinking back on it, I shouldn't have been surprised. Growing up, my father had always been a man who was respected by other men as a man who could hold his own in most any situation – which I now realized included the use of his fists.

Finally, after being beaten until his face looked like it had been hammered with a meat cleaver, Mister Denton had enough and raised his hands, palms forward. "I yield," he said. "I've had enough. You, Mister O'Shea are the better man."

I can't remember ever being prouder of my father than I was at that moment. I knew he was doing this because of me and his fear that I had come close to being shot by Mister Denton, and he wanted to punish him for what he attempted to do.

Before deciding whether or not to take Mister Denton down to the police station for what he'd done, my father dragged him over in front of me and told Big John to apologize – and when he did, my father told me if I wanted to press charges for attempted murder, we would take him to the police station.

I watched as Big John swallowed and sweat began to show on his forehead. "I wasn't trying to shoot you – just scare you. I guess when it comes right down to it, I was lucky I didn't hit you. I couldn't have lived with that. I'm sorry, lad. I truly am."

He stood there like a whipped dog, staring down at his feet. I knew if I brought charges against him, he would go to jail and his business would be ruined, his family torn apart and in general, be a marked man, which I didn't want to see happen. Basically, Big John Denton would normally be considered a decent man, if not for his always wanting to be the best at everything he did. He held the heavyweight boxing championship of the county, and had won every team pull he'd ever entered. No one could stand up to his huge team of horses, which he refused to tell anyone where they came from. So, it stood to reason, he would want to win the cross-country horserace and finally beat father at something, but he just didn't have a horse that could beat Beauty or Hurricane. Of course, he shouldn't have gone to such extreme measures to see what he considered to be his only competition eliminated from the race by shooting at me and Conner, trying to scare us off.

I stared at him for a long time, letting him drown in the silence. After an insufferable time, I said, "I won't prosecute on one condition and it isn't negotiable."

I could see in his eyes that he was trying to figure out what that condition might be and if it came to it, I would bet a hundred pounds that he would never guess the condition.

Finally, he asked, "What might that condition be, lad?"

"That you put in one day a week of hard labor, free of charge, helping build the new hospital until it is completed."

Two months ago, my father and I, under the guise of O'Shea Stables and O'Shea Freight Company, had put up the money to build a new hospital. The money came from some of the bounty I had acquired, but that part was never mentioned. There were some stuffed shirts living in Boston who would have frowned at using ill gotten money for anything – even though it was for the greater good of the community.

The mayor and town council were thrilled at the prospect of getting a new hospital with all the latest equipment and lavished us with praises.

When word got around, several other wealthy men in Boston came up with the money to furnish all the beds and things necessary to run the hospital, which, in reality, wasn't necessary, but since they offered, we couldn't say no. We knew they had done so to get the publicity and their names on a plaque attached to the front of the hospital, but neither of us cared. Getting a new hospital with all the up-to-date equipment was all we cared about. And the best part was that patients would only have to pay what they could afford. As the owners of the hospital, we set the rules. For sure, a few greedy people disliked the idea, but we didn't care. We were building the hospital to help people, not get rich off of them.

Mother, being a social person, found a doctor - recently arrived from England, who was more than qualified to be the chief of staff, and convinced him to take the job.

The mayor and city council had wanted to name the hospital after us but we refused, although we did allow a plaque to be mounted on the front wall next to the entrance with our names included along with the others who had contributed. We named the hospital, The People's Hospital, and we were proud to be a part of it.

One of the reasons for my decision about Big John Denton serving time helping build the hospital, instead of going to jail, was that he was an excellent carpenter.

When he heard my demand, he sighed. There were tears in his eyes when he looked at me and said, "Thank you, lad. It will be my honor to help with the building – and I'll even throw in some supplies... and at no charge, mind ya."

"And one more thing," I told him, which brought a questioning look back to his face. "And what might that be?" he asked.

"That you look around and find a horse worthy of challenging Hurricane and we'll race again – just you against me."

Big John looked at me skeptically and said, "I hope you mean with my jockey up – not me."

Big John Denton stood a good six and a half feet tall and weighed closer to three hundred pounds than he did two hundred. With him riding, he would have lost the race before it started. The only horse capable of carrying so much weight would have to be one of the big, slow moving draft horses that he normally rode. They were the only ones big enough to carry him, and for sure not able to jump fences and run fast.

"With your jockey on the saddle," I said and stuck out my hand.

When we got home, my father told me how proud of me he was. "You're growing into a fine young man with a good head on your shoulders, lad. Yes, a fine young man indeed."

That night, I climbed onto my bed, feeling very proud of myself, not realizing my comfortable life was about to change.

Somewhere around three in the morning, my uncle, King Neptune, came to me in my dreams.

CHAPTER THREE

"Well, Brody, lad, are you rested?" he asked. "You've been on land for close to five months and I'm betting you're getting anxious to get back out to sea and the excitement of another mission."

I woke up and swung my legs over the side of the bed and sat up, rubbing the sleep from my eyes. "Mission? I have a new mission? So soon?" At this moment it seemed like it had been only a few days since coming home, not five months. "What 's the new mission about? Not my birth father, I hope…" I said out loud, praying it wouldn't be. I knew the day would come when I would be asked to seek him out, but I dreaded to see that time come. I was still trying to process what it would take to go against Malimar and all the power I was told he had.

After a burst of chuckling, my uncle said, "No, Brody, not yet. It seems there is a man, who is not a wizard, that fancies himself a fearful pirate and has decided to take over Abigor's territory now that his is gone. He's even gone so far as to state that he was in the process of bringing down Abigor, but you, with more luck than a genie can offer, got there first. He's also been saying you were fortunate, and caught Abigor when he was asleep, but if you dare to face him, you'll find yourself feeding the fish in Davy Jones' Locker."

Had my uncle not been so serious I would have laughed out loud. "Are you telling me you want me and my crew to go back to the Mediterranean Sea and hunt down this blowhard and make him eat his words? This mortal who thinks he is more powerful than a wizard?"

"I know," my uncle chuckled. "Him facing you and having no powers will be an unfair fight, but I have no other choice but to ask you to end his reign of terror. And to answer your question, yes, that is exactly what I'm asking you to do. And… with all his raiding and posturing around, I doubt you'll have much trouble finding him. But please don't underestimate him. A blowhard like him can be very dangerous. He actually believes he is unbeatable, and if you're not careful, he could get lucky and we don't want that."

From what past experience I've had at dealing with both mortal and wizard pirates I hope I'll never let my ego get the best of me like every one of the men or wizards I have so far encountered. Always proceed with caution and use common sense is my motto, which I related to my uncle.

"One other thing," my uncle said, "Before we get into the details of your mission, there's something you need to know. Malimar knows about you and all you've accomplished, but thankfully not that you're his son. To him you're nothing more than a new young wizard who has been creating an uproar and a pain in his… what should I call it?"

"Neck," I said. "I'm a pain in his neck."

"Yes, neck works quite nicely," my uncle said. "He is searching for you, but so far he hasn't been able to find you because you're not at sea or using your powers, which is frustrating him to no end. Your last known whereabouts were the Mediterranean Sea when you had your episode with Abigor. So, it's very possible he may go there, searching for you, now that Abigor is no longer in power, thinking you are the one trying to take his place, which makes me reluctant to send you back to the Mediterranean area."

This took me back a little bit and I said so. "I have to admit, I'm a little reluctant, myself. I don't know if I'm ready to face him just yet, plus, at the same time, chase down this mortal pirate. It may be more than I can deal with all at once."

There was a long pause before my uncle spoke again. "Are you still there?" I asked, wondering if he'd closed off our communication. I couldn't always tell. Sometimes he would stop our communication in mid-sentence and I would have to wait until the next time he came to me. Then, at other times, he was just taking a pause in the conversation.

"Yes, lad, I'm still here. With Malimar on the rampage, and possibly headed for Abigor's old territory, I'm now torn about asking you to go on this mission, even though it did seem quite necessary a few minutes ago."

I wasn't quite sure how to answer him, but found myself saying, "I guess the decision is up to you, but if you believe it's important, I will go. The decision is yours."

There was another long pause, then, after a sigh, he said, "This new pirate has already taken several lives and enslaved close to a hundred men and women. He's raising havoc all up and down the coast of Spain, France, Italy, Greece and Turkey. Given time, he will raid every coastal town and city all the way up to Russia if he isn't stopped."

"I will gather up my crew and go, then," I said with more conviction than I felt.

"Thank you," my uncle said very softly, in almost a whispered sigh. "I will give you all the information I can find out, as soon as I get it. And Brody – stay alert at all times, please. I will pray that your father doesn't arrive before you've completed your mission and gotten safely away."

After promising I would leave as soon as possible, my uncle told me goodbye and wished me good luck. Then, with a flash of light, he was gone, leaving me alone with my mind swirling like a small boy swishing a stick in a tub of water.

Sleeping the few hours left until daylight was no longer an option, so I packed my bag and was ready to leave by the time the sun came creeping through my bedroom window.

I have kept in communication with my men while we have been ashore, for they work for the O'Shea Trading Company when not out chasing pirates. I knew it would take very little time to assemble them and get the ship ready for travel. In my absence, Mister Logan and Mister O'Callaghan kept the ship busy, making short delivery or pickup runs for our company, and as luck would have it, the ship had just returned two days ago and was sitting in the bay, getting cleaned and restocked.

At breakfast, I made my announcement to my parents and said my goodbyes, promising to take care of myself.

My mother always hated it when I was called for a mission, but had reconciled herself to the fact that I was an agent for King Neptune and his word was law, at least until someday when she hoped to convince me to give up sailing the high seas and chasing bad people, while staying ashore to help run our businesses.

That might have been nice, but I was afraid it was never to be – at least not for a long, long time.

The one part about my relationship with my uncle, King Neptune, was that my mother, so far, didn't know that one day I was to take his place as ruler beneath oceans and seas. So, with that in mind, I always smiled and patted her hand and said, "Maybe one day, Mother. Maybe one day soon," Knowing, or at least hoping, that it would be years before we had to face my becoming the newest King Neptune…

On the way down to the wharf, I went in search of Kathleen and found her at the small medical center, doing what she did best, treating patients.

She was surprised to see me and said so, then frowned. Her female intuition took over and she knew something was up. "What's wrong?" she asked, taking my hand and pulling me into her small office that looked like a windstorm had just gone through it. Papers were piled everywhere. I looked around and realized she needed help; someone to take care of the paperwork because with as many patients as she had, she had no time for the bookwork.

Large teardrops formed in her eyes and rolled down her cheeks when I told her I would be leaving, again. After wiping the tears from her cheeks and taking a deep breath, she said she would patiently await the day of my return. We hugged and kissed, with me promising not to be gone long. At least a part of me was hoping that would be true.

As much as I loved going to sea, leaving Kathleen seemed to get more difficult each time I was called into duty. I wondered if someday she would agree to becoming Mrs. King Neptune, queen of the seas.

I found Mister Logan and Mister O'Callaghan in a place called *The Boar's Head* having a leisurely breakfast.

"Good morning, lad," Mister Logan said as I approached the table. "To what do we owe the pleasure?"

I sat down and ordered tea, then told them of the mission ahead of us, leaving out the part about Malimar possibly being in the area and what piled on trouble that would bring us.

They agreed to have the crew assembled within the hour. One of our crewmen was on the dock and I asked if he would row me out to the ship where I could store my gear, chart our course, and get my cabin in order.

I was about to step down into the longboat when I heard Corey Anne's voice filling my head. "Stop! Don't leave yet! I need to talk to you!"

I looked toward the far end of the wharf and saw her running toward me. I tossed my seabag into the longboat, and waited.

She hadn't been at breakfast when I announced my leaving, so I assumed she wanted to say goodbye, but to my astonishment I could see she was carrying a bag. "I'm going with you," she announced as she stopped in front of me.

I looked in her eyes and could tell she was serious – but there was no way I could allow her to go. Especially with the possibility of running into Malimar, and him wanting to do away with me. There was no point in both of us becoming fish food. It took me the better part of an hour before I convinced her she needed to finish her violin training and only when she agreed, did I promise we would discuss the possibility of her one day going with me, once I returned.

She finally agreed but only if I kept in touch with her through our mind talk, so she would know where I was and to make sure I was still among the living, as she put it.

"Agreed," I told her, just as father's buggy pulled onto the wharf with mother sitting next to him. Mother jumped out and hustled Corey Anne and her luggage into the buggy, telling her God only knew what. Whatever it was, I knew she wouldn't be going to sea with me anywhere in the near future.

Once she had Cory Anne in the carriage, she rushed over and gave me a last hug, saying, "You take care of yourself, and make sure it's coming home to us soon, you'll be doin', you hear?"

I kissed her on the cheek and said, "Yes, mother."

CHAPTER FOUR

Malimar's ship was sailing a northeasterly course across the Atlantic Ocean, just a few hundred miles southwest of The Straits of Gibraltar when he made a decision.

"Ten degrees to starboard!" he called out to Henry Ragsdale, his helmsman, an elderly, gray haired, bedraggled looking man, who stared at Malimar with eyes filled with fear. His back still stung where Malimar had taken a whip to him just two days prior. He had been tied to a post and, before he was allowed to be cut down, Malimar forced one of the crewmen to rub salt into the wounds.

He'd been humiliated in front of the entire crew just because he had been slow to react to one of Malimar's orders. The old wizard pirate had been a holy terror for several months now – even moreso than normal, and he knew he wasn't the only crewmember to suffer Malimar's wrath. Several others had been whipped and one had drowned after being thrown overboard by the captain during one of his rages. Another nearly died from being keelhauled over some small infraction no one was sure what it had been.

The latest to suffer Malimar's wrath was Harley Pike, one of the ships deckhands and part time galley helper. He was serving a bowl of soup to

Malimar when a rat ran across his shoe and startled him. The sad part was that he dumped the entire bowl of soup in Malimar's lap. The old wizard reacted by dragging Harley over to the cutting board where he grabbed a meat clever and threatened to throw him overboard.

Harley pleaded for his life, promising such a thing would never happen, again.

"Get out of my sight and see that it doesn't!" Malimar roared, sending Harley scurrying for someplace to hide. Malimar left the galley, screaming curses as he headed back to his cabin to change his pants.

Everyone agreed, that in the mood Malimar was in, Harley had been lucky to survive.

Then there had been Tugger. Tugger was in his twenties and strong built. He'd been brought aboard just a few months back by some men who shanghaied him while he was walking along the wharf, and sold him to Malimar for a few shillings, which Malimar took back shortly after taking Tugger aboard his ship. Malimar had turned himself into a giant troll with arms like trees and dragged the two men into an alley where he smashed their heads together, knocking them unconscious, then took back the money he'd paid them, along with relieving them of what other few dollars they had.

Because of his size and strength, Tugger was made a deckhand who tugged on the halyards when the sails were being set. On that particular morning it was raining and the lines and deck were both slippery. It was Tugger's misfortune to be pulling on a line just as Malimar was walking past.

Tugger was engrossed in what he was doing and didn't see Malimar. A gust of wind pulled at the sail and caused Tugger to pull extra hard on the line. His feet slipped and he lost his grip on the line and fell backwards into Malimar, who was knocked to the deck.

Before Tugger could help Malimar up and apologize, Malimar was on his feet with a look of pure evil in his eyes. He raised his right hand toward Tugger and the crew watched in horror as he was lifted into the air and tossed over the side of the ship like nothing more than a piece of trash.

Malimar glared at the crew, daring any of them to make a sound; then stormed off down below deck. He'd just disappeared down the hatch when they heard Tugger's screams. The sharks were making short order of him and there was nothing the crew could do but go about their business like nothing had happened.

Henry turned the wheel to ten degrees – not one more or not one less, and held the wheel steady. He knew they were now headed toward The Straits of Gibraltar, but said nothing. He'd been one of Malimar's slaves now for the past six years, and in all that time they had never gone to the Mediterranean Sea. Why, all of a sudden were they going there now, he wondered, but knew better than to ask any questions. Especially when the old wizard was still walking around, talking to himself and acting like he'd gone completely daft. Henry held their course steady and kept his thoughts to himself, but decided their going to the Mediterranean Sea must have something to do with Malimar's angry disposition.

It had been a spur of the moment decision for Malimar. The Mediterranean Sea was the last known place I had been. It was where I had won the cat and mouse game with Abigor, and there were rumors of a new pirate taking over Abigor's domain. So… it stood to reason that Malimar wondered if it could be me who had taken over and was now the new ruler of the Mediterranean?

If that was true, he wanted to find me and make a mockery of me by sending me to spend eternity at the bottom of the Mediterranean Sea. At least that's how I guessed he saw things.

After watching his helmsman make the turn and the deckhands adjusting the sails, Malimar walked to the bow and stared toward land, all the while, talking to himself.

"Once I rid the waters of this new rapscallion, then, maybe, I will take over as ruler of the Mediterranean Sea. After all, the wind is pleasant. The water is warm, and there is still so much plunder, I will never want for anything," Malimar told himself.

As his ship sailed toward the entryway to the Mediterranean Sea, the Atlantic Ocean suddenly turned into a torrent of massive waves, up to forty feet in height that came crashing down on Malimar's ship, nearly capsizing it. It was the worst and most terrifying storm the crew could ever remember. It was worse than any Malimar had created when overpowering his prey.

With shortened sails and all hatches battened down, the ship continued to struggle its way up one gigantic wave, then crashing down the backside, pitching and rolling so hard the men down below believed the ship would sink at any moment and they would drown.

Malimar did his best to will the stormy seas away, but the power causing them was stronger than his own, which meant it could be only one person – his older brother, King Neptune!

Malimar was lying, prone on his bunk, holding on with all his might – yelling at his older brother, calling him by his given name. "Artimus! Stop this! Stop this instant! Why are you prying into my affairs?"

Suddenly the interior of Malimar's cabin was filled with a bright light, then the image of his older brother appeared and the storm ended as quickly as it had come. The waves returned to normal and the ship settled down.

"You want to know why I'm interfering with you going into the Mediterranean Sea? Why you should ask a question like that, is beyond me - because I think you already know the answer. You're hunting the young wizard. You think he's trying to take over Abigor's domain, but I'm here to tell you, little brother, you are mistaken. The one you seek is nowhere near the Mediterranean Sea, so stop throwing your tantrums and back away. Go back to your beloved Caribbean islands that you love so much!"

"Then where is he and if it is not him, who is pillaging and plundering in Abigor's old domain?" Malimar asked, sitting up and glaring at his brother.

"The person trying to take over Abigor's domain is just a mortal; a man – not a wizard. He thinks with Abigor gone; he can do as he pleases. He goes by the name of Ezekiel Bolingbroke and claims to be a descendent of Henry Bolingbroke who was the grandson to King Edward III. The truth is, he is a nobody. Oh, yes, he is from England, but he's been in and out of jail most of his life, mainly for theft. He escaped prison and hid away on a merchant ship – then murdered the captain and took over his ship. He then sailed the waters around the coasts of Ireland, Scotland, England and France, trying to make a name for himself as a pirate, at least, he did until it got too hot for him and he ran to the Mediterranean Sea just after Abigor's demise. When he found the area without a pirate, he decided to assume that position. The man has an ego bigger than his ship. He even goes so far as to call himself, King Bolingbroke."

Malimar received this information with several nods of his head. "Then where is the young wizard I seek? I have business with him," Malimar said.

"What business might that be, little brother" King Neptune asked.

Malimar stood up from his bunk and said, "That will be between him and me, and is of no concern to you."

"I beg to differ," King Neptune said. "I'm making it my concern."

Malimar looked his brother in the eyes and asked the simple question, "Why?"

There was a long silence and Malimar could hear a whispered voice in the background but he couldn't decipher what the person, whom he assumed to be his sister-in-law, Marbella, was saying.

What Malimar couldn't hear was, in fact, Marbella warning her husband not to reveal that Brody was Malimar's son.

When King Neptune finally spoke to his brother, he said, "Let's just say, I have his best interests at heart, and let it go at that."

Malimar was confused. This was totally out of character for his older brother. Normally he left everyone above the water alone and stayed out of surface affairs. So, what was so special about this young wizard that would cause his brother to champion him?

"Leave the boy alone and let it go at that!" King Neptune said, strenuously.

Malimar looked into the eyes of his older brother and said, "All right – at least for now, but someday, I will find out why this young wizard is so important to you."

"And one day you shall, little brother. One day you shall." King Neptune said with a sigh.

And with that, Malimar's brother vanished, leaving him sitting alone in his cabin with a thousand questions racing around in his brain. One of which was what to do now, since the young wizard was no longer in the Mediterranean Sea as he'd thought.

As he paced the interior of his cabin, another thought filled his brain. What if maybe what his brother had said was just a ruse to keep him away from the Mediterranean and the truth of the matter was that the pirate ruling the Mediterranean was really the young wizard he was looking for. His brother could be quite devious when he wanted to be. Malimar placed both hands on the table near his bunk and said, "There is more here than meets the eye, and one day I will have the answers, one way or another. But for now, I have decisions to make. Even if the pirate controlling the Mediterranean Sea is nothing more than a mortal, he needs to be taken down. No mortal pirate should rule any of the surface waters. That honor should be for a wizard and only a wizard. But what if it is the young wizard I seek…?" Malimar smiled at the thought.

After going topside and assuring himself his ship was still seaworthy in case they had to fight, he ordered his crew to continue on. He would put the fear of the Devil into this mortal rogue pirate who claimed to be of royal blood, if that is who he really is - which would also rid himself of some of the tension that was tearing his insides apart.

And as for his brother, Malimar knew he could create storms to slow him down, but he was not able to come above the surface of the water to confront him face to face.

Malimar knew he might suffer what few indignities his brother might throw at him, but in the end, he would overcome - for he was the mightiest wizard above the surface of the water.

Malimar stood on the bow of his ship, eagerly awaiting his next victory. He would then settle down and await my return, for he was sure I could not resist coming back. In his mind, the Mediterranean was much too inviting for me to stay away for too long.

CHAPTER FIVE

I knew nothing of what was going on between King Neptune and his brother Malimar. Nor did I realize he was actually on his way to the Mediterranean Sea to deal with the same man I was. Yes, I had been warned he might be, but had I known for sure, I'm not sure I would have even left Boston Harbor.

But, as they say – *Que sera, sera*. What will be will be.

It was a glorious Monday morning when we sailed out of the harbor and into the Atlantic Ocean. The sun was shining brightly and not a cloud anywhere to be seen. A stiff wind pulled us along and as I stood on the bridge with Mister O'Callaghan, Mister Logan and Mister Collins, our helmsman, the smell of salt filled our nostrils. The crew was singing some bawdy song as they adjusted the sails to get the most out of the wind that was to power us toward our destination. The sound of the waves crashing against the side of the ship as it plowed its way through the water sent a feeling of strength and giddiness coursing through my veins. I had nearly forgotten how glorious it felt to be at sea. At least for the moment, I felt like I was king of the world.

Had I known fate would soon be shaking us around like a piece of rag in a cyclone, I might have elected to turn around and go back to Boston where life was comfortable and somewhat safe. But that was not the case. I assumed the mission would be rather simple and we would be back in Boston in just a few months at the longest. What is it they say about the best laid plans of mice and men? I don't recall, but I'm sure it related to us.

We'd been at sea for three days when I once again received a face to face with my uncle, King Neptune. I was in my cabin, checking the charts when his face appeared. I was in the process of taking a sip of my steaming hot tea when the words, "Brody, are you there?" reverberated throughout the cabin, causing me to not only choke, but to spill the hot tea on my pantlegs. I sat the cup on the table, grabbed a rag and quickly soaked up the tea from my pants, and then and only then did I look up at the ceiling. My uncle was staring down on me with a look on his face that said he was about to tell me something I wasn't going to like.

"Yes, I'm here, uncle," I told him, picking up my cup and taking a much-wanted sip of what was left of my tea, then setting the cup on the table again. "You have information for me?"

"I do, and I don't," he said, causing me to get a questioning look on my face. How can it be both ways, I wondered?

"I've been debating on whether to contact you yet because I don't have all the details I need for a visit."

"Then why are you contacting me?" I asked, knowing that, at least the part he did know, must be important.

I could see his face on the ceiling, as clear as I could have had he been standing just a few feet away from me. And I could see the indecision in his eyes. Finally, he nodded his head and said, "I did say I would pass on any information I got as soon as I received it – and I have at least some."

I knew he was expecting me to ask what it might be, but I decided to just wait for him to tell me. And sure enough, after a short pause, he said, "Malimar is in a snit and he's headed for the Mediterranean Sea. He's convinced you're the one who has taken over Abigor's domain – even though I tried to tell him differently."

I ingested the information like swallowing a spiny sea urchin, while trying to stop my heart from pounding like a convict breaking rocks with a huge sledgehammer. After a long silence, I looked up at him and asked, "So, what am I to do now - turn around and go back to Boston? Or shall I sail around in circles until he runs head on with the pirate that is there and decides I'm not the one he seeks and deals with him, then leaves? And… If he's already dealt with this pirate you call Ezekiel Bolingbroke, why do I still need to be out here, sailing around in circles, chasing the stern of my ship?"

After another pause and some background prompting from his wife, Marbella, my uncle cleared his throat and said, "I think you should continue on. You're still a long way from the straits that will take you into the Mediterranean Sea and possibly running into him head on. In the meantime, I will do my best to figure out what my brother's next move will be. And you're right, if he deals with Bolingbroke, then there will be no reason for you to go on. If that happens, I will contact you. If, at that time I think you're getting too close and my brother is still in the vicinity, I will instruct you to turn back - but, please, don't turn back – at least not yet."

I agreed to do as he asked and when he'd gone, I went topside. I needed some air.

To take my mind off my immediate problem, I decided to do a little fishing. After an hour, I guessed the fish knew my heart wasn't in it and decided to just swim around and around, staring at my bait before continuing on.

"Something on your mind, lad?" Mister Logan asked as he stepped up next to me.

I looked at him and sighed. I guess I was wearing my emotions on my face.

He nodded his head and pointed at the water. "I can tell it's something other than catching fish."

I pulled my line in, removed the bait from the hook and tossed it overboard, where it was gobbled up almost as soon as it hit the water. How did they know, I wondered?

I looked out over the sea and stared at the water as I repeated to Mister Logan what my uncle had told me, then looked at him and said, "So, here we are – at the request of my uncle, still sailing toward who knows what kind of danger with Malimar, who just happens to be the most powerful and evil wizard on the seven seas - and who is out there just beyond the next wave - searching for me with the intent of sending me to a watery grave - and not that I believe he would give a whit even if he found out he is my blood father."

Mister Logan grinned and slapped me on the shoulder, saying, "Relax lad, I think you may be over-thinking this. Look at it this way; this Malimar takes care of the pirate in the Mediterranean Sea that we were supposed to chase down. He'll do our job for us, then more than likely head back to the Caribbean where he likes to hang out, leaving us free to get some time doing what we love to do – sailing and fishing, with very little danger to spoil the trip."

I didn't have a comeback for that so I just shrugged my shoulders. Even though I wasn't totally convinced, I would try and see things his way – but still keep a wary eye out for I knew things could change in the blink of an eye. Murphy's law is always out there somewhere, lurking about, waiting for his chance to spoil everything.

I called a meeting of all hands and filled them in with what information I had. I reminded them we still had a great many miles to cover before having to come to some kind of decision. "We will deal with whatever happens to come our way when it comes, but in the meantime, I want all of us to be ready to fight if we have to, which means tomorrow morning we begin training again. Misters Logan and O'Callaghan will once again see to your training."

Over the next several days, I trained alongside my men, limbering up my muscles that were sorely in need of exercise. Being the captain of a ship doesn't always allow for much time to exercise like I did back on land, training horses or mucking out stalls, which keeps you very busy.

The men enjoyed seeing me train along beside them. It gave them confidence; which can go a long way toward winning a battle.

The days were warm and pleasant as the ship skipped over the water to everyone's delight. Fishing was bountiful and the nights were cool, which made for comfortable sleeping. Fighting with pirates and wizards just seemed to drift away into nothingness; replaced with dreams of Kathleen Maquire.

CHAPTER SIX

When Malimar passed through the Straits of Gibraltar without incident, he found himself feeling warmth in the air, which in turn, much to his surprise, calmed his temper just a little. He seriously doubted he'd ever been completely calm in his entire life, but he had to admit it felt good to relax, even a little.

He strode up to the bow and let his eyes search for another ship, but saw none. Next, he did a mind search for any powers that might be in the near vicinity and came up empty there, also. By now it was late afternoon and would be dark soon. After checking his charts, he told the helmsman to veer the ship to port five degrees and within less than an hour, he could see lights along the coast of Spain beginning to show.

After directing the helmsman to steer toward the lights, Malimar turned himself into an Egyptian Vulture and lifted into the night sky. It felt good to be doing something besides pacing the deck of his ship, or worrying about the young wizard. The wind felt good against his face as he glided across the water toward land. A strong wind current lifted him even higher and he could see the lights of what appeared to be a town.

The Egyptian Vulture is a small vulture called a white scavenger that can fly over the area without attracting much attention, especially in the darkness of a moonless night. Malimar wanted to see what kind of place his ship would be entering and very quickly vetoed the idea of stopping here. It was nothing more than a fishing village, and not worth taking the time to stop. Oh, he could anchor just off shore and allow his crew to go ashore and find whatever pleasures they might, but for himself, he had no interest in this village. There would be no money or treasure to find here. No power to oppose him. These were just peasants – fishermen, who at best, barely scrapped together a living.

Circling around, Malimar quickly found a southernly air current and flew back to his ship and once he'd landed on the deck, and turned himself back into a man, he gave new directions to his helmsman. There would be no place to pillage during this night.

The sun was halfway up in the sky when Malimar stood on the bow of his ship and scanned the shore through his long glass. There, in the distance, he saw what looked to be a fair-sized city – something more in line for what he had in mind.

After anchoring in the small bay where three other ships were at anchor, Malimar instructed his men to go ashore and bring the city to its knees. "Do whatever it takes to let the people know they are at the mercy of Malimar, the greatest wizard of them all! I want their money and any treasure you can find. What else you do; I don't care as long as the city is mine. Now, go and do my bidding!" he yelled.

Out of pure fear, the men raced to the railing and climbed down into the longboats that had been lowered over the side as soon as they'd set the anchor.

Left to their own, the men might have caused a little havoc with their drinking, fighting and carousing, but as far as looting and pillaging the town, they probably wouldn't have gone that far. But they had their orders – orders like the ones they'd carried out in other places where Malimar wanted to make a statement - a statement that would quickly spread to other towns and cities. Malimar reveled at being a powerful wizard who could not be defeated, and could take whatever he wanted, whenever he wanted it. And using his men to do his bidding was less tiresome.

Malimar stood on the bow of his ship and watched as his men climbed up onto the pier and headed into the city, knowing they were afraid to disobey him.

Suddenly, he got an idea and just the thought of it made him lean his head back and laugh. After catching his breath, he raised his hands in the direction of his men and yelled, "To you who are my crew, from now until you have completed the task before you, you shall be trolls doing my bidding! Now go and destroy the city!"

And just like that, the pier was filled with ugly looking, massively built, trolls. Malimar could hear the screams of terror as they entered the city and began their mission. He'd chosen trolls because they have huge muscled bodies, small brains and absolutely no compassion whatsoever. Trolls were the perfect warriors in this kind of situation.

Turning, Malimar saw men scurrying around on the three other ships sitting at anchor. They were gathering weapons to go ashore and do battle with the hideous creatures invading the city.

"No, no, no," Malimar said as he raised his arms and turned himself into a huge, fire breathing dragon, some thirty feet long and fifteen feet high, with a wingspan of twenty feet. He then lifted into the air and flew to the closest ship, where he spit out long flames of fire, setting the ship ablaze. As he flew toward the next ship, he could hear the men screaming and heard splashes as they leaped overboard and into the hungry mouths of the sharks, Malimar had summoned.

Within minutes, the three ships were raging bonfires with many of the men trapped below deck. All of the men who were on deck and jumped overboard to keep from being burned became the victims of ravenous sharks sent there by Malimar.

Still as a giant, fire breathing dragon, Malimar landed on the dock and in short order set all of the buildings along the wharf on fire as his hideous laugh filled the air.

All through the night the trolls ravished the town and the only ones to escape were those who had seen what was happening and had sneaked away into the mountains to hide before the trolls got to them.

Come morning when Malimar's ship sailed back out into the Mediterranean Sea, there was little left of the town called, Almeria. It was nothing more than a pile of blackened wood, with whiffs of smoke still rising into the sky. It would be years before they could even consider doing any serious fishing or feel like urging ships to anchor in their small harbor to do business.

Malimar stood on the bridge of his ship, knowing word of what he'd done would spread faster than a forest fire, and by the time a few more towns had fallen under his raids, the man who had taken Abigor's place would be looking for a place to hide, for he would know Malimar was looking for him. But it would do him no good. He would find him and make a laughingstock of him before he fed him to the sharks, or maybe something more hideous. If the man tried to stand up to him, he might consider giving him a quick death, but if he ran like the coward Malimar guessed he would be, then he would make him suffer a long, slow, painful death. He abhorred cowards.

Shortly after Malimar and his crew of cutthroats entered the Mediterranean Sea, a kind of darkness seemed to engulf the entire area, with gray and black clouds filling the sky and the air becoming chilly instead of warm and balmy. Cold rain fell. The people weren't used to this kind of weather and tempers soared, causing a great unrest to cover the entire region. People were afraid to leave their homes and when they did, it was in fear of being killed or severely beaten and robbed, so they carried weapons and became the very essence of what they feared. There was an evil feeling in the air that bore itself deep inside them and they didn't know what to do about it, causing many innocent people to be needlessly killed.

Malimar raided and pillaged as he pleased, with no opposition from the pirate who claimed to be an ancestor of King Edward III and new ruler of the Mediterranean Sea. Neither this Ezekiel Bolingbroke nor anyone else dared to stand up against this new power whose desire for destruction seemed to have no end.

Along with everyone else, Ezekiel Bolingbroke heard the stories of this new pirate who was leaving a trail of broken and torn cities in his wake. He'd even visited one along the coast of Italy and after seeing the destruction, he set sail for the Straits of Gibraltar, hoping to get far away before he was detected by this evil pirate called, Malimar.

Ezekiel believed Malimar had to be a wizard, to create such destruction - and he had no intentions of going against him. Besides, he had enough treasure on his ship that would allow him to go anywhere in the world he wanted to go. He would change his name and everything about his past. No one needed to know about his time as a pirate. Maybe he would cross the Atlantic Ocean and sail over into the Pacific Ocean where he'd heard there were hundreds of islands where a person could hide. The idea was very appealing to him and as soon as he cleared the Straits of Gibraltar, he would chart his course.

Once he'd made his decision and his crew had trimmed the sails, Ezekiel felt himself relax, at least, a little. He knew he would not be able to become completely relaxed nor get rid of his anxiety as long as he was still in the Mediterranean Sea, or maybe even the Atlantic Ocean for that matter. No, he knew he could only relax once he was safely hidden on an island somewhere in the Pacific Ocean.

Ezekiel paced the deck of his ship, always looking behind him. He would go to the stern of the ship and put the long glass to his eye, searching for a ship that might be chasing him – and sighed heavily when he saw no one.

At night in his cabin, he would try to get some much-needed rest, but after only a short while, he would go back up onto the deck and look behind him with his long glass, even though he could see only a short distance in the darkness. His nerves were becoming raw. Why was the wind so light? Why couldn't it be stronger so they would have more speed? As he paced the deck, Ezekiel came to realize how his victims must have felt and didn't like the feel of it. If he could get free, he promised himself to become a recluse on some island in the pacific, where he would be safe from Malimar and the rest of the world.

CHAPTER SEVEN

While all of this was going on, unbeknownst to me, my crew and I sailed on toward an unknown future. It had been some time since my uncle had brought me any information on Malimar and his doings and I was feeling a bit anxious. I felt confident we would spot the entryway into the Straits of Gibraltar by sometime late tomorrow afternoon - and I needed to know what was happening before we sailed into what could be more trouble than I could handle.

I told Mister Collins, our helmsman, who informed Mister Finn, the chief bosun's mate, that I wanted to drop all sails and hove to until I could figure out what we were going to do.

With that done, I went below to my cabin and hailed my uncle, whose face appeared almost immediately. He looked aggravated and worn down and when he spoke, I could hear the tiredness in his voice.

"I know why you've contacted me and I'm sorry for not contacting you, sooner. But... the truth is, my brother has gone into the Mediterranean Sea area and has been causing so much trouble that it's been difficult to keep up with him. I think he's been trying to lure Ezekiel Bolingbroke out into the open so he can destroy him, but Bolingbroke is having none of it. He knows he can't go against my brother and have any hopes of winning. Bolingbroke has seen the destruction my brother is leaving behind and he is running for his life. The problem is, I haven't the faintest idea where the man is running to?"

Uncle Neptune sighed. "All I know is, his ship is sailing in the direction of Spain. Where he will go from there, I just don't know. I suspect he will leave the Mediterranean, but I don't have the slightest idea where he might go? On the other hand, he could just as well be hunting for a place to hide in Spain. There is too much going on and not enough information to back it up or make a prediction on what might happen next."

"I can understand why this Bolingbroke is running, indeed I can," I told my uncle, "and I don't blame him. We should be able to see the entryway to the straits by late tomorrow afternoon, and if he's coming through, we should be able to see him," I said with a certain measure of assuredness. "And if we do run into this Bolingbroke, am I to do battle with him? And what am I to do if Malimar shows up? I can't do battle with both of them at the same time."

The thought of what might happen in the next few hours was overwhelming and my body began to shake. Taking a deep breath, I willed my nerves to calm down.

The image of my uncle was standing only a few feet in front of me and I watched as he put his thumb and first finger up to the bridge of his nose as he considered my questions. After some time, he released his nose and blew out some air. "I'm not sure what to tell you lad. I wish I did. One side of me wants you to chase both of them down and bring them to justice, while the other side of me wants to keep you safely away from at least Malimar. After seeing all the damage he's caused, I'm afraid his powers have grown even stronger than they have been and his mind sicker than it's ever been."

I swallowed. I certainly didn't like the sound of that. But now was not the time to get all squeamish inside again. That would never do. "Do you at least know his location?" I asked, hoping he would know.

My uncle nodded his head up and down. "To the best of my knowledge, he is raiding along the coast of Greece, heading north toward the Aegean Sea, so you should be safe to enter the Mediterranean Sea and engage with Bolingbroke, if you can; but do so with great caution. I no longer know just how strong my brother's powers are. He may be able to detect your presence from that far away if you have to use your powers, or maybe he can't, I'm just not sure."

I could see the weariness in my uncle's eyes and the slump to his normally powerful shoulders, and I felt sorry for him.

By now, coming in contact with Ezekiel Bolingbroke was the least of my problems. He was a mere mortal, and of no real threat to me or my men as long as I kept my head.

My next question was because of my need to feel reassured. "With these stronger powers you say Malimar now has, do you still think I can stand against him?"

At that, my uncle ran his fingers through his hair and sighed – then looked at me and smiled. "Brody... Lad... as I've told you many times, you don't know the full extent of your powers yet. And I'm guessing you won't know until you have a need to call upon them. But to answer your question directly, yes. You have more power in you than he'll ever have. Your power is nearly equal to mine, but again, as I've said before, you need to strongly believe in yourself. That's where your true strength and power lies."

I awoke the following morning to the sound of waves washing against the side of my ship and I felt better than I had since embarking on this new venture. I felt certain we would encounter Bolingbroke, overpower him and be gone before Malimar knew we were anywhere near him. I swung my feet over the side of my bunk and stood up. I was hungry and could hardly wait for breakfast.

But... had I known what was about to happen, I might have pulled the cover back over my head and stayed in bed, which, of course, I would not have been allowed to do. Fate and Murphy's Law has a way of sneaking up on you and changing all of your carefully laid plans.

Horatio T. Hollingsworth was sixty-one years old. He stood five feet tall and weighed a little over two-hundred and thirty pounds. The top of his head was as void of hair as a sandstone but he still had, thin, stringy hair on the sides and back of his head, which was grey and hung down close to his shoulders. Not only was he vain, but had illusions of grandeur concerning his abilities to command a ship going into battle. Over the past forty years while working as a bookkeeper for the ministry of the navy, Hollingsworth had studied everything that had been written about naval warfare and deemed himself ready for command, even though he had no actual experience.

He had his workday planned down to the minute and would finish his bookwork early so he would have time to study seamanship and dream of someday being the captain of an English warship. In his mind, he could see himself standing on the bridge of his ship, bringing war to one of her majesty's enemies, then coming home to a hero's welcome.

One year ago, his dream had somewhat come true. A Spanish warship called El Diablo had been captured by one of her majesty's warships named *The Conqueror*. And indeed, the captain had come home to a hero's welcome.

Horatio was from a wealthy, and by now a very influential family, whom he hounded on a daily basis to help him get his commission. Horatio's kindly mother was particularly sympathetic to his whining and nagging, and put pressure on his father to pull his weight and help their son become an officer in her majesty's navy. Three months later, he was made a captain and given command of the captured Spanish ship, El Diablo, which no one in naval command gave a whit about, or wanted to serve aboard. And, if the truth was known, should Horatio and his ship go missing, no one in the ministry would mind one tiny bit.

Horatio strutted around like he'd just been made the King of England. At last, his dream was coming true, and with his mother's help, he created a uniform that made him stand out like a huge, ugly pimple on one's nose.

The El Diablo was a gaff-rigged Spanish Galleon, weighing in at twelve hundred ton. It was one hundred sixty feet long and had a beam of thirty-two feet. At the time of her capture, El Diablo was a cargo hauler and carried no weapons of any kind. Of course, as the ship's new captain, that was about to change.

Over the next six months, El Diablo was converted into a battle seeking ship, with a whopping hundred and fifty guns being added.

The crew was not at all to Horatio's liking, but there was little he could do about it. They had been selected by the ministry themselves, which Horatio guessed was to be a test of his ability to command. They were the dredges of the earth who, for one reason or another, had been sentenced to long prison terms. Fifty of the vilest men to ever walk the deck of a ship were released to go aboard El Diablo as its crew; with only a handful ever having stepped foot aboard a ship, before.

Horatio took one look at them and vowed to make fighting sailors out of them - whip them into shape. *Whip* being the operative word. Within the first half an hour of going aboard, Horatio called out a man who snickered at him in his shiny new uniform. He ordered the man to be strung up where, he, himself administered twenty lashes – then marched up onto the bridge and said, "I am Captain Horatio T. Hollingsworth and I will not tolerate disrespect for me or my authority. From this day forward, I am your Lord and Master. Anyone who challenges my authority will taste the whip, or, if I deem, be keelhauled. Any that might survive the keelhauling will be sent back to the prison you came from, to serve out a life sentence. The choice will be yours.

Follow my rules and you will be well taken care of. Disobey them and you will suffer the consequences. Any of you who might try to do me harm because you do not like my rules or methods will automatically be hung by the neck until dead, and your remains thrown to the sharks. Do I make myself clear?"

At that point, Horatio motioned for his four handpicked officers to step forward. They were men who had all been passed over for command and had a grudge against the ministry. They were armed with pistols and swords, and there was no doubt as to their duty and allegiance.

Horatio had chosen them because of their grudges against the ministry, and had paid them good money, along with other gratuities, to be determined later, to be not only the officers aboard El Diablo, but also his personal bodyguards.

The crew stood, staring back at their new captain, and Horatio could see the fear in their eyes. No man in his right mind wanted to face the whip. Nor did any man want to be keelhauled – which meant a man was tied to a line looped beneath the ship and dragged under the ship's keel and up the other side. Few men survived – depending on the speed he was dragged. And no one had ever survived being keelhauled the length of a ship. Nor was going back to prison an option any of them wanted to choose. At least here, they were somewhat free men. And, from what they'd seen so far, they had no doubt their new captain would hang a man for the slightest infraction. Tough and mean as they were, their lives were in the hands of this Horatio T. Hollingsworth, and they knew it. And, even if they were to disobey one of his orders, where could they hide? Nowhere. They would be on a ship in the middle of the ocean.

Strutting back and forth across the bridge, with his hands clasped together behind his back, Horatio continued his oratory. "I do not mean to be a harsh captain, but as I said, I will not tolerate insubordination. You are here because you are the dredges of society and were serving a life sentence in prison. I, Horatio T. Hollinsworth, secured your release to serve under my command, for I believe in giving a man a second chance," which was a lie, but the men didn't know the difference, and he wanted to instill at least a small amount of confidence in them. He'd read that in the book on commanding a ship about how to gain the trust of your crew, and making them feel obligated to their captain was number one on the list.

He stopped and placed his hands on the railing between him and the men below. "Why, you ask? Because I want fighting men, not sissies like some I've seen. It is my job to seek out the Queen's enemies and destroy them –

which is exactly what I intend to do. This ship and its crew will go down in history as the mightiest warship in her majesty's navy. We shall conquer any and all enemy ships we meet! When we return to port, it will be as, heroes – free men - not convicts!"

A cheer rose into the air and Horatio knew he'd done exactly what he'd planned to do – make them afraid of his wrath while craving the rewards he offered.

At that point, Horatio waved to a man standing on the pier and four men came marching up the gangplank, carrying kegs of rum.

"Enjoy the night - for come morning, we set out to seek our fame!" Horatio called out to the sound of more loud cheers. Reprobates they may be, Horatio thought to himself, but they are my reprobates and will do my bidding.

Horatio went below to allow his crew their night. Tomorrow they would begin what he hoped would lead to his being knighted. Such a small gesture as rum would insure their loyalty.

CHAPTER EIGHT

For some reason, I awoke feeling like this was going to be a wonderful day. The sky was clear and the sun was shining brightly. There was enough wind to make our sailing an easy task. Even the crew could feel it and were singing a lively tune when I came up from below.

"Beautiful day, ain't it, Captain?" Mister Finn shouted as I went up onto the bridge.

"Aye, that it is, Mister Finn. That it is," I called back, waving my hand in the air.

Mister Collins had just taken over from the night helmsman and looked as though he too had a good night's rest.

"If we continue on this course, we should see the entryway to the Straits of Gibraltar within a few hours," Mister Collins told me.

I nodded for him to continue. I then left the bridge and walked toward the bow of the ship where Mister Logan was standing with a long glass to his eye, staring off the port bow. I thought that was strange because our destination was to be slightly off to the starboard side.

"See something interesting do you, Mister Logan?" I asked as I approached him.

"Aye, that I do," he said, lowering the glass and handing it to me.

As I raised the glass to my eye to see what he'd been looking at, he said, "To me it looks like a Spanish Galleon, but she's flying a British flag, and she's heading toward us with all sails up. And if you look closely, you'll see cannon barrels sticking out of her port side. I think it's a ship that's been captured by the English and turned into an English warship."

I looked at the oncoming ship and had to agree with his evaluation. Suddenly, the great feeling I was having disappeared like a whiff of smoke. We were flying an Irish flag and to the best of my knowledge, England and Ireland were not on good speaking terms. As a matter of fact, an Irish ship captured by the captain of an English ship, would bring that captain a great honor.

I swung the glass to my right to see if we might reach the Straits of Gibraltar before the English ship could catch us, but was instantly distracted and took in a large gulp of air. I handed the glass back to Mister Logan and said, "I have a feeling our day is about to get somewhat complicated."

He lifted the glass to his eye and let out a long whistle. He'd seen the same thing I had - a ship that looked to have just left the straits, and was flying a skull and crossbones flag.

Mister Logan lowered the glass and handed it back to me and said, "It looks to me like we're between ah rock and ah hard spot, captain."

He was right. We were caught right between the two ships and neither of them would be extending an olive branch of peace.

Mister O'Callaghan joined us and Mister Logan apprised him of our upcoming situation. Mister O'Callaghan made a clicking noise with his tongue, then cleared his throat. He looked at me and asked "Do you think it would be cowardly for us to come about and maneuver ourselves away from this head-on disaster? And if we're lucky, the two of them will battle it out, without us having to get involved?"

It was funny because that is exactly what I was wondering. If the captain of the English warship saw both our flags, who would he be inclined to do battle with first? My guess would be me. The English have no love for the Irish and capturing one of their ships would be a big feather in his cap; whereas, a pirate ship might also be a feather in his cap – but not as big a one as an Irish ship.

I turned to Mister Collins and called out, "Come about! And be quick about it. We have an English warship bearing down on us from the port and a pirate ship coming from the starboard!"

As soon as I finished my order, I watched as Mister Finn started to call out my orders, then turned and ran up next to me, his eyes all sparkly and a wide grin spread across his mouth like he'd just committed some mischief.

I looked over my shoulder at the two oncoming ships, then turned back to Bosun Finn and said, "You look like you have something on your mind, Mister Finn. What is it?"

Mister Finn looked past me and figured we still had time, so he said, "Just the other day I heard you talkin' ta Mister Logan about you still wonderin' how powerful you might be?'"

"That's right, I did mention that to Mister Logan. So, what has that got to do with what's going on now?" I asked him, glancing over my shoulder again, looking at the advancing ships.

"Well-sir - them two ships comin' at us just might be ah way for you ta find out?"

"What in blue blazes are you talking about, Mister Finn? Don't you realize they both are planning on attacking us?" I asked him.

"Aye, Captain, I do. But what if you was ta try some of yer magic on 'em? You know, test your powers…"

"And what if they don't work?" I asked, glancing over my shoulder again and saw both of the ships were closing in on us.

"Well, lad, then you'll know and Mister O'Callaghan can see ta the cannons and Mister Logan can see ta the swords, rifles and pistols, and we'll give 'em ah right good fight, doncha know.

As I was trying to make up my mind about this hair-brained scheme, both Mister Logan and Mister O'Callaghan were issuing orders of their own, to ready the cannons and bring up all the weapons needed for hand-to-hand fighting, just in case.

"You can do this, lad," Mister O'Callaghan called out as he helped shove the barrel of a cannon out through the firing hole on the starboard side of the ship.

While that sounded like good advice, I wasn't sure if I was up to it, but I also knew I had to make a decision very quickly or plunge headlong into a battle with two ships at the same time. While the men seemed confident, I wasn't so sure. We were outgunned by both ships and there would be no catching them by surprise.

CHAPTER NINE

Captain Horatio T. Hollingsworth had been standing on the bridge, enjoying the morning when the man in the crow's nest called out, "Ship flying an Irish flag off the port bow, by five degrees, Captain!"

Horatio looked up, then ran, or rather *wobbled* as quickly as he could to the bow of his ship and put the long glass to his eye. Sure enough, there it was! And it was headed in his direction! Excitement rose up inside him like a child at Christmas. He'd been at sea for almost two months now and had yet to see another ship! Now, right in front of him was a prize worth waiting for – an Irish ship for the taking! He couldn't believe his luck. He would sail back into England with a prize that just might win him a knighthood.

"All sails unfurled and full speed ahead!" he yelled. Then turning to face his crew, he put both hands to his mouth to form a circle. "Battle ready the cannons and all hands ready for combat! We have an Irish ship to take, so, look lively, lads!"

As his orders were being carried out, Horatio made his way back to the bridge where he would oversee the taking of the Irish ship. He could picture it in his mind, their masts lying on the deck from being struck by his cannon balls; his men slashing their way through their motley crew, the Irish captain surrendering to his superior force, and him, personally binding the Irish captain's hands and taking him prisoner. He could even see them bringing the Irish ship back into port with people lined up on the wharf, cheering…

With all the excitement of capturing one of England's mortal enemies, the pirate ship off in the direction of the entryway to the Straits of Gibraltar had gone unnoticed.

The man in the crow's nest had his eyes glued on our ship and called out, "They're still coming, Captain! We'll overtake them in less than an hour!"

As Spanish Galleons go, they are by far one of the slowest ships to sail the sea, and because of their size and tonnage, they hold their own in high winds and storms, but seven knots, which equates to a little over ten miles per hour, is about as fast as they can safely go. And that is with all sails unfurled and a strong wind at their back.

"All sails unfurled!" Horatio yelled. "Run them down!"

The helmsman looked at Horatio's back and shook his head. All sails had been unfurled for some time now. The only reason they would get within firing distance was because they were heading toward each other. If the Irish ship decided they didn't want to fight, and turned away, there was no way they could ever catch up to them.

Horatio was about to have a heart attack with all his frustration at the slowness of his ship. His only consolation was the fact that the Irish ship was coming toward him, and all he had to do was give it a little time!

The man in the crow's nest turned to look around and almost had a heart attack when he saw the pirate ship headed toward both their ship and the Irish ship. "Pirate ship!" he called out. "Port side fifteen degrees!"

Astonished and surprised, Horatio was facing his first time in actual battle and he was about to have two battles going on at the same time. His breathing was coming in rasps and his brain was having a hard time coping with everything that was happening all at once. He tried to yell out orders, but nothing came out but a wheezing sound.

Fortunately, the few old salts in his crew came to his rescue as the helmsman swung the ship sideways, giving the port cannons a chance of retaliation against either or both of the ships coming down on them.

The chief bosun called to the cannoneers to ready their guns and when the ship was in position, he fired at the oncoming pirate ship, which was the closest, but because of being overly excited, the cannonballs fell into the water, well short of their targets.

Ezekiel Bolingbroke had seen both ships and recognized the English flag and the ship for what it was. But the ship flying the Irish flag confused him. There was no reason an Irish trading ship shouldn't be in these waters, but he'd never seen a trading ship with cannon ports. And why would an Irish war ship be here unless it was looking for an English ship to try and sink?

Had he accidently sailed into a battle zone, which at this point seemed to be the only conclusion he could come to. Ezekiel's first mate, a grizzled looking old man with only one eye who was known only as Peke, eased up next to him and said, "What say ye, Captain, do we back away and wait for them two ships ta do battle with each other, then take on the winner, if there is one?"

Ezekiel folded his arms across his chest and stared at the two ships for a long moment before saying, "I like that idea, Peke. Bring the ship hard to starboard, and move away from the immediate battlesight, then come back around so that we might observe the fight. But at the same time, ready the cannons and the men in case they are needed."

At this point, Ezekiel Bolingbroke could care not a whit who won the battle because the winner, if you could call him that, would more than likely be severely wounded and not able to put up much resistance, and he could then capture both ships.

Horatio stood on the bridge of his ship and watched as the pirate ship moved away from the upcoming battle. He was confused and couldn't believe what he was seeing. He felt his heart begin to pound with excitement. He could conquer the Irish ship without having to worry about the pirate ship, and when he was finished with the Irish ship, he would turn on the pirate ship and force him to surrender as well. Two ships in one day! They would return to England in style, and show that uppity naval ministry a thing or two!

Looking across the water in the direction of the Irish ship, he made his decision and called out to his first mate, Lieutenant Charles Brawley – "All cannons ready! Fire on the Irish ship on my command!"

"Aye, aye, Sir!" the lieutenant called back, hoping the captain knew what he was doing. He had never been to sea before, let alone be involved in a battle. The only reason he'd been made second in command was that he was the biggest and toughest man on the ship, which made him important to the captain as a bodyguard who could rule over the crewmen.

Horatio T. Hollingsworth knew he wasn't a brave man, but losing this battle and having to return home defeated, or being taken captive and made a slave, was not an option. He had to defeat both of these ships and return home the victor where he might live out his life as a hero. His mind was racing, trying to remember what he'd read in his manuals about battles at sea and as he did, he felt his confidence rise.

He could see it in his mind, coming into port with two captive ships and being greeted as a hero; everyone cheering. The ministry standing there with their mouths hanging open - then sitting around the fireplace at the club with his fellow club members hanging on every word as he recalled the bloody battles that brought him fame and fortune. Ahh, that would soon be his life; the one he'd dreamed of since he was a young man.

He stood on the bridge, watching as his ship and the Irish ship narrowed the gap between them. Very soon he would show the Irish what it meant to go up against an English warship. Yes, very soon he would hear their captain yell out, "I surrender!"

CHAPTER TEN

I had been standing on the bow of my ship, watching as the pirate ship moved out of the line of fire, along with watching the English ship come around, showing her port side guns to us – all the while, contemplating the idea of how to use my powers. Mister Finn had suggested I try out things I'd never done before. "Have some fun, lad," he told me.

Have fun. What a novel idea. With that in mind, I hurried back to the bridge and instructed our helmsman, Mister Collins, to bring the bow of the ship so that we faced the port side of the English ship, allowing them a narrower target to shoot at.

While the ship was coming around, I ran back to the bow and stood, waiting for us to get into position. By now, I could see the captain of the English ship standing on the bridge of his ship and I chuckled. He reminded me of a large, brightly colored ball sitting on top of two spindly legs.

I glanced over my shoulder and saw my men standing, staring at me, wondering what I was going to do. I nodded my head and said, "Let's have some fun, men."

"Yes, indeed, let's have some fun, Captain." Mister Finn called back, spreading his arms wide.

I turned back and waited until I saw the English captain raise his arm, readying his cannons for firing. At that point, I raised my hand in the air and waved to him, which caused him to pause and look at me like I'd gone completely daft. A large scowl replaced the confident look he'd had on his face. Then his look turned to one of anger. He dropped his hand and yelled, "Fire!"

We heard the roar of his cannons and saw the puffs of smoke rise from each cannon. At that point, I raised my hands out in front of me, hoping I could do this. I sent out a force that caused the cannonballs to stop and hang in the air for a moment before they fell into the ocean, not more than twenty feet from the English ship. And after they fell into the water, I bowed at the waist in the direction of the English captain, who was standing there with his jaw hanging open and his eyes as big as the bottom of a two-gallon bucket.

Next, I looked at the sky and created a huge black cloud to hover just above the English ship and without warning, dump water on the captain. No one else, just the captain – drenching him and his shiny new uniform.

Laughter erupted behind me and I glanced over my shoulder to see my men falling on the deck, laughing. Of course, neither the English captain nor his crew saw the humor in what I'd done. Ezekiel Bolingbroke had witnessed the whole thing and realized I was no ordinary Irish trading ship. And as the realization hit him that a wizard was commanding my ship, he also knew he would be helpless to defend himself against me.

"Come about! Come about! Run for the straits!" Ezekiel yelled, hoping he could get away while I was dealing with the English ship.

I saw what he was doing and sent my thought waves in his direction, and just as the bow of his ship was turning in the direction of the straits, four big, blue whales came to the surface and surrounded him, swimming a circle around his ship making it impossible for him to go anywhere.

I stopped the rain on Horatio and made the black cloud disappear, allowing him to get his wits about him once again. Standing there, dripping wet, he stared across at me with hatred in his eyes. I could tell he realized I was not an ordinary seaman, and wasn't sure what he was to do next. He was about to leave the bridge when I saw him stop and suck in a huge gulp of air. He had seen the whales come to the surface and surround the pirate ship, keeping it at bay.

Still frozen where he stood, Horatio was brought out of his reverie when he heard Lieutenant Brawley say, "I ain't never actually seen one, but I'm guessin' the one in command of that Irish ship, is ah wizard."

"That's what you think, do you, Mister Brawley?" Horatio said, trying to act brave, when in truth, his knees felt so weak he could hardly stand and his heart was racing like a greyhound chasing a fox.

"Don't seem ta me that he can be anything else, Sir. Not after what he done to us and now that pirate ship with them whales comin' up like that. Only ah wizard can do them things, and that's the truth of it."

Horatio's breathing was getting back close to normal and his heart had calmed down to jogging instead of racing, and he was about to say something when he heard a voice coming from the clouds.

He looked up to see the face of the most ferocious monster he'd ever seen. The thing had fire coming from his mouth and eyes that could burn their way into your very soul. The face was visible to both ships and, when it came, the voice sounded like it was coming from somewhere deep inside a cave.

"Drop all sails and surrender and I will allow you to live," the monster said, then blew fire at the ocean, causing a giant wall of water to go several hundred feet into the air.

"Resist, and I will see that you are all, one by one, eaten by sharks, or maybe by a giant octopus," the voice said.

I watched as both captains turned and looked in my direction and when I had their attention, I filled the ocean around them with sharks and a giant octopus.

I did it this way to put a scare into them they wouldn't soon forget, because the face of a fifteen-year-old boy didn't do much in the way of putting fear in them.

I left the monster's face staring down at them, waiting for their answer. After a minute, when there had been no response, the monster asked, "Cat got your tongue? What say you?"

The captain of the English ship was the first to speak. In a weak voice that sounded almost childlike, he said, "My name is Horatio T. Hollingsworth and I am the captain of this vessel. What... what is it you want us to do?"

Mister Logan, Mister O'Callaghan and Mister Finn were all now standing next to me as I continued to make the monster in the clouds, speak my words.

"I want you to put your longboats over the side. Then, you and your men climb down and get into them; then row away from your ships. Take nothing with you! No weapons, no treasure, nothing. Just the clothes you're wearing," the monster said.

Almost immediately the men in the pirate ship did as the monster commanded and I counted five longboats, with the man I presumed to be Ezekiel Bolingbroke, standing in the bow of the lead long boat. They rowed some distance away from their ship and stopped, hauling the oars inside the boats, then waited for the English crew to do the same.

While they sat there, the longboats bobbing up and down on the waves, I dropped a wall of fog over the ship. When the pirate ship was completely incased in the fog, I waited a long minute then lifted the wall of fog, leaving the ocean void of the pirate ship. It had vanished along with the fog.

The men from the pirate ship seemed to be talking to their captain all at the same time, and I knew I had made an impression on them.

I was having fun. My powers seemed to come at will and I felt no boundaries.

The men on the English ship lowered nine longboats and had climbed into them; waiting for their captain, but the English ship's captain stood proudly on the bridge, refusing to leave.

This disturbed me somewhat. I didn't want to see anyone drown. So, the monster said, "Captain, I will not wait forever. Get into the longboat with your crew, and be quick about it!"

I could see tears running down his face as he stood firm. And after only a few moments, he looked directly at me and I heard him say, "I am not a brave man, nor am I a coward. But... I am the captain of this ship and I will not leave her. The manual says the captain always goes down with his ship."

At that, I had to shake my head and wonder if I would have the courage to do that if I were in his position.

"Very well," the monster in the cloud said, then, looking down at the crew of the English ship, he said, "Move away from your ship. Go and join the others."

They did as the voice told them and I looked back at Horatio T. Hollingsworth, who still stood, stalwart, in his conviction to stay aboard his ship, no matter what.

A thought struck me and once the crew was far enough away, I raised my hands and lifted the ship into the air, then turned it upside down. Horatio grabbed ahold of the wheel and held on, but his weight was too much and his fingers slipped loose and he was dropped into the ocean, not far from his men.

This got chuckles from the men in my crew as Horatio floundered around in the waves until the men in his crew hauled him aboard one of the longboats.

Then, in a flash of light, his ship also disappeared.

I counted a total of fourteen longboats now adrift on the ocean and wondered what to do with them. If I left them alone, there were several possibilities. One, the men in the English longboats might attack the men in the pirate longboats, or vice versa. Either way, I doubted there would be a winner since they had no weapons and the fight would be with their bare hands. And, if that happened, the survivors would be left to their own devices, trying to make it back to land. There was always a chance, but a slim one, that they would make it. We were at least fifteen miles or so from land and the waves were anything but small. The second option would be for me to take them aboard and carry them to the nearest port? If I did that, should I release the English crew, who had taken a shot at me, or turn them over to the authorities with charges of trying to sink my ship? As for the pirate crew, I felt assured the authorities would be more than happy to get their hands on them. I stood there with these thoughts roaming through my brain.

Mister Logan had been standing a few feet away, watching as I stared out across the water in the direction of the longboats. He stepped closer and asked, "Made up your mind yet, captain?" The monstrous face was still glaring down from the cloud.

I waved my hand and the face disappeared, as did the black cloud.

I turned to look at him and saw my entire crew looking at me, waiting for my answer. I knew they would go along with whatever I decided, but instead of answering Mister Logan's question, I said, "As I have said before, on this ship, every man has a say. So, with that in mind, the decision isn't mine. We'll discuss our options, then take a vote. The final decision will belong to the majority."

Mister O'Callaghan stepped up next to me and whispered in my ear, "Ah, lad, you're becoming quite the diplomat, aren't 'cha?"

I looked at him and grinned. "I hope so. I could have made the decision as what to do with the men in the longboats, and everyone would have gone along with my decision, but in truth, I felt you men should have a vote as to their fate."

At that point I suggested the men give me their thoughts, but before their suggestions could be voiced, something happened that I had not given consideration to.

One of my men pointed toward the longboats and said, "Captain."

We watched as the men in the English boats, raised their hands in the air as though they were surrendering to the pirates.

I looked at the pirates who had pulled weapons from inside their coats and was pointing them at the English sailors. Then, in horror, we watched as the men in the pirate boats began firing their pistols at the English sailors. It happened so suddenly the English sailors had no chance to react and were all killed. While we were standing there, stunned, they turned their weapons on us and began firing at us. Two of my men were wounded before we could duck behind cover.

Anger welled up inside me like a raging tornado. I wanted to send down my wrath on them and send them screaming to Davey's Locker. And I would have, too, if not for the hand laid on my shoulder and the soft words of Mister Logan. "Take a deep breath, lad. Calm yourself before doing something you'll regret, later."

Through gritted teeth, I hissed, "Did you not see what they did?"

"We all did. And not a man of us would blame you if you do whatever it is you're thinking about doing. But remember this, sending men to their death during war time is one thing but technically, we are not at war with these men. You are a young man with wizard powers, and murdering men who don't stand a chance, is something that will eat at your conscious for the rest of your days. It would be mass murder, and speaking for all of us, we don't think you are that kind of young man."

I looked down and could see our doctor checking the two men who had been shot by the pirates and he nodded his head and gave me a thumbs up so that I would know they would be all right.

The pirates were still taking random shots at us as they rowed toward land, but they were now too far away to do us any harm.

I looked at Mister Logan. His words had an effect on me and I felt my nerves beginning to calm down. "Then, what do you and the men propose we do with them? We can't let them get away with a thing like that. We're all witnesses to their blatant murdering of men with their hands in the air, surrendering."

Mister Finn, my chief bosuns mate, and an old salt with most of his life being spent on a ship, raised his hand. "Permission ta speak, Captain?"

"Permission granted, Mister Finn. What do you have on your mind?"

"Well… it's like this, sir, you bein' the captain and all, well, you have the same power as a judge. Whatever you say, goes. So, I guess what I'm purposin', is, bring 'em aboard the ship and hold a trial. Call as many of us as witnesses as you feel you need to, cause we all saw what happened, then make your decision as to what's ta be done with 'em. Then it would have been done all proper like, and no one could say a thing against ya."

I looked at my men and asked, "All in favor of that idea, raise your hands."

To the man, every hand was raised.

As our ship got close to the pirates in the longboats, they looked up and saw at least twenty rifles pointed at them. They knew they didn't stand a chance and tossed their weapons over the side of the longboats.

Standing in the bow of one of the longboats, glaring at me, was the man I'd been sent to destroy, and I have to admit, I was looking forward to it. There was no doubt about his lack of compassion for his fellow man.

As we took them aboard, Ezekiel Bolingbroke remained sitting in the longboat, with a small trunk filled with treasure sitting in front of him. "I do not wish to be rescued. I will take my chances and row myself to land in this boat," Ezekiel said as though he had a choice.

I looked down at him and smiled. I had to admit, he was trying to brazen it out, but I would have none of it. "Nice try," I said. "I see you disobeyed your orders to leave everything behind and chose to keep weapons hidden inside your coats, and try and sneak away with some of your treasure. Tsk, tsk, tsk," I said, shaking my head. "But, as I consider myself to be fair, I will give you two choices. Your first choice is to come aboard and stand your chances at the trial I will be conducting. And your second choice is to stay in the boat and have my men sink it with you in it, after giving us that chest and whatever is inside. So, what will it be?"

Ezekiel looked at me with hate in his eyes. I had left him no real choice. If he came aboard my ship, he would be found guilty of his crimes and sentenced to death by whatever method I chose. Plus, I would have all of his treasure. And, if he chose to stay in the longboat, my men would sink it and he would die by drowning, or being eaten by sharks.

After a moment, with a defiant look on his face, Ezekiel lifted up the small chest of treasure and tossed it over the side of his boat, looking at me to see what I would do, but I did nothing. His treasure meant nothing to me. After a long while with us staring at each other, he began to row the boat toward the shore.

My men raised their rifles to their shoulders and waited for my command, but I said nothing. Instead, I pointed my hands in Ezekiel's direction and watched as his boat was lifted out of the water and deposited onto the bow of my ship, to more astonished gasps from the men of his crew.

I walked over and stopped next to his boat and said, "You didn't think I would let you get away and leave your men to suffer for your crimes, did you?"

The pirate captain stood up and stepped out of the longboat and glared at me. "So, you are a wizard, are you? I should have known. But how would you fair standing against me as a mere mortal? Do you think you could defeat me without your magic, man to man, with a sword in your hand?"

I knew he was searching for a way that didn't include a trial and a sentence of death. Choosing to die in combat, with a chance of defeating one as young as me was in his mind, the best chance he had.

I could understand his reasoning. I would never like to go to the great beyond by being hanged from a yardarm, either.

I turned to Mister O'Callaghan and said, "If you will, Mister O'Callaghan, make room here on the deck and have one of the men bring two rapiers."

While I waited for Mister Finn to bring the rapiers, I instructed my men to move the long boat from the bow and secure it somewhere. I was trying to act very nonchalant about this whole fencing affair, knowing it would make Ezekiel Bolingbroke nervous.

I also knew that being challenged; I had the choice of weapon, so, I chose the rapier because it was much lighter than a broad sword and I had become quite adept at fencing rather than hacking away with a heavy sword that quickly depleted my energy.

By the time Mister Finn showed up with two rapiers, the pirate captain and I had taken our coats and hats off, and were ready to do battle, which, to be honest, I wasn't looking forward to. I enjoyed fencing, but not when it meant I had to kill someone in order to win the match.

Mister Finn handed each of us a rapier, then stepped back and told us to touch our sword tips in preparation of the fight. We did, then waited for Mister Finn to drop his raised hand.

The pirate captain was surprisingly quick on his feet and almost immediately went for the kill, which I parried easily and flicked the tip of my rapier against his cheek, making a long, shallow cut that immediately turned red.

Stunned by my move, the pirate captain became more cautious with his moves, and it was evident he was an experienced dueler, which is why he challenged me, thinking he would have an easy kill - me being so young.

As we danced around, sizing each other up, he tried several moves against me that only a seasoned dueler would know about. But I was able to parry them, causing a look of concern appear on his face. It was obvious I was much better at dueling than he'd expected. Even with all his practiced moves, I felt I had the upper hand and began to cut him in various parts of his body with just the tip of my rapier. I could have killed him at any time, but as I said earlier, I do not like having to send someone to the great beyond. Besides, what I had in mind was to show him up. I wanted to see him disgraced in front of his men. Show them he wasn't the powerhouse he claimed to be.

Anger and frustration finally got the better part of Ezekiel and he began swinging his rapier like a broadsword, leaving himself wide open to be finished with just one thrust of my blade. Instead, I watched for the right opportunity and flicked his rapier from his hand and touched the tip of mine to his chest in a mock kill, then backed away.

I looked at Mister Logan and Mister O'Callaghan who were standing nearby, each with a pistol in their hand, and told them, "Tie him up, along with the others. We will commence with the trial first thing tomorrow morning – after breakfast."

If looks could kill, the glare I received from Ezekiel Bolingbroke would have ripped out my heart and fed it to the sharks.

CHAPTER ELEVEN

While I slept a night filled with horrific dreams, we sailed into the Straits of Gibraltar and then into the Mediterranean Sea, where my night helmsman decided to hove to and wait for me to come topside and decide what we should do.

I woke up, groggy and unrested. The thought of hanging men from the yardarm troubled me to no end, even though I had the authority to do so and I believed they deserved such punishment for all the evil they'd done.

I stumbled into the galley and got myself a cup of tea, then went topside, where I found the sky to be overcast and a chill wind blowing across the deck. The prisoners were standing, tied to one another near mid-ships, with their captain, Ezekiel Bolingbroke, tied to the main mast.

I had just taken a sip of tea and the sight of the prisoners and the thought of the trial ahead of me almost made me run to the side of the ship and empty my stomach over the side, which would have been absurd because I had nothing in my stomach to throw up.

Instead, I swallowed and willed my stomach to quiet down, then I made my way up onto the bridge, just as the night and day crews were trading places.

Mister Collins looked at me and said, "You don't look so good, captain. Maybe you should try to eat something and get some rest until you feel better. The trial can wait."

Before I could make a reply, Mister Logan appeared at my side and said, "Good morning, Captain," all respectful like, including a salute to impress our prisoners.

I returned the salute and he leaned in close and asked, "Can we go to the stern, lad?"

I nodded my head and followed as he led the way.

At the stern of the ship, we were out of earshot of the prisoners and after glancing over his shoulder, Mister Logan said, "I wanted to talk to you in private about what we're to do with the prisoners?"

"What are you talking about?" I asked, puzzled at his concern. To me the outcome was obvious...

"Well, you see, it's like this – it's been a long night and..."

I understood where he was going with this and I raised my hand to butt in. "Yes, of course. We are civilized. Please take care of it."

Mister Logan turned and gave a nod to Mister O'Callaghan who immediately began taking the prisoners, five at a time, allowing them to do their unmentioned business.

Turning back to me, Mister Logan asked, "What about food? Are we to feed them?"

With all my worrying, I hadn't given thought to the fact that it had been some time since they'd last eaten. As I recalled, even a condemned man is granted a last meal.

At the same time, another thought was racing around in my brain – one that might make me feel better about this whole situation. "Yes, feed them. The trial will commence once they've been fed."

And since I liked the idea that had come to me all of a sudden like, my stomach began to make noises, saying, "feed me."

I had breakfast brought to me in my cabin so I could sort out the details of my new plan, knowing that once I had things thought through, I would feel much better which allowed me to enjoy my breakfast.

Sometimes the storm isn't quite as bad as it first looks. But as it turned out, it took the rest of the day to sort things out, and during lunch, I instructed Mister Logan, my second in command, to remain where we were until I had things figured out. "Put the prisoners to work cleaning the decks or such other jobs you can think of, with our men overseeing them, of course."

And with that, I went back to my cabin to think.

My encounter with the English Captain, Horatio T. Hollingsworth, who wanted to become a hero by capturing me, but instead lost his life at the hands of the pirate Ezekiel Bolingbroke and his band of cutthroats, put the idea in my brain. In the end I finally decided I could pass judgement on the pirates for their crimes without having to administer the punishment.

As I sat at my table, feeling good about myself, another thought filtered its way into my head; one that would take more thinking about. By the time the candle had burned down to a nubbin, my brain felt exhausted and my eyes were having a hard time staying open, I went to bed thinking about my new problem, Malimar and the trouble I would have to face if we ran into him during my plan.

Malimar was not a happy man, or wizard, or whatever you wanted to call him. People were suffering because of his anger. He had searched the Mediterranean Sea and had found neither me, nor the pirate Ezekiel Bolingbroke. By now, he would be sailing north into the Aegean Sea, creating devastation and destruction everywhere he went because of his anger at not finding me. In my dream I could see the huge storms that washed over small coastal villages, turning them into nothing but scrap scattered across the beaches.

As it turned out, Malimar was in the northern part of the Aegean Sea, between Greece and Turkey when he felt a jolt of power slam into his brain. It was only a small jolt, but a jolt, nonetheless, which caused him to turn and look toward the west. Straining to understand where the jolt had come from, he felt it again and this time, he could pinpoint the direction, but not the exact spot. It was coming from too far away – somewhere far to the west.

Running to the bridge, he screamed at his helmsman, "Turn around! Turn around! Head for the Straits of Gibraltar, immediately!"

Both excitement and anger flooded his body. Excitement at finally locating the young wizard who had eluded him for so long, and angry because he was so far away!

Unable to wait for the long voyage back to the Straits of Gibraltar, Malimar ordered his crew to continue to sail with all sails unfurled, then turned himself into a sea eagle and lifted into the air, flying across land – Greece to be exact, in hopes of locating me.

He wasn't sure what he would do once he found me, but find me he must. There would be plenty of time to make that decision once I was within his sight.

CHAPTER TWELVE

I must have been exhausted because I slept the sleep of the dead. By the time I got up, the sun was nearly straight overhead when I made my presence known on the deck. As I walked up onto the bridge, I could see the nervous pirates staring at me, wondering if I was making them wait, on purpose – causing them to suffer the silence.

Prior to coming up to the bridge, I had instructed Mister Logan to see to gathering each man's name and a little about him, so I could decide his fate as fairly as I could.

While I stood on the bridge so all the prisoners could see me clearly, I called each man before me individually and listened to his story, making notes next to his name, before calling up the next man.

The process was intentionally a long one, forcing each man to try and guess his fate. They stood, watching and listening to each other's story. Sadly, not a one of them said anything worthy enough to entice me to lighten their future sentence. Most had been at sea a good part of their lives and had known little but pirating, which lent no grounds for leniency. Not one man said he was sorry and wanted to change his lifestyle.

Finally, I came to Ezekiel Bolingbroke, the captain of this band of rogues. "Have you anything to say?" I asked him as he stood, staring daggers at me.

He looked up at me and spit in my direction. "That's the only thing you'll get from me!" he yelled. "You've already made up your mind about my future. That's why you've brought me here, to see me hanging from the yardarm so you can take my place. If you're wanting to see me beg for my life, I'll not give you the satisfaction. But know this, young wizard - had you not come loaded with your wizardly powers, I would not have been so easily taken. So... do as you will, for I cannot stop you. But hear me, on this day I curse you to be imprisoned in a place so vile it is beyond description. May you have to watch as snakes and bugs of the worse kind, defile your body with infectious bites, while all you can do is scream from the pain."

And with that, Ezekiel Bolingbroke leaned his head back and laughed.

As I stood there, looking down at him, a chill ran down my spine. I didn't know whether the man had the ability to guarantee such a curse would be fulfilled or not, but just the thought of it created images in my brain that would definitely cause me to have terrible nightmares for some time to come.

Trying to brave it out, I smiled and said, "If I was inclined to believe in curses and such, I would be shaking in my boots, but, unfortunately for you, I do not believe mortals such as you can do anything but spout ineffective threats."

I looked out at my prisoners and told them, "It is the judgement of this tribunal that each of you is guilty of multiple crimes- and it is within my right to hang each of you."

An audible groan filled the air.

I waited until they quieted down, then said, "But... I have decided not to invoke my power to do so.

An audible sigh of relief filled the air, again, and when it subsided, I shared my plan with them.

"No... no one will hang on my ship today. Instead, I have decided to take you all to Greece, where I'm sure they will be more than happy to take you off my hands and dole out punishment for the many crimes you've inflicted on the people there.

This information brought about more loud groans. The atrocities they had inflicted on the people of Greece had been devastating, leaving a trail of death and destruction on both the east and west coastlines. They knew hanging would not be an option. That would be too quick. No, they knew they would suffer beatings and hard labor for the rest of their miserable lives, which is the way the Grecians did things.

I felt good about my decision. I had completed my mission without killing anyone. I felt sorry for the loss of the English sailors, but their demise had not been from my hands. That was on the shoulders of the pirate, Ezekiel Bolingbroke, which I planned to inform the authorities in Greece about.

I was about to give the order to set sail for Greece, when I felt a coldness engulf my body and looked up to see a sea eagle circling my ship. It was staring down at me with eyes the color of rubies with bright rays shooting out of them. I could feel them piercing my very soul. I swallowed and wanted to do something to defend myself, but my body felt paralyzed. Malimar had found me!

CHAPTER THIRTEEN

I watched as the sea eagle circled the ship a few more times, then landed on the bow and turned himself back into a man. For what seemed an eternity, he stood glaring at me. Then, with an arrogance about him, he walked up onto the bridge and stopped within a few feet of me, without anyone confronting him, including myself.

I could feel a force surrounding my body like a cocoon and I didn't like the feel of it. It reminded me of what people must feel like when I did it to them – wrapping them in a sort of cocoon so they could do me no harm.

I could see Malimar standing there, examining me from head to toe and I was amazed to find I wasn't afraid. Although I knew him to be the most powerful wizard in the air-breathing world, to me, he looked like nothing more than a normal man. And as I studied him back, he was only a few inches taller than me, and a few pounds heavier, but other than that, we looked very similar.

Suddenly, I'd had enough of being enshrouded in whatever was wrapped around me and gritted my teeth and exerted power to free myself. With a burst of energy that set me free, I saw him step back and stare at me with a curious look in his eyes. I was free of whatever spell he'd cast on me and I grinned at him, causing him more confusion.

He squinted his eyes to study me even closer as I just stood there, staring back at him, saying nothing. I didn't know what to say or do. I wasn't prepared to do battle with him, at least not yet – or ever, if I could figure a way out of it. He was my blood father, after all.

Finally, I guess the suspense got the best of him and he said, "So, we finally meet."

I said nothing. I just shrugged my shoulders and stood there, grinning like an idiot.

"You have given me some restless nights, young wizard. Do you know that?" he asked.

I continued staring at him with my foolish grin and again, just shrugged my shoulders. I wasn't sure how much he knew about me, if anything, and I wasn't about to reveal anything about myself until I had more information. I wished my uncle was here. I didn't know what he could do, since he had no powers above the surface of the water, but I wanted him here anyway. Maybe he could reason with his younger brother.

"You have broken the spell I cast upon you, so that means you do have a certain amount of power, but is it strong enough? That remains to be seen, doesn't it?" he said as a matter of fact, then sent a bolt of energy at me that knocked me back against the railing. I retaliated by sending a bolt of energy at him and watched as he was thrown against the opposite railing.

For the better part of an hour, we fought – raising each other into the air, then slamming each other down on the deck. At one point, we even turned ourselves into trolls and hammered on each other until we were both exhausted. At that point, panting, each of us changed back into ourselves.

I looked around and saw that my crew and the prisoners were still under his spell, and wondered if they could see and hear what was going on as I had been able to.

"You fight good," he said, "which makes me wonder who you are and where you came from?" he asked, bringing my attention back on him.

So, he didn't know I was his son. He didn't see the likeness, or did he? Was he trying to bait me into revealing my true identity? After a moment, I made a decision and said, "My name is Brody O'Shea and I am from Cork, Ireland. Who are you and where are you from?" I asked right back at him.

He leaned his head back and laughed a bone chilling laugh, then brought his attention back on me with those ruby red eyes. "I should do away with you here and now, but you interest me, young wizard. I want to know more about you before I cause you to die a horrible, gut wrenching, death."

It was my turn to lean my head back and laugh. I was playing a dangerous game and I knew it. If I pushed him too far, he might in his anger do away with me and my crew, and maybe even the prisoners, as well. But... for some reason, I wanted to brazen it out and not let him see the fear that had my insides doing summersaults.

"From what I have seen, you too, are a wizard, but you have yet to reveal your name. Should I have heard of you?" I asked him, puffing my chest out like a banty rooster.

This caused his eyes to go wide and he said, "You are an insolent pup, aren't you? Yes, you remind me a lot of myself in my younger days. But to answer your question, my name is Malimar. I am the mightiest and most powerful wizard in the world."

I thought by now he should have put my resemblance to him and my power together to realize who I really am. But apparently, he hadn't, so I continued with the farse.

"Really? I wonder why I've never heard of you?" I lied.

"What do you mean, you've never heard of me? I am known throughout the seven seas, Mister Brody O'Shea; which is more than I can say for you! And by the way, Brody O'Shea is no name for a wizard. Humph, Brody O'Shea, indeed. No matter because in the end, it isn't going to make any difference because by the time the sun goes down, you will no longer be a thorn in my side."

His words cut deep into my conscious brain. This was what I had always been afraid of; that when we met, I would cease to exist and I wasn't sure what to do about it. I had actually just fought with him using our powers and been able to stand up to him on equal terms. Neither of us had won, but neither of us had lost, either. I wondered if he had thrown his strongest powers at me, or had he just been playing with me. Maybe I should challenge him to a mortal type duel – with rapiers, maybe. At least that way I might stand a chance – a small one, albeit, but at least a chance.

The way I saw it, he more than likely used his powers to do battle for all these years and maybe, just maybe, he wouldn't be so good doing battle as a man.

Maybe I should try and reason with him? No, I didn't think that would work. To him I was a threat and his only recourse was to dispose of me. I wondered if I told him the truth - that I was his son, would that change anything? There were so, so, many questions bouncing around inside my head that I couldn't think straight.

He interrupted my thoughts by saying, "I'm getting bored. Say your goodbyes to whoever it is you pray to, if you indeed pray to some deity, young wizard."

And with that, he stepped back a few paces and waited. And when I just stared at him, he nodded his head and said, "So be it." He then raised his hand and sent a bolt of energy toward me, thinking I would just stand there and be blown apart. Instead, I raised my hand and sent a bolt of energy of my own out to meet his.

The two forces met in the middle, creating a giant ball of light as each of us held our ground, trying to overpower the other. I was standing face to face with him and holding my own. Something inside me seemed to grow and suddenly, I began to believe in myself and felt I could stand up to him. At least I hoped I could. But no matter what the outcome, I would not go down without a fight.

Malimar raised his other hand and sent a second bolt of energy at me, which I also repelled.

We stood, each sending bolts of energy at each other, with neither of us conceding. Not only did we send bolts of energy at each other, we changed ourselves into vicious animals and then trolls, again, that hammered away at each other, neither of us giving an inch.

How long this went on, I don't know, but as we stood there, testing each other's powers, a wall of water rose into the air and we heard a voice yell, "Malimar! Stop it right now! You don't know what you're doing!"

Malimar stepped back and looked at his brother and I did the same, our bolts of energy disappearing. I was never so glad to see anyone in my entire life. I felt exhausted.

I looked over and saw my uncle, King Neptune, standing on the back of a gigantic whale that was floating on the surface of the ocean.

Malimar looked at his older brother with a huge scowl on his face. "What are doing here, Artimus? This is of no concern of yours. Now go back down where you came from and play with your fish."

"Oh, but is very much my concern, little brother. You, Malimar, are about to make a grave mistake."

"Oh?" Malimar said, never taking his eyes off of me in case this was some sort of trickery. "And why would you say that?"

I could see the hesitation in my uncle's face and when our eyes made contact, I nodded my head for him to continue, and watched as he nodded back, wondering if he was going to tell him the truth about me?

"Destroying this young man would be the biggest mistake you've ever made and you have made a great many of them, little brother," King Neptune said with his hands planted firmly on his hips.

My uncle took a deep breath, then said, "Take a good look at him and tell me what you see?"

Malimar stepped to within inches of me and looked deep into my eyes for what seemed to be a long time – then stepped back and eyed me from the top of my head to the soles of my boots, tilting his head from side to side.

He then looked at his brother and said, "I see a young wizard who is full of himself and thinks he can take my place as the king of the wizards. That's what I see. What else is there to see?"

My uncle shook his head from side to side before saying, "Oh, there is a lot more to see, if only you would put away your bitterness and take the time to look."

"What kind of nonsense is that?" Malimar yelled. "I have looked at him! All I can see is an overzealous young pup who is full of himself who wants my throne."

"Yes, I suppose that's all you would see, isn't it? Yes, the only thing you can see is a threat to your livelihood. And you want to destroy that threat. Right?"

Malimar began to shake his head, then looked at my uncle and asked, "What is this all about? Why have you come to the surface? Why are you butting into my business? Talking nonsense."

Again, my uncle looked at me for a long moment, then turned his attention back on his brother. "I came here to stop a tragedy. For your information, he wants nothing to do with replacing you because, one day, he will be replacing me."

Malimar took two steps backward and sucked in a large breath of air. "What? Have you lost your mind? This whelp can never take your place, or mine. How can you say such a thing? Only I, as your brother and only heir, can do that."

"Oh, but he can, little brother. He can, and will, someday." King Neptune said with a smile.

"But that's impossible," Malimar sputtered. "He could only do that if he was your son, or mine - and I know you have no children, sons or daughters, and neither do I."

Both I and my uncle stood there, staring at him, saying nothing - and when he finally realized the implication of what had been said, he backed up even more and put both hands out in front of him. "Oh, no! No, no, no. There is no way this young rapscallion is my son. I have no sons. So whatever sort of scheme you've cooked up, it won't work on me. Now go away and leave me alone!"

My uncle stood firm on the back of the whale and waited for my father to stop his fuming before he spoke again. "Think back, Malimar, to the time some, sixteen years ago when you were raiding and pillaging along the Irish coast and the young lady in Cork you took a fancy to? Like so many other places you raided, you left with no regard as to what you'd done, only this time, you left something behind."

Malimar looked from my uncle over to me, and then back at my uncle. "No. That can't be," he said, with less conviction that he'd previously had.

My uncle just stood there, shaking his head up and down – a small grin on his face.

Malimar walked over close to me and reached out and ran his finger across my cheek, glaring at me with those ruby red eyes.

After a minute of being under his scrutiny, I said, "Hello, father. I've wondered when and if this day would ever happen."

He stepped back, shaking his head, still unsure about what he'd just heard. He wiped his hand across his mouth and said, "That would explain a lot; your having power and enough tenacity to stand against me. But that does not give you the liberty to try and kill me so you can take my place," he hissed.

Feeling braver with my uncle here, even though I knew he had no powers above the surface of the water, I looked at Malimar and asked, "What are you talking about? When have I ever tried to kill you?"

Malimar studied me for a moment, then replied, "What about just now, here on this very ship?"

"Who landed on my ship, imprisoned my crew and threw a bolt of energy at me, hoping to kill me quickly? I was only defending myself. Not once did I try to kill you, although there were a few times I believe I could have, if I had wanted to."

Lost for a rebuttal, Malimar looked at me, then over to my uncle, who just shrugged his shoulders. Slowly, Malimar turned back to me, and when our eyes met, I felt inclined to continue. "Just so we can get the facts straight, I never asked to be your son, nor did I ever desire to replace you or my uncle. None of this was my choice. But hear me now. I do not like what you have become and I will do everything in my power to see you dethroned. I do not wish you to die, just put in a position where you can no longer force your will on others. So, before this goes any further, please, stop. With all your power, could do so much good, if you would only do it, instead of being mad at the world all the time."

Malimar stood there, looking at me like I'd lost my mind, the anger welling up in his ruby red eyes. And after a long silence, he spat out, "You have no idea why I am the way I am!" His breathing was labored and he was clinching his fists open and closed. Finally, he yelled, "This is not over!" And with that, he turned into a sea eagle, again, and flew off toward the eastern shore.

I looked over at my uncle, still standing on the whale's back and saw the sadness in his eyes. "I'm sorry things had to end this way," I said.

He nodded his head and said, "You did all you could do at this time. But beware, Brody. Now that he knows, I have no idea what he will do, and you may still be in danger."

"I understand, and I will," I said, hearing mutterings of oohs and aahs. I looked down onto the deck and saw that the men of my crew, along with the prisoners, were awake again and were staring at the man standing on the back of the whale.

Before things got out of hand, I raised my hands and put them to sleep, again.

"They won't remember a thing when they wake up," I told my uncle just before the whale dove back down into the ocean, taking my uncle with him.

Even after my uncle had disappeared beneath the water, still, I waited for a few more minutes before awakening the men on the deck of my ship.

When they awoke, I was standing on the bridge, looking down at them just as I had been when Malimar had arrived in the form of a sea eagle.

The men were, all looking around, staring at each other, confused, knowing something wasn't right, but not sure what it was.

The sound of my voice brought their attention back to me.

"As I was saying, instead of wielding out the justice that I am entitled to do, I will be taking you back to Greece to be turned over to the authorities there. I feel sure the punishment they will come up with will be far more agonizing than the quick death of swinging from a rope."

Once again, I heard the loud groans and other remarks coming from the prisoners, but pretending not to notice, I looked down at the members of my crew, who still stood guard over them, and said, "Mister O'Callaghan, will you and Mister Finn, see to the securing of the prisoners? And when they are secure, I want us to get underway for Greece."

"Aye, aye, Captain," Mister O'Callaghan called back, raising his hand again, in a salute for the benefit of the prisoners. I smiled and headed for my cabin. I had had enough excitement for the day.

Once I got down to my cabin, l plopped down on my bunk. Every muscle in my body hurt from the battle I'd had with Malimar. My body was pleading for sleep, but just before it came, I suddenly realized I hadn't said anything about having a twin sister, and for some reason, I was pleased I hadn't done so. There was no telling how he would have reacted to that? I would save that bit of information for a later time – if there was to be a later time... And with that, I smiled and drifted off into a deep sleep.

CHAPTER FOURTEEN

Not only was Malimar flabbergasted at the thought of having a son, he became very upset with the thought of me taking my uncle's place as the ruler beneath the seas. That should have been him, and the only way that wouldn't happen is if he was somehow dethroned. Generally speaking, having a son meant very little to him. I was just the after effect of a dalliance he'd had during one of his raids. But, now that I had come to his attention and had basically the same powers he did, I was much more than just his son. I was a threat against all he'd been hoping for, which was my uncle's death so he could take his place as the rightful heir as King of the Seas.

He paced the inside of his quarters; his mind in a tither. Had he known about my birth and taken me with him – raising me and training me to be the next in line after he'd gone, might have been different. But that had not been the case. Others had raised me; mortals, with all their high and fancy morals. Then his own brother, who he despised, had gotten involved and only he who knew what nonsense he'd put in my mind. So now, he had not just his brother to contend with, but me, also, and I was a bigger problem than his brother was. Some way – somehow, he needed to take me out of the picture.

Unable to rest, Malimar went back up onto the deck of his ship and lifted himself up into the crow's nest, and stared for a long time at the sea, knowing rest would not come until he had this whole whelp thing under control.

Willing himself into the air again, he lowered himself back onto the deck. He paced the deck from bow to stern and back again, several times, wondering what he was going to do. Could he murder his own son? He wasn't sure, and that bothered him. Taking the lives of people he didn't know was one thing, but his own son?

He knew his brother's powers could only cause him minor setbacks, like causing an ocean storm to slow him down, or maybe whales ramming the side of his ship. Things that would cause him only mild distress. He could deal with that, and had done so for many years. It was having a son with power, he feared. I was real and on the surface with powers that could someday mean his dethronement. No matter what I or his brother said, Malimar was convinced I meant to dethrone him and take his place, which in his mind meant only one thing... I was sent by his brother, King Neptune, to kill him.

Standing on the bow of his ship that continued to sail toward the entryway of the Straits of Gibraltar and then the Atlantic Ocean, my father talked to the empty sky. "You may think you have outsmarted me, brother of mine, by enlisting the aid of my whelp, but you have yet to see what I am capable of. You have not won the day. Not by a longshot."

He knew what he needed to do. He looked toward the bridge and yelled, "I want all sails unfurled! Do it now!"

And when his orders had been obeyed, Malimar walked to the stern of the ship and looked out across the water. He raised his hands in the air and shouted, "Come, strong winds. Speed my ship to its destination!"

And with that, a heavy wind filled the sails and the ship was propelled at a speed much faster than it was designed to go.

When the ship seemed to be literally flying across the water, and all members of his crew were hunkered down, holding on for their lives, Malimar stood with his legs spread wide and his fists on his hips. He leaned his head back so he could see the sky, and let loose with an evil laughter that caused every man on his ship to shutter with fear.

Only when most of the Mediterranean Sea was behind him and the Straights of Gibraltar only a few miles away, did he allow the winds to drop and allow his ship to continue on at a pace consistent with the normal sailing speed.

During the night, Malimar awoke with a feeling that made him hurry up on the deck and allow his mind to search for me. Smiling, his powers found me and he knew I was headed in his direction. As he stood there, his plan began to take form in his mind and he called for the winds to come from the starboard side of the ship. When all sails had been adjusted, he told the helmsman to head for the city of Algiers.

Algiers was a city on the coast of Algeria that was noted for its wide-open wildness. He would allow the men to go ashore for a couple of days to take their aggressions out on the people they came in contact with. He calculated it would take me that long to get into the Mediterranean Sea, allowing him to come in behind me and keep a close eye on me and what I was up to.

As for me, I realized none of this and had no way of knowing what trouble I would be facing in the near future.

Being anxious to get my prisoners deposited with the authorities in Greece, we were a good forty miles away from land when we sailed past the lively city of Algiers and all that was going on, there.

Little did I know the dolphin swimming along beside us was Malimar.

CHAPTER FIFTEEN

The trip across the Mediterranean Sea was slow and uneventful in comparison to what we'd recently gone through. A few days later, we were happy to see the port of Athens, Greece; a city where our prisoners had raided and pillaged enough times that they were more than happy to take them from me. We were assured their punishment would be long and filled with agony for the many crimes they had committed.

We spent the next three days resting and recuperating – enjoying the hospitality of the mayor of Athens, who it seemed couldn't thank me enough for stopping the reign of terror Ezekiel Bolingbroke and his band of thieves had bestowed on them and other cities along the shores of Greece.

The men of my crew were more than happy to join in the merriment that was heaped upon us by the local citizens. There was singing and dancing; along with enough wine to sink a ship. More than one beautiful young lady tried to tempt me from my loyalty to Kathleen, but I held steadfast to my promise to her and went to sleep in my bed each night with a clear conscious.

In all this merriment, what I didn't notice was the tall, aristocratic looking man who was always somewhere nearby wherever I seemed to be. Oh, I'd noticed him a few times, but he looked like he belonged there and he never approached me, so I just assumed he was a local who liked to be out and about. You'd think by now I had learned to be more cautious and suspicious, but apparently, I hadn't.

After three days, I was beginning to feel homesick and tracked down Mister Finn, surprisingly, not in a bar, but at an outdoor music concert. He was sitting near the front row, holding hands with an attractive woman near his age, and when I took the seat next to him, his face turned pink. Stammering, he introduced me to her.

As it turned out, she was the owner of a bakery Mister Finn had wandered into and after a little chit-chat, they had felt an immediate and strong attraction to each other. I was more than a little suspicious when Mister Finn asked if we could speak privately.

He excused himself and we walked away to a place under the limbs of a huge apple tree. Mister Finn reached up and plucked two juicy looking apples, and handed one to me.

"I feel there is something on your mind, Mister Finn, and you seem a bit reluctant to say what it might be," I told him straight off, then took a bite of the apple and waited for his reply. To my great delight, the apple was one of the best I'd ever bitten into and I was content savoring the juices. I took a second bite and chewed contently as I looked up at the sky, waiting for him to speak.

I smiled when I watched a shooting star cross the night sky.

Mister Finn still hadn't bitten into his apple and was toying with it like he was holding a ball - tossing it back and forth, from hand to hand. Finally, he stopped tossing the apple back and forth, made a big sigh and said, "Well sir, it's like this... Lisa, that's her name, Lisa."

He'd already told me that during the introduction and now here he was, repeating himself, which caused my stomach to grumble. I thought I knew what he was going to say, but waited for him to say it, and to prompt him to reveal his real meaning for bringing me out here. I said, "Yes, you said that when you introduced me to her. And that she owns a bake shop down on the wharf that you accidently wandered into. And, since you've brought me out here, I can only assume there is something else you want to say. Something you don't want to say in front of Lisa?"

"Well now, yes, sir, there is, lad," he said, putting the apple in his pocket.

"And what might that be?" I asked, watching him squirm.

"Well sir, ya see, sir..." He took a deep breath and said, "I've decided I want to stay here, with Lisa, and well, I'm askin' yer permission to abandon ship."

I wasn't surprised by his statement, but tried to look like I was. With a surprised look on my face, I asked him, "And may I ask, just what are your intentions with this nice lady? I hope you aren't planning on taking advantage of her…"

"Oh no, sir, nothing like that, sir. We've taken ah shine to each other and we're plannin' on gettin' married. That's the other reason I brung ya out here. You, bein' the captain and all, well, it's my understandin' that as the captain of a ship… well, you can marry people. And yes, lad, I'm hopin' you'll allow me ta leave the ship, but it would mean ah lot to me if'n you'd marry us before I go ashore for good and become ah landlubber."

The thought of being the one to marry them was a gigantic surprise to me and I wasn't quite sure what to say. On one hand, it was a great honor to be asked, but on the other hand, I had never performed a wedding before and I wasn't sure what I was to do, or how to go about it? And the truth of the matter was, I didn't know if it would be legal for me to marry them.

After a long silence, Mister Finn was the first one to speak. "Are ya all right, lad? This whole thing is a surprise ta me too, ya know. Never thought I'd ever find ah woman who would want the likes of me. It was her that done the askin', and well… that's when I realized I have feelings for her, too, so I said, yes. But I also told her I would be needin' yer permission ta leave the ship. The part about you marryin' us is my idea," he said, beaming from ear to ear.

"Yes, I'm fine. Just a bit surprised and overwhelmed, by it all," I told him, trying to get a grip on myself. Finally, I grinned and reached out and shook his hands. "If you're sure about this, then you have my permission to leave the ship, and congratulations."

"And what about the marryin' us part?" he asked with a questioning look in his eyes.

"About that. Before I can commit to anything, I'll need to check the book and see what all it entails," I told him in all earnest.

Mister Finn shook his head up and down and said, "I was on ah ship, oncest where the captain performed ah weddin' and as I recall, he said they had ta be out ta sea at least three miles afore he had the authority ta marry anybody. And fer the words, I ain't got no notion of what yer supposed ta say, but I reckon its somethin' along the lines of if'n we care about each other and want ta live ah life tagether from now til we go to the great beyond? It would be something like that."

I agreed to look into it and get back to him early tomorrow.

I hurried down to the wharf, and went out to my ship, forgetting about my urgency to get underway and go back to Boston. I searched one of my books and low and behold, I found a section that discussed a captain's right to marry people.

I had just climbed up onto the wharf when I saw Mister Logan and Mister O'Callaghan coming toward me. I quickly told them about Mister Finn and his lady friend.

They both seemed genuinely happy for him and Mister Logan suggested we make it a big party with all the crew invited. "After all," he said, "it's like one of the family leaving the ship to retire."

Of course, the entire crew would be invited. Afterall, they would need to be aboard to sail the ship since we would be going to sea to perform the ceremony. So, the following day, without disclosing all that was to happen, we brought Mister Finn and his bride to be, aboard the ship. I put her in my cabin, for the time being and we set out to sea.

After we got underway, with the permission of the crew who allowed since she was to be married to one of their own, she would not be a curse, I allowed Mister Finn to bring her topside.

Of course, Mister Finn, being our Chief Bosun's Mate, wanting to show his position on the ship, stepped up and began shouting orders, which the crew hopped to straight away – wanting to make him look important to his bride to be.

By mid-afternoon, we were several miles out to sea, well past the three-mile limit when I asked Mister Finn to hove to, which he saluted me and turned and began shouting orders, like he always did.

The men, wanting him to look good, jumped to and in quick order, the ship was rocking gently on the water. I then ordered Mister Finn and Lisa to go below and put-on whatever clothing they were to be married in, and not come topside until I sent for them.

As soon as the two of them were out of sight, the crew commenced to decorate the bridge, even to building a giant arch where the ceremony would take place. Earlier, I had laid out my captain's uniform down in the galley, since Mister Finn and Lisa were using my cabin. When the decorations were finished, I went below to get dressed. I wanted to look the part for the bride and groom.

There were oohs, and aahs when they came back up onto the deck. Lisa looked very beautiful in her wedding dress and flowers in her hair. She informed us it was the same dress her mother had been married in. It was snow white and filled with lace. She wore a lace shawl and a veil over her face. As for Mister Finn – well, all I can say is I would never have recognized him. He was bathed and clean shaven and smelled like he'd just stepped out of a men's parlor. He was dressed in a black suit that fit him like a glove, making him look just like a dapper gentleman.

With knees rattling like a rattlesnake's tail buzzing, I somehow stumbled through the proceedings without hearing half of what I said, and sighed a huge sigh when I heard myself say, "As the captain of this ship and by the powers vested in me, I now pronounce you, husband and wife. You may kiss the bride."

And as Mister Finn stepped forward and took her in his arms and kissed her, there were loud whoops and hollers from the crew.

The party lasted well into the night. One of the crew brought up his concertina and another, a fiddle. Far into the night there was music and dancing and more toasts than I could count.

Finally, Mister Finn, who had remained somewhat sober, made his way up onto the bridge and raised his hands for quiet. And when the only sound was the waves washing against the side of the ship, he said, "There ain't enough words ta express my feelings right now but I think you all know how I feel. And I want ta thank each and every one of you from the bottom of my wicked old heart, [which got a hardy laugh] for doin' this for me. I will never forget any of you, or the times we've had tagether. But there comes ah time…"

"Oh, hush up!" one of the crew yelled. "We know how you feel and we feel the same way but if you don't take your new bride and get outta here, she might change her mind!"

And with that they headed down below to my cabin, to cheers and pats on the back.

The following morning, I met with Mister Finn privately and gave him not only his wages, but the money I'd been setting aside for just such an occasion, when he was ready to retire. "You'll not have to go into this marriage without funds of your own," I told him.

Mister Finn looked at the pile of money and jewels lying in front of him, then up at me, and with tears in his eyes, he said, "This is more money than I've ever seen, lad. And you're sure it's all mine?"

"Aye, that it is, Mister Finn, and as far as I'm concerned, you've earned every farthing."

"I'm a rich man, then – thank you," he said standing up and putting his hand out to me.

After shaking hands, he hefted the bag of jewels and gold, he said, "Thanks to you, my Lisa will never lack for anything."

Feeling a bit embarrassed, I jokingly slapped him on the shoulder and shoved him toward the passageway. "Get out of here and go start enjoying your life before I change my mind."

Two days later, we left Athens, with all hands waving goodbye to their shipmate, Mister Finn, now a married man and landlubber. Lisa stood next to him, all smiles with one arm around Mister Finn's waist.

As the wind caught the sails and the ship began to move slowly toward the ocean, I glanced over my shoulder and off to the side, I saw the tall man, dressed in black, that I had seen several times before. But this time, a cold chill ran down my spine. He had never said anything to me, nor had he spoken to any of my crew, but suddenly I got the feeling something about him was not right. Being always in the background, along with being distracted with the wedding, I never associated him with being Malimar and that he was keeping an eye on me.

CHAPTER SIXTEEN

Prior to the wedding, at the suggestion of Mister Finn, Nolan Burke was brought aboard the ship. Before bringing him aboard, Mister Finn had stated, "Nolan is a long-time friend and a chief bosun in his own right – him bein' a son of the sea for some sixteen years now, with the last nine as chief bosun on ah tradin' ship out of Dublin. As fate would have it we ran into each other at Lisa's bakery and went to the tavern next door where we shared a pint or two, and well… as it turned out, the ship he was on is bein' retired here in Athens and he was about ta go lookin' fer a position on another ship. Well, lad, I couldn't believe my good luck. With yer permission, I know Nolan will make ah good replacement fer me."

And with that he clamped his mouth shut and folded his arms across his chest, waiting for me to make a decision.

Grinning, I accepted Nolan aboard as the bosuns mate, subject to the men accepting him too. And now he shouted orders as we sailed into the wide Mediterranean Sea with a southerly breeze coming from our port side.

We were all excited at the prospect of going back to Boston, and somewhere along the way, Malimar had been completely forgotten.

Shame on me, for as soon as we left the harbor, the tall man in the dark clothes made his way to the jail where Ezekiel and his cutthroats were being housed and put the guards to sleep. He then went in and made a deal with Ezekiel. "If I turn you and your men loose and provide you with a new ship, you have to promise to share any and all of your spoils with me, forever – and be at my beck and call, should I need you."

Of course, Ezekiel eagerly promised. Anything to get out of the lifetime of hard labor he'd been sentenced to.

Malimar stared at him through the bars and knew exactly what kind of man he was dealing with – a lying, backstabbing crook who would agree to anything to get out of prison. "Hear me and hear me good, mortal. If you try in any way to welch on our deal, I will find you and the things I will do to you will make this place look like heaven."

Ezekiel studied the man in the black clothes and ruby-red eyes and realized who he was and what he was capable of. He took a large gulp of air, and finally said, "I will do as you say. You have my word as one pirate to another."

Malimar leaned his head back and laughed. He'd never known a pirate's word to be worth a farthing. They were all liars and thieves who would do anything to get what they wanted. "Just do as I tell you and you will live to be a rich old man, for I will also protect you if you come under attack. But... try to cheat me and you will never know peace, ever again."

And with that, Malimar dissolved the locks on the prison doors.

Out on the wharf, they looked over the several ships at anchor. "Choose the one you wish to leave on and I will get it for you," Malimar told Ezekiel.

Licking his lips, Ezekiel looked the ships over and saw one sitting away from the others. It was a caravel that looked fairly new, and it caused his heart to pound when he saw it was already equipped with cannons. She was long and looked like she would have speed enough to run down any of the trading ships he would attack and if need be, out run any warship chasing him. "That one," he told Malimar. "The caravel in the far corner of the bay."

Malimar eyed the ship with a critical eye and smiled. "You have chosen well. Wait here. I shall go and acquire the ship for you."

And with that, Malimar turned into a sea gull and flew out and landed on the deck of the ship. And when one of the seamen tried to shoo him away, he turned himself into a troll and tossed the man overboard.

Ezekiel and his men watched as Malimar ejected the crew from the ship and when the captain came rushing up onto the deck, Malimar turned himself back into a man and spoke to the captain. "You have two choices, Captain.

You can sign your ship over to my friend, Ezekiel Bolingbroke, and I will allow you to jump overboard and swim for shore. Or, you can refuse and I will cause a hundred crows to swarm down on you and peck on you until you scream for me to allow you to sign the papers. The choice is yours."

The owner of the ship, within the past week, had inherited the ship from his seafaring brother. He, himself had never been to sea, nor had he ever had a desire to go to sea. He was comfortable being the overlord of his fairly good-sized farm. He had only come aboard to see what the inside of a ship looked like and had it in mind to sell the ship, but now, with this wizard staring down at him, threatening his life, he signed the ship over to this, Bolingbroke – whoever he might be.

In a very short time, the papers had been signed and the man was swimming toward the shore, thankful he'd been allowed to live.

Malimar climbed over the side with a smile on his lips and stepped into the longboat tied there. With a wave of his hand, he commanded the longboat to take him to the shore, where he handed the ownership papers to Ezekiel, saying, "Remember our deal, mortal."

A chill ran down Ezekiel's back and his tongue felt thick. All he could do was nod his head up and down, whispering, "I won't forget. I will keep a log and your share will be ready for you anytime you want it."

Satisfied with himself, Malimar jumped into the water and turned himself into a dolphin again, and swam away to the stares of Ezekiel and his men.

Again, being ignorant of what Malimar had done, I stood on the bow of my ship and watched as the miles sped by, never realizing that my journey was far from being over.

We had cleared the entrance to the Straits of Gibraltar by half a day and was now back in the Atlantic Ocean as I came up onto the bridge to give Mister Collins our helmsman a new course.

When I came topside, the sky couldn't have looked more beautiful – a bright blue with a few white puffers floating lazily across the blue background. The wind was out of the north and we were on a starboard tack. "Come to…" I said, just as the sound of thunder rumbled across the air and the sky turned black as night. Lightning struck the water causing it to churn up, tossing my ship around like a rag doll being shaken by an angry dog.

Then, out of nowhere, Malimar appeared in the form of a giant. His eyes were flashing bolts of light and flames were coming out of his mouth, scorching everything they touched. "You didn't think I'd forgotten about you, did you?" he hissed!

He stuck out his hand and I was lifted into the air, wrapped in a web like cocoon.

As I floated in the air, some thirty feet aside and above my ship, I watched as Malimar blew into the sails of my ship, sending it on its way, with my crew standing in horror – watching me being lifted even higher before being sucked into the black cloud.

I tried as hard as I could to break this spell, but to no avail. I now realized that earlier, he had just been toying with me to see what kind of power I had. Now, he was showing me that I still had a long way to go to dethrone him.

CHAPTER SEVENTEEN

I don't know how long I sat in the dark, wet, stink of the hold of Malimar's ship, but it seemed like an eternity. I was given nothing to eat or drink for what I guessed to be three days, and I could feel my strength evaporating a little more each day.

At first, I had tried to loosen myself, fight back, extract myself from the cocoon, but all I did was tire myself out. Next, I tried contacting my uncle, King Neptune, to ask for his help, because technically the hold of the ship was beneath the surface of the water, but again, I came away exhausted, with nothing to show for my effort but a throbbing headache.

Finally, I tried to send my thoughts out to my twin sister, Cory Anne. We had always been able to speak to each other with our minds, but this time, my efforts were once again, all for naught.

After several more days and nights of feeble attempts to break free of my bonds, or contact someone, I gave in to exhaustion; knowing if I was to survive this ordeal, I needed to conserve my strength. And with that, I did my best to relax and sleep as much as I could in case the impossible happened – that I somehow was able to free myself.

The sky was a brilliant blue and a cool breeze loafed its way across the green pastures where Kathleen and I were riding side by side. She was riding Beauty and I of course, was riding Hurricane; but we weren't racing. The horses were just sauntering along at their own pace. Kathleen and I were close enough that we were holding hands. I must have said something funny because she leaned her head back and laughed, and it sounded like an angel singing.

That's when I felt something smash against my ribs and a harsh voice yell, "Wake up!"

Stifling a groan, I opened my eyes and looked up into those fiery ruby-red eyes of none other than, Malimar.

"On your feet, boy!" he yelled, kicking me, again with the toe of his boot.

I looked down and could see I was no longer wrapped in the cocoon. Rolling over onto my stomach, I pushed myself up and found that after being wrapped in the cocoon for so long, I had a difficult time getting to my feet – and when I did, I had to grab ahold of a crate next to me to steady myself. Every joint in my body ached and I felt far too weak to try anything.

Even in this dark, damp place, I could see Malimar's image standing in front of me from a light coming from the passageway that led up to the deck and fresh air. He folded his arms across his chest and glared at me.

I seemed to have lost all my powers and I wasn't sure how much longer he was going to allow me to live, so I gritted my teeth and stared right back at him.

Slowly, a scowl crossed his mouth and he said, "I don't know what kind of scheme you and that soft-hearted brother of mine have cooked up, but I'm here to tell you that I don't believe a word of it. You are not my son! I have never sired any whelps! But if I did, he would be nothing like you! He would be like me! Strong of will and would never allow my brother to brainwash him, like he did you!"

I just stood there, trying my best to regain my strength, but with having no food or water for such a long time, it wasn't easy. I even tried willing my strength and power back, but nothing happened, and that's when I realized how much power my father really did have. He had somehow stripped me of my powers and had taken complete control of me. I was at his mercy, if he had any in him.

Still, I would not allow him to feel any victory over me, so I just stared at him, saying, nothing.

"I could kill you, here and now and never lose any sleep over it," he said with a snarl.

I could see the disappointment in his face when I chose to say nothing in return. I think he wanted me to grovel in fear and beg for my life, but I did none of those things. I just stood there as if what he said meant little to me.

"Have you nothing to say for yourself?" he asked.

I straightened up as close to my full height as I could and said, "You can deny me all you want, but the truth is, I am your blood son and you will never be able to change that no matter what you say or what you may do. And, the truth is, I don't like you any more than you like me, because I believe you are an evil man. And because of who you are, I never want to be like you, nor do I dream of someday taking your place."

I could see his eyes getter redder and hear the raspy breathing as his chest rose and fell. I could see his jaws tightening - and I could feel his anger, which at any point could erupt, causing my death, but, unrelenting, I plunged on.

"The truth is, I was happy believing I was just a mere mortal. Life was much simpler and the people who raised me are fine, decent people. It was your brother who told me the truth and asked me to help him make the world a safer place – a world where people like you no longer exist, and someday will be spoken of as nothing more than mere myths. That I may someday replace my uncle as the ruler of everything beneath the ocean is yet to be determined. I'm not so sure I care much for that idea, either."

We stood for a long time, staring at each other. I'd said my piece and would wait, letting him make the next move, whatever that might be.

After a while Malimar nodded his head up and down, as a slight grin spread across his face. "You are strong of will, I will give you that," he said, unfolding his arms. "Even if I believed all you've told me, it would still make no difference to me. You are a threat to my way of life – a life of my choosing. And I will not allow you or my brother to interfere. Granted, I could kill you now, but my brother would eventually find out about it and if you recall, I reluctantly promised him I would not do so. But… I did not promise I would not make sure you could no longer be a threat to me or those of my kind. What I have in store for you will be a long, slow death that will be filled with pain, but not coming from my hands. I will, however, from time to time, come by for a look at your despicable decaying body."

And with that, he leaned his head back and laughed that bone chilling laugh he had.

Just as quickly as the laughter came, it stopped and he raised his hand and snapped his fingers. The passageway was darkened by someone coming down the steps and in less than a minute, food and water was set down in front of me. After setting the food and water in front of me, the frail little man turned and scurried back up the ladder and disappeared.

Malimar looked at me and said, "Eat. You will need all the strength you can muster for what I have in mind for you."

As quickly as he'd appeared, he was gone.

I dropped down on my knees and looked at the food in front of me. The aroma almost caused me to pass out. There was leg of lamb, boiled potatoes with some kind of gravy over them, three kinds of vegetables and in a bowl next to the platter was what looked like an apple creation of some kind. I wanted to cram it all into my mouth and fill my empty stomach as fast as I could, but knew if I did, it would make me sick. So... with great restraint, I took my time and nibbled on the food until I felt full, then took a small drink of water, saving the rest of the food and water for later when hopefully, my stomach wouldn't reject it.

Hours later, with a full stomach, I could feel my strength returning, somewhat – but not my powers. Whatever spell he'd cast on me was much stronger than anything I could do to undo it.

As I sat there in the darkness, my mind was filled with curiosity over what he had in mind for me. He said I would need all the strength I could muster, which could be a thousand different things.

Several hours after feeling nourishment for the first time in I don't know how long, I was able to stand up and walk around a little. But when I tried to go toward the open passageway, I was blocked by an invisible wall. Even though I could walk around - any way you looked at it, I was still imprisoned. I sat back down and picked up the leg of lamb bone and nibbled at the small bits of meat left on it.

There was nothing I could do but wait for his next move because worrying about what he had in mind for me would do no good. "What I need to do is concentrate on getting my strength back and then, my powers," I said into the darkness.

CHAPTER EIGHTEEN

Cory Anne O'Shea sat cross-legged on her bed with her fingers pressed against her temples and said, "Brody, where are you? Brody, I need you to answer me. Brody, can you hear me? Answer me! Oh, little brother of mine, you are so in trouble when you return if you don't answer me right this minute! Brody! Please, answer me!"

Dropping her hands into her lap, Cory Anne sat staring out of the window of the flat she rented during her time in New York studying the violin. She wasn't supposed to know it yet, but one of the ladies in the office let it slip that Cory Anne had finished as the top violinist in her class and was going to be rewarded by being asked to play a solo at the governor's mansion during the birthday bash they were holding for him next week. Cory Anne was thrilled. It would look good on her less than impressive resume once she was out looking for places to play. Since I was far away and she couldn't spill the beans to anyone else before she graduated, she wanted to share her news with me. She was becoming very upset and frustrated not being able to contact me.

And especially right now, I have to tell you, I would have been very happy to receive her mind talk, but sadly, I was not able to. Malimar's hold on me was very strong - much stronger than I ever imagined it could be. How at my young age, could I possibly have believed I could go up against him and win? All of this, you have all the power you need, you just have to believe in yourself, was just so much hooey. For several days now, I have been believing I could break free of Malimar's hold on me, but that did about as much good as trying to punch harder than a giant gorilla.

Cory Anne climbed off her bed and paced around her room. Something was wrong – she could feel it in her bones. She knew I wouldn't intentionally shun her mind talks. But whatever was keeping us apart was beyond her grasp. She had come up with several scenarios that could prevent us from speaking to each other, but one by one, she tossed them aside as not true. "Then what is it?" she cried out loud.

Suddenly, she felt the impulse to go home. Maybe her parents would know something. As much as she wanted to, she knew she couldn't leave until she graduated, which was still three months away.

"Oh!!!" she screamed as she stormed out of the flat; and that was the day she began to run. Besides playing the violin, running became the second-best thing she loved to do. Running helped relieve the stress and anxiety over not knowing about me or her future. Part of her stress was finding out most of the great violinists had to go back to Europe to make a living as a musician.

Here in the new world, people loved hearing her play, but there just wasn't enough places that would hire her. She loved playing the violin and knew she had a real feel for it, but she didn't want to move back across the ocean. She loved this new land and she loved the ranch and stables her father had built up. As she ran, she wondered if living with her parents and working there, with a chance to play here and there once in a while would be enough? From time to time, she would concentrate on sending a thought wave to me, hoping I would answer, not knowing I was a thousand miles away, locked in the hold of a ship with an invisible shield around me, keeping her mind probes from getting to me.

Had she known about my predicament, I honestly believe nothing else would have mattered, not graduating, not upcoming concerts, nothing. She would have found a way to try and find me. After all, we were twins.

What she could have done once she found me, I don't know? She was my twin sister and we were bonded to each other in a special kind of way, but did we share the same powers? I had yet to encounter a female wizard.

CHAPTER NINETEEN

Mister Logan, Mister O'Callaghan, and Mister Collins, along with the rest of my crew, eased my ship into the Boston Harbor and dropped the anchor as quietly and as inconspicuously as they could, not wanting to face anyone just yet. My not being with them was not going to be easy to explain since it involved wizardry and magic. They were aware my parents knew about me and my powers, but how would they explain to them that they had to just stand there and endure what was happening to me without trying to do something about it?

"Who's going to tell them?" Mister Collins asked of Mister O'Callaghan and Mister Logan who were both standing on the bridge, staring at the front door of our shipping company, hoping my father had gone home for the day. But of course, such luck was not in their favor.

In fact, my father had just stepped out of the front door, intending to close up for the day. After locking the door, he turned to go to the stable where he kept a horse, and in doing so, noticed a ship coming into the harbor. After satisfying himself that it was my ship, he turned back and went down to where a man sat in a row boat, fishing and offered to pay him to row him out to the ship.

The man agreed and the men on my ship grimaced when they saw him approaching the ship and groaned when he began to climb the rope ladder and come aboard.

Mister Collins looked at Mister Logan and Mister O'Callaghan and said, "Looks like you need to make a decision, and soon."

As soon as my father climbed aboard my ship and saw the look on everyone's faces, he knew something was wrong. "What has happened? Where is Brody?"

Mister Logan, being the second in command, stepped up and said, "It's a bit of a story, Sir, and I'm thinking it will be better told down in the captain's quarters."

Reluctantly, my father nodded his head. He wanted to know right now, but knew it would do no good to argue, so he followed them down to my cabin.

Once there, Mister Logan and Mister O'Callaghan poured out the whole story, knowing my father knew about me having powers, but not sure Malimar had ever been spoken about.

Father sat quietly listening to every word and when Mister Logan finally said, "And I'm sorry to say, that's all we know."

"But he was alive the last time you saw him?" my father asked.

"Yes, very much so. And like we said, we spent two weeks looking for any sign of him or Malimar's ship, before sadly returning to Boston," Mister O'Callaghan replied.

"Thank you," my father said, standing up. "And the rest of you are unharmed?" he asked.

"Aye," Mister Logan said. "And if it's alright with you, we'd like to replenish our supplies and go back out."

"And just where would you go?" my father asked.

"To the Caribbean. That's where Malimar is known to spend a lot of time," Mister O'Callaghan said. "There's rumors he has a home in Jamaica. Maybe that's where he took him."

My father gave this some consideration and after thinking about it, he said, "Come by tomorrow and I'll see to giving you what you need."

Back up on the deck, Mister Logan told one of the crew to take my father back to shore in the longboat, then announced that the crew could have shore-leave, but only for the night, explaining come morning, they would be restocking the ship and he would need all hands. He went on to assure them they would have two full days' leave once the ship had been restocked, before heading off to the Caribbean to search for me.

What they thought they could do to stand against Malimar and his powers if they found me, was yet to be discussed... And I can only guess they'd decided to cross that bridge when they came to it.

My mother was working in her flower garden when my father rode in and went directly to the barn. She'd looked up and waved, but he didn't seem to notice her, which seemed strange since he was always delighted to be home and always waved at her if she were outside. Suddenly a feeling came over her and she put her hand over her mouth and stood up – then ran toward the barn. Mother was big on premonitions.

When she entered the barn, she saw him standing with his hand raised and pressed against the wall. Tears were streaming down his cheeks. She silently walked up next to him and stopped; afraid to say anything because she thought she knew the answer, but also, because of her need to know, she was afraid not to ask.

My father must have noticed her because he turned and took her in his arms, saying, "It's going to be all right. It has to be."

"What's going to be all right?" she whispered, afraid of his answer.

He guided her into the kitchen and sat her down at the table, then made a cup of tea for her before spilling out everything he'd been told. And when he'd finished, he sat, staring at my mother, who sat in silence for what seemed to be an eternity. Finally, she stood up without a word being spoken, went over and began preparing the evening meal while stealing herself from breaking down and crying. While she worked, her mind drifted to Cory Anne and she wondered if somehow, her daughter knew what was going on?

As the days had passed, Cory Anne struggled her way through the festivities, including her graduation. As the top student in the class there had been a lot of pats on the back and congratulations, without much enthusiasm on Cory Anne's part because of worrying about me and not being able to contact me. Making a decision, Cory Anne canceled two events where she was to play, saying she was needed at home, hoping they would understand – and if not, they needed to understand that family came first with her.

She packed her bags, closed out her flat and bought a ticket on the first passenger coach headed for Boston, which was being loaded as she came out of ticket office. She knew the trip would take four days with nightly stop overs to change horses and give the passengers a reprieve from being jostled back and forth all day long. At her young age and the urgency of her trip she would just as soon gone straight through – stopping only to change horses and grabbing a quick bite to eat. But that was not how the passenger coachline worked. "You'll be stopping every night for your comfort and well-being," the stationmaster had told them, to the delight of the other three passengers.

Her growing concern for my well being kept her from eating much or getting a decent night's sleep. And during the day it was all she could do to keep from yelling for the driver to go faster.

It was late afternoon when she reached Boston and lugging her suitcases, she headed down to the wharf to see if her father was still in his office. That's when she saw my ship sitting at anchor and her heart began to pound. Maybe she'd been worrying for nothing, she thought as she opened the door to the freight office and rushed inside.

Father looked up and saw Cory Anne but had conflicted feelings. First and foremost, he was happy to see her – but, secondly, he wondered why she'd come home unexpected and unannounced. And lastly, because of what he needed to tell her.

One look at father was all it took to read his face and feel her anxiety return. "What has happened to Brody?" she blurted out, even before they'd hugged.

Father knew how close we were and knew he couldn't whitewash anything to keep the truth from her. Plus, he knew of our telepathic communication. "Have you heard from him through that mind thing you do?" he asked.

"No!" Cory Anne blurted out. "That's the problem; he doesn't answer me! Is he here? Is he hurt and can't answer me? He is alive, isn't he? Oh, I know he must be. I would have known if something that bad had happened to him. Can I at least go to him?"

Father let her ramble on until she'd exhausted all the questions built up inside her. He guided her over to a chair and sat her down, then explained all he knew, and when he'd finished, he said, "They're loading the ship as we speak, and will be leaving in just a few days – as soon as the crew has rested, at least a little. They've been through quite an ordeal, themselves."

"I see," Cory Anne said, the wheels in her head spinning like a leaf in a windstorm.

Now that she knew the reason, she hadn't been able to contact me, she was determined to do something about it. Just what, she didn't know, but she knew the ship wouldn't be leaving without her.

CHAPTER TWENTY

Once again, I was sleeping when I felt the toe of a boot slamming into my ribs and a gruff voice yelling, "On yer feet, boy!"

Taking a large breath to try and alleviate the pain, I opened my eyes and looked up at a face covered with a scruffy beard and weary eyes that had seen far too much evil and destruction since his shanghaied arrival on the ship. "The Master wants you topside. Now get on yer feet and get movin'," he yelled.

I did as I was told and when we got to the bottom of the stairs leading up to the deck, I got a whiff of him and turned my head back. He was filthy dirty and stunk as bad as I did since not having a bath during all this time. Absently, I reached up and ran my hand over my own face and felt the makings of a beard, myself. I had been shaving every day for over a year now because I didn't like the look or feel of a beard on me.

My slight hesitation warranted me a hard blow between the shoulder blades. "I told you to get movin'! Now, move!"

I wanted to reach out and smash him in his ugly face, but even though I'd been allowed to eat for some time now, my strength wasn't what it should be, so I shielded my eyes and slowly climbed the stairs.

I felt a certain excitement as I stepped out onto the deck. My being able to come up from the hold meant the shield that kept me down there, had been lifted. My next thought was whether my powers had returned now that I was free of his hold on me.

It took a minute or so for my eyes to adapt to the brightness of the sun, and when I peeked between my fingers, the first person I saw was Malimar. He was standing not three feet in front of me. He had his fists on his hips and hatred in his eyes. I felt a shudder run up my spine. I expected him to say something, but he pointed to the bow.

Finally, I was able to drop my hand and look around. Less than half a mile directly in front of the ship was brown water flowing into the ocean as far as I could see from north to south.

"That is the mouth of the Amazon River," Malimar told me. It was discovered a few years ago by a Spaniard named, Vicente Yanez Pinzon."

"If this truly is a river, then why do I not see land on either side of it's opening into the ocean?"

He smiled one of his rare smiles and said, "Because it is well over two hundred miles wide here. Even one hundred miles into the interior of this country which is called Brazil, the river is still six miles wide."

This was hard for me to believe. I had never seen a river so wide you couldn't see across it, and I said so. "You expect me to believe there are rivers you cannot see across?"

The smile left his face and he said, "I do not care one whit what you believe or do not believe. I am only telling you this so you will have some information about your new home."

I felt my chest constrict and I heard myself saying, "My new home?"

The smile returned to his face as he said, "I understand that, where you will be living there are snakes more than thirty feet long that can swallow a three-hundred-pound pig without any trouble. And the spiders... I don't think you really want to know about the spiders... And of course, there are hundreds of stinging bugs that love to suck the blood out of you."

He raised his index finger in my direction and said, "I'm told there are giant red colored ants as big as my finger. I'm also to understand that when they go on a raid, they clear everything in their path for a half a mile wide – including humans."

His smile increased when he saw the look in my eyes. I hated snakes, spiders and bugs. I looked back at the brown water rushing out into the ocean and becoming a part of it. He must have noticed what I was looking at because he said, "I'm told there are man eating fish in this river. I don't know the name of them, but I'm assured they are there."

Man eating fish? Did he mean sharks? I didn't think so, but I couldn't determine how much of what he was saying was the truth and how much was lies to scare me.

As we came closer to entering this mighty river, I could feel the heat and humidity filling the air and it made my nose sting. I suddenly realized this was the place he'd spoken of some time back when he was telling me of my future.

"Do people actually live here?" I asked, and watched as his eyes began to twinkle.

Spreading his arms wide, he said, "Oh yes. There are many tribes in the vast jungles and you will need to be very cautious. I'm told they do not like intruders, especially ones with light skin, like yours. There are several tribes who are eaters of men, and if they catch you, you will wind up sitting in a pot of boiling water as their next meal."

And with that, he leaned his head back and laughed at his little joke. When he'd finished, he continued. "Most of the tribes, if they catch you, will brand you as a slave by tattooing snake-like lines on your face. The men will force you to do their work and the women will beat you with sticks if you don't do it the way they want it done – that is, if you survive the snakes, ants, bugs, spiders, and wild animals."

Again, he leaned his head back and laughed, then said, "Oh, did I forget to mention the man-eating plants? Ghastly things. If, while traveling through the jungle, you happen to pass by one, it will reach out and grab you, then drag your screaming, fighting body into its folds and that's the last anyone will ever see of you."

As Malimar's ship entered the rushing water of the Amazon River, Malimar had to use his power to cause a strong wind to push the ship forward. I was taken back down to my prison with the invisible wall that kept me there and was left to my fear of what was going to happen to me.

I watched the passageway, counting the days we sailed up the Amazon River and counted nine sunrises before I was summoned once more onto the deck to meet with Malimar.

The ship had come to a stop and sat idly in the water. Here, the river wasn't as wide, maybe a half a mile at the most. The heat and humidity were overwhelming. I guessed it must be well over a hundred degrees on land, and not much better, here in the middle of the river.

Two men had come for me this time and when I was close, they shoved me toward the railing. I stopped just short of going over the side and looked at Malimar, who was holding a wooden bowl that held several pieces of meat.

"I want to show you that I was not lying about the man-eating fish. Look over the side of the ship," he ordered.

I stepped near the railing and looked over at the brown, muddy looking water. Malimar stepped over near me and tossed a few pieces of meat into the water.

I jumped back at the almost instant churning of the water. There were hundreds of the fish, all fighting for the pieces of meat. Malimar tossed the rest of the meat in, and within seconds, it had been devoured by these little creatures no more than four to six inches long.

Malimar looked down at me and said, "What do you think will happen if I toss you over the side of the ship and tell you to swim for shore?" Do you think you could make it?"

I stared down at the now still water and knew exactly what would happen if I tried to swim for shore. I would last less than a minute.

Malimar shook his head and said, "No, lad. That would be far too quick of a death. As I told you some time ago, you will have a slow, tortuous death. Many times, will you beg to die before you go to meet whatever deity you believe in."

"Why are you doing this?" I asked.

"Why? I think you know why. I promised my brother, the man you seem to care so much about, that I would not kill you outright. But that does not mean I cannot, somehow, be a contributing factor. I thought long and hard about how to dispose of you without doing it myself and as you can see, I found the solution I was looking for."

I heard a snarl coming from the shore and looked in that direction. Standing on a tree limb near the shore was a very large, black cat. He was looking at us with no fear in his eyes. His snarling left no doubt in my mind as to what would happen if we were to meet. With no weapon or powers, I would be his next meal.

"Are you telling me you are putting me on the shore, leaving me to fend for myself?"

"Very astute, you are," Malimar said, nodding his head. "Yes, the jungle you see, will be your home for so long as you can survive. And from the stubbornness I've seen in you, you will find a way to keep from dying – at least until you are too weak to fight any more."

The jungle looked dark and forbidding, and I was afraid. I looked at my blood father and from the look in his eyes, I knew he wasn't lying about leaving me here. "Will I be allowed to take any weapons with me? Knife, broadsword, hatchet, anything?"

"You will be allowed the clothes on your back and one knife. That will be all," Malimar said with a snarl.

"And what about my powers? Will those be returned to me?"

"NO!" he screamed. "I have taken your powers away, forever!"

"Then why are you abandoning me here in this God-forsaken place? If I no longer have any powers, what danger to you can I be?"

He stared at me for what seemed to be a long time. Finally, he said, "If, and I say, if, what my brother claims to be the truth, that I am the father of a whelp like you, I cannot allow you to grow to manhood and someday be taken down to one of my brother's cities and given the throne that rightly belongs to me. Even with your powers gone, you still are a threat to me. I don't believe you are my son, but I shall take no chances. You will die, here in this jungle - and that will be the end of it."

Malimar turned and motioned to his men, who lowered a longboat into the water and forced me into it, then rowed me to the shore and tossed me unceremoniously onto the muddy ground. I climbed to my feet and watched as Malimar's ship left me standing there, all alone.

So, this was how it was to end. For the first time in my life, I felt weak and vulnerable. I looked around and could barely see a few feet into the dense jungle, that waited for me with at least a hundred different ways to see to my demise. I would die here with no one to mourn my passing – devoured by whatever flesh-eating creatures lived here. Maybe, someday my bones would be discovered, but even that was highly unlikely. As Malimar wished, I would just disappear, never to be seen or heard of again.

"No!" I screamed. "I will not give in that easily!"

CHAPTER TWENTY-ONE

It was close to midnight. All the shops and stores and offices were dark inside when Cory Anne creeped down along the wharf. She was dressed in dark clothes and carried a satchel wrapped in waterproof canvas.

My ship had been tied up to the wharf so it could be cleaned and loaded with supplies for the trip to try and find me. At supper last night, my father made the announcement that the ship would be leaving with the morning tide, and Cory Anne had made up her mind to be on it when it sailed out of the harbor.

Her only problem was that she couldn't make her presence known until they were too far out to sea to turn back. If she were found she would unceremoniously be put ashore.

Cory Anne also knew all of our ships had night watches. The harbor was relatively safe at night, but a night watch was added insurance that temptation didn't get the best of someone.

Cory Anne had kept to the shadows and was now within just a few feet of the ramp leading up to the main deck. In the moonlight, she could make out the man on watch. He was standing near the ramp, puffing on a pipe and looking up and down the wharf.

Cory Anne stood in the darkness near the front of one of the buildings, wondering how she could create a distraction that would take him away long enough for her to sneak aboard.

The powers that would be must have been smiling down on her for at that very moment, two men came running down the wharf, one chasing the other. When they were close to my ship, the man in the rear called out, "Nate! Are you on watch? This man stole my wallet. Give ah hand." The voice was none other than Mister O'Callaghan.

The man smoking the pipe must have been Nate, because he rushed down the ramp and ran toward the man running in his direction. The thief turned and tried to go back, but Mister O'Callaghan was blocking his way. He stood there, only a moment when he made his decision and ran over to the edge of the wharf and dove into the water.

The night watchman, Nate, dropped his pipe on the wooden floor of the wharf and dove into the water – along with Mister O'Callaghan.

Cory Anne wasted no time. She picked up her satchel and made her way up the ramp and immediately headed down below. She had been aboard my ship enough times to know where she was going, and in no time, she stepped cautiously into the galley and filled a sack with food, then made her way down into the hold and was quickly, hidden behind some crates. She chuckled to herself as she spread her bedroll on top of a long crate, where she could sleep comfortably. She had a place to hide, food and water enough to last until they were at least a week out to sea. She smiled as she lay down.

Meanwhile, Mister O'Callaghan overpowered the thief and held him under the water long enough to make him give up and hand the wallet back.

Normally, he carried very little money on him and hardly ever paper money. So, if a thief should happen to steal his wallet, he wouldn't think much about it. But this was not just ordinary money he was carrying. It was the money given to him by my father to pay for the trip, and for extra supplies, or any other need they may have – like paying for information.

With the wallet in his possession once more, he turned back and swam for the shore, with Nate not far behind. Mister Logan had heard the noise and had climbed out of bed and got dressed to go find out what all the commotion was about, never realizing he had just barely missed seeing Cory Anne sneaking down the passageway.

After meeting up with Nate and Mister O'Callaghan, and getting an explanation, he went back to bed, shaking his head. Mister O'Callaghan, on the other hand, had to shed his wet clothes and boots and dry himself as best he could. The stove in the galley still had some smoldering coals and was hot enough for him to make some tea and leave his clothes nearby to dry. He was in the process of putting on dry clothes when the cook, who ironically was named Cook – Jack Cook, came through the door and halted. When he recognized Mister O'Callaghan, he asked, "Hungry are ya?"

Mister O'Callaghan smiled and said, "As a matter of fact, I am, but that's not the reason I came in here in the first place," then went on to explain his reason for being there.

Mister Cook looked around and got a questioning look on his face. "If you didn't come in here to eat, where's the missing food?"

"Missing food? What missing food? I don't understand," Mister O'Callaghan told him.

"It's as plain as the nose on your face, Mister O'Callaghan. I don't suppose you would notice a thing like that, you not bein' the cook and all. But I could tell right away. That block of cheese is some shorter than it was when I went to bed. And there were four loaves of bread sittin' on the counter, and now there's only two. So, what do you make of that, sir?"

Mister O'Callaghan scratched his head and said, "Maybe one of the other hands came in before I got here and was hungry and helped himself to something to eat."

"I suppose that could be it, but… I'm not so sure. That much cheese and two loaves of bread is a lot for one person to eat. Plus, there might be other stuff missin', too."

"Maybe there were several hungry people here tonight," Mister O'Callaghan said.

Mister Cook thought for a moment, then nodded his head. "Spose you could be right."

Lying comfortably on her blanket, deep down in the hold of my ship, Cory Anne never knew she came very close to being discovered.

First tide came early the following morning, with the sun just barely creeping over the horizon, and when the tide went back out to sea, my ship went with it.

My ship had just cleared the entryway to the harbor when my father pulled his horse to a stop near the end of the wharf. The horse was panting from running hard all the way from O'Shea Stables, to where he now stood. My father stepped down and rubbed the horse's wet neck, saying, "You did all you could."

Earlier, my father had stopped at Cory Anne's bedroom door and knocked, calling for her to come down to breakfast, and when he got no reply like he usually did, he opened the door just wide enough to stick his head in. "Cory Anne?"

And when no response came, he stepped inside her room and looked around. The chest where she kept some of her clothes had two drawers standing open.

At the thought of what that meant, he shook his head, saying, "No, no, no!"

My mother heard him and came into the room asking, "What's wrong, dear?"

My father turned and stared at her for several moments before he said, "I'm afraid Cory Anne has done something stupid."

"What on earth are you talking about? You're making no sense."

My father pointed at the empty drawers and then the bed, saying, "I'm afraid she's gone down to try and sneak aboard the ship and go with them to try and find Brody."

Mother's hand went immediately to her mouth and, after a moment, she said, "You need to go after her! Surely, they won't let her go with them, will they?"

Father shook his head and said, "I don't think they will – but what if they don't know she's aboard. She could have sneaked aboard during the night."

Mother pushed my father on his shoulder, then said, "Go! Get her off that ship before it sails! Hurry, you've no time to waste!"

He hadn't even taken time to saddle his horse and rode him hard, but it hadn't been enough. The ship was too far gone by the time he got to the wharf. All he could do is stand and watch as it sailed out into the ocean.

As he stood there, he prayed when they found her, and surely they would, that they wouldn't toss her overboard because of the superstition that a woman aboard was bad luck.

With a heavy heart, my father rode slowly back to O'Shea Stables. He was dreading telling my mother that he had failed to stop their headstrong daughter from going off on a wild goose chase that could possibly cost her life.

Once out in the Atlantic Ocean, Mister Logan gave the order to turn south toward the Caribbean Islands, Jamaica, being their destination.

Still unnoticed, Cory Anne was sitting on the crate she was using for a place to sleep, eating a piece of cheese and bread when she saw the cover to the stairway go back and heard someone coming down into the hold.

Very quickly, she hunkered down behind several barrels nearby, and waited on baited breath that she wouldn't be found yet. She wanted to wait until they were several days at sea before she would present herself to Mister Logan or Mister O'Callaghan, hoping they would see the right of what she'd done.

The man who came down into the hold rummaged around, walking right past her within two feet, but in the darkness did not see her sitting behind the barrels, holding her breath.

Finally, he found what he was looking for and went back up the stairs, closing the hatch behind him.

Once again in the silence and solitude of the hold, Cory Anne sat up and finished eating her breakfast.

CHAPTER TWENTY-TWO

Malimar's ship had barely disappeared down the river when I was attacked by a swarm of mosquitos. They covered my face, neck, and arms, biting and drawing blood from every bit of exposed skin on my body. My first instinct was to jump in the river to get rid of them, but my brain put a stop to that very quickly – knowing the deadly man-eating fish would be waiting.

Instead, I bent down and grabbed a handful of mud and began smearing it on my exposed skin. And in a short time, the mosquitos flew away, looking for another victim.

I looked around and could not see into the thick jungle more than a few feet – it was that dense. As I stood there, feeling lost and without much chance of survival, I began to get angry. Not at Malimar, but at myself. I wasn't some weakling who couldn't take care of himself. I was Brody O'Shea, captain of my own seafaring ship and all those who sailed with me – and an agent of King Neptune, himself. Some foul-smelling jungle with all of its potential dangers was not about to get the best of me.

The first thing I would need was shelter for I could see dark clouds coming toward me, which I guessed would bring rain. There were long pieces of branches with leaves on them, lying all about, and after hacking my way a few feet in from the river's edge, I found a suitable place to make my camp and set about clearing a space. When I was finished, I tore some of the long palm leaves into strips to make pieces of rope with which to attach the limbs with leaves to the branches above my head and down the trunk of the tree, creating a shelter of sorts. Next, I piled limbs high enough off the ground so I would have a place to sleep without getting wet. When that had been accomplished and I was satisfied with what I'd done, I set about my next tasks – a fire and food.

Here in the jungle, food shouldn't be too difficult to get. I am surrounded by all kinds of creatures, along with what I conceive to be edible plants. Starving was not my big concern. It was figuring out how to start a fire that I was concerned about. The thought of eating raw meat was not something I looked forward to. With the hopes of finding a way to create a fire, I found some rocks near the water's edge and with them, I made a small circle just inside the shelter roof, then found some relatively dry grass, along with some damp pieces of wood and placed them inside the circle of rocks.

Satisfied I was ready, I sat down and pondered on my situation – how do I go about creating enough heat to cause the grass to catch on fire. I'd read somewhere about rubbing two sticks together, and gave that a try – but the wood around here was far too damp to create enough heat to start a fire. I'd also heard something about striking a piece of flint, which would create sparks that would start the grass to burning, but I had no flint, so that wasn't even a consideration. I looked around and found some small pieces of rock and tried striking them together, but stopped after a short while. I hadn't been able to get even one spark.

Just then, the heavy rain began to fall and with it came a bolt of lightning that knocked me onto my back and I felt like a thousand bees were stinging me all at the same time. The insides of my ears hurt like someone had pierced them with a needle. And that's when everything went dark.

When I opened my eyes again, my body hurt all over and it took all my strength to sit up and look around. I must not have been unconscious for very long because through the rain, I saw a burning tree!

After a wobbly start, I was able to gain my balance and made my way to the tree where I tore a burning branch off the tree and using a piece of leafy branch to keep the rain off my burning branch, I hurried back to my shelter and laid it on the grass. It seemed to take forever to heat the grass enough for it to catch fire, to which I added more wood.

Soon, I had fire! Fortunately, I had collected a good-sized pile of wood and stacked it near the far corner of the shelter to let it dry out. I would have enough wood to hopefully last through the night. I knew I could not let the fire go out – ever, knowing a lightning strike wouldn't come along any time I wanted it to.

I was bathing in the warmth of the firelight when I saw something move on my left – and when I turned my eyes toward the movement, I almost jumped up and ran into the night.

Coming toward me was the largest snake I had ever seen. It had to be at least ten feet long and eight inches in diameter. It came slithering into my shelter with its head a few inches off the ground and its long tongue darting in and out of its mouth.

Instead of running, my primeval instinct took over and I grabbed up one of the rocks from the fire ring and threw it at the snake, striking it on the head – dazing it. Next, while it was still halfway unconscious, I jumped on it and with a quick slice of my knife, I cut its head off. I had never eaten snake before, but then again, I had little choice. I was stranded in a jungle where no eating establishments were to be found.

Actually, it wasn't bad. It tasted somewhat like chicken. I added more wood to my fire and watched as smoke drifted up into the night air. The rain had passed by and the sky was filled with stars, much like when I was standing on the deck of my ship out in the middle of the ocean.

Suddenly I was very thirsty, but I was afraid to drink the water from the river. If it had man eating fish, what else might there be? I had read somewhere that many rivers carried sickness.

Stepping out into the moonlight, I noticed that several of the long leaves had rainwater sitting in their folds. It took at least a dozen leaves to satisfy my thirst, and after my thirst had been quenched, I looked around and found an extremely long leaf and sat it inside my shelter, and after many trips I was able to fill it with water from the smaller leaves. I would have water come morning.

With my stomach filled with meat and water, I added more fuel to the fire, then curled up to the warmth of it and went to sleep.

CHAPTER TWENTY-THREE

Cory Anne knew that several days had passed and last night, she had eaten the last of the cheese and bread. She'd been fortunate to find a keg of fresh water, so water had not been a problem. But sitting day in and day out in the dark, damp, hold of my ship was beginning to grate on her nerves.

She gathered up her blanket and stuffed it back into her satchel, then stood up. After taking a deep breath and building up her courage, she made her way up the stairs and stopped at the hatch. Then, after taking another deep breath, she slid the hatch back and stepped out onto the deck.

The first person she saw, and who saw her, was Mister Hauge, one of the deckhands. Not believing his eyes, he swallowed and called out, "Mister Logan! We got us ah situation here."

Mister Logan and Mister O'Callaghan had been standing on the bow, discussing the trip when they heard Mister Hague's voice calling out to Mister Logan. "Yes, what is…" and that's when he saw Cory Anne, standing there big as life itself, grinning at him and waving her hand in his direction.

Mister Logan and Mister O'Callaghan both hurried down to where this slip of a girl was standing. "What in blue blazes are you doing here?" Mister Logan asked.

Cory Anne took a deep breath to fill her with courage, then said, "I've come along to help find my brother."

"But… but… how did you get on board? And do your parents know where you are? Because they never said a word to me about you coming along." Mister Logan's voice was getting higher and higher the longer he talked. Frustration was washing over him like standing under a waterfall.

Mister O'Callaghan heard the frustration in Mister Logan's voice and he laid his hand on his friend's shoulder. "Maybe this will be better discussed down in the galley. The poor lass looks to be starved and frightened, and we wouldn't want the boss to feel we were unhospitable to his sister. would we?"

Mister Logan looked at his friend who was grinning like a fox that had just stolen a chicken. He then looked at Cory Anne and said, "Please, come with us down to the galley where we'll get you something to eat, and then you can explain how you got aboard without anyone seeing you."

Both Mister Logan and Mister O'Callaghan, along with our cook, Mister Cook, watched in fascination as Cory Anne ate everything put in front of her and washed it down with four cups of tea without a word spoken by any of them. When she finally sat back and wiped her mouth, she grinned and said, "Thank you. I guess I was a little bit hungry."

"A little bit, you say! Girl you ate as much as any four men we have on this ship! But I must say, thank ye, for payin' setch ah high compliment to my cookin'," Mister Cook said.

Suddenly, Cory Anne felt embarrassed. "Oh," she said, "I didn't mean to take food away from any of the crew. I…"

Mister Logan cut her off by raising his hand and saying, "Shush. We'll hear no more such talk. We have plenty of food and you're not taking any away from us. Now, can we get down to business?"

Cory Anne nodded her head and said, "Yes. What do you want to know?"

Mister Logan smiled and said, "Let's start with why you sneaked aboard and how?"

My sister began with her attempt to speak to me through our mind speak, and explained how she had become very worried about me and had come home to find out I had been taken hostage by our blood father, Malimar. The thought of what he might do to me was what prompted her to stow away on the ship until she felt certain they wouldn't take the time to take her back.

The part where she had sneaked aboard while the night guard and Mister O'Callaghan were in the water chasing down the crook who had stolen Mister O'Callaghan's wallet, got a loud gee-haff from Mister Logan and a flushed look on Mister O'Callaghan's face.

When everything had been told by my sister, Mister Logan sat back and asked, "So, now that you're here, what are we to do with you? How will I explain to the crew that you won't jinx our mission?"

The galley was filled with silence as they pondered Mister Logan's questions, until finally, it was Mister Cook, who said, "Why not tell them the truth and see what they have to say. After all, it does make since she would try to help rescue her twin brother if she could, don't it?"

Mister Logan looked at him and said, "Sometimes the hardest things to think about are the simplest things to do." And so, after Cory Anne, herself, explained why she was aboard, the men huddled together for no more than two minutes before our bosun mate, Nolan Burke, stepped back and looked up at Cory Anne, and said, "We know you and yer brother were like two peas in ah pod, and it's understandable that you'd want ta go along and do what ya can ta try and save him. So, with that in mind, we've decided ta allow ya ta stay on the ship, so long as you don't bring us no bad luck. But mind ya, lass, at the first sign that you're ah jinx to us, we'll be droppn' you off at the nearest port."

Cory Anne looked up at Mister Logan and asked, "Jinx?"

"The men on ships have many superstitions," Mister Logan told her. "They've been around as long as I can remember and most sailors take stock in them. I don't believe in them, myself, but the crew…?"

"Well, that's just plain silly. How can grown men believe in such things? Don't they know they're only superstitions, not anything real? Can't you…"

Her rapid-fire questions were halted by Mister Logan's raised palm. "Miss O'Shea, if you will please give me a moment, I think I can explain."

Cory Anne realized she'd fallen back into her normal way of dealing with things and shut her mouth, then reached up and ran her fingers across her lips as if she was sealing them, allowing Mister Logan to continue.

"Had this been any other ship, you might have been thrown overboard or at least put into a longboat and set adrift. But… since being with your brother and witnessing his powers, the crew has changed their attitude some; which is why they're giving you this chance."

Cory Anne just stood there, digesting Mister Logan's words until Mister O'Callaghan asked, "Is there any chance, you being his twin, and all, that you might also have powers?

Mister O'Callaghan's question caused Cory Anne to gasp at the thought. "I… I… don't know?" she said, shaking her head. "I've never given it much thought. Oh, I confess I've thought about it a few times, but I've always been afraid to try and find out."

This caused Mister Logan to scratch his neck. "But I thought the two of you could talk to each other by just using your minds."

Cory Anne smiled at the thought. "Yes. Yes, we have, but not recently. I've tried and tried but each time I send a mind probe, I get no answer, which is why I'm here now. I'm afraid something very bad has happened to him. He would never not answer me if he was all right."

"Could he just be too far away?" Mister O'Callaghan asked.

"That's what I thought at first," Cory Anne said, "But then I got to thinking about it, Brody and I were able to mind talk when he was in the Mediterranean Sea and I was in New York City, which is pretty far, isn't it?"

Mister Logan and Mister O'Callaghan both grinned and Mister O'Callaghan said, "Yes, lass, it is very far, several thousand miles."

"So why can't I contact him now? You don't think he's hurt and can't answer me, do you?"

Not wanting to scare her more than she already was, Mister Logan said, "The last time we saw him, he was under some kind of spell put on by this Malimar. But, to the best of our knowledge, he was all right."

"Maybe he's still under that spell and that's the reason he can't answer you," Mister O'Callaghan said, trying to comfort her.

Cory Anne thought about this for a moment and decided they may be right. But how long would this spell last? Would he be released sometime in the near future? she wondered, giving her a ray of hope. After a moment of thinking, she asked, "Do you think I should continue to send out thought waves in the hopes he will at some point be able to respond, so we can at least know where he is?"

Both Mister O'Callaghan and Mister Logan shook their heads, with Mister Logan saying, "Of course, you should keep trying – every day. And if at some point we get lucky and you do make contact with him, your worries about being a jinx will be gone."

Cory Anne smiled and said, "Of course, I will try several times each day."

Mister O'Callaghan posed the question – "And would you be up to coming down here in his cabin and trying to create some small powers, with us here to help you like we did with your brother?"

After thinking for a moment, Cory Anne gave a sigh, and said, "Yes."

CHAPTER TWENTY-FOUR

While Malimar was off doing God only knew what, and maybe my uncle, King Neptune, too, I was left to fend for myself in a jungle so dense I couldn't see more than five or six feet in front of me at high noon. At night, it was so dark I couldn't see my hand in front of my face, which made traveling at night impossible. Which, of course, I didn't want to for fear of stepping on or running into something dangerous to my health.

I had the good sense to find a long stick and, each day, cut a notch in it so I could count the days. So far, I had been here, sixty-three days. I had built up my shelter into a small, one room affair that was at least mostly watertight. I had built up my fire pit and had enough downfall to keep the fire going around the clock. I had been extremely lucky to have had a wild pig come into my cleared-out space – I believe by accident. He was turning to go back into the jungle when I jumped on his back and plunged my knife into his neck. As for vegetables, I found many things I had no name for, but tasted all right – such as a certain tree root that when boiled or baked tasted just like the potatoes we had back home.

Of course, the only reason I hadn't tried to move further into the interior and build a more permanent structure was the hope of seeing someone in a boat, coming up or down the river – which, so far, I had not had the pleasure. Even if I had seen someone, I'm not sure they would have even stopped.

To keep the mosquitos and bugs from biting me incessantly, I kept myself smeared with a coating of mud. I probably looked more like a native than a white man, although, so far, I had not seen anyone to have something to compare with. With being here alone for so long, without hearing another human voice, I was starting to get just a wee bit lonely. At night, I thought about my family and what they must be thinking, wishing I could see them at least, one more time.

I awoke on the morning of my sixty-fourth day of exile, with a new thought in mind – to go into the interior and try to find the people who live here and try to make friends with them. And, if per chance we could somehow communicate, they might know how I could get back down to the entrance of the river. As I recalled, Malimar mentioned a town built there.

I was filled with hope as I sat eating my breakfast of roasted pig and fire cooked roots that tasted like potatoes. The only thing missing was salt. I missed having salt and other spices I'd grown to like. I was reaching for a gourd I had found and hollowed out to make a water container when I heard a rustling on three sides of me. I picked up my knife and stood up, ready to defend myself against whatever creature was wanting me for his or her breakfast.

During my many excursions, I had seen large cats, both black and tan colored, that from nose to the tip of their tail had to be eight or nine feet long. I had seen spiders as big as a plate and other creatures I can't find the words to explain. And to them I was nothing more than a meal to be pursued. The clearing was suddenly filled with natives; all carrying long spears that were aimed directly at me. There had to be at least twenty of them.

They were shorter than me, wearing nothing more than a piece of animal skin around their waists. M y first thought was why weren't they covered with mosquito and bug bites?

They all had tattooed faces, and some had tattoos on their arms and the upper part of their bodies. Not a one of them stood more than five feet tall, but they seemed to be well muscled – and all of them had long, straight hair that was as black as the jungle at night.

One of them stepped forward and threatened to throw his spear at me, motioning for me to drop my knife. If I still had my powers it would have been funny to see their reaction when I did something unexplainable, like turning myself into a troll, or maybe an elephant. I was sure they'd never seen an elephant or a bird that flew away.

But, since I no longer had any powers, I dropped my knife and raised my hands in the air.

I'm not sure how they knew I was there, but my guess would be they saw the smoke from my campfire and came to investigate. The one who had approached me poked me with his spear and nodded in the direction he wanted me to go, as half of the natives led off into the jungle.

By now, my clothes were tattered and rotting off my body, and weren't much protection from the thorns that seemed to reach out and scratch me as we pushed through the dense jungle following a path only they could see. Once, when unexpected, a giant spider ran across in front of me, I jumped back to keep from stepping on it, and my reward was a jab in the back with a spear and muffled snickering from my captors.

We fought our way through the dense jungle for hours without a word from any of them and when I turned and looked over my shoulder at the man just behind me and asked, "Do any of you speak the Queen's language?" My answer was another a jab in the back with his spear. So much for communication.

With the canopy of the jungle being so dense, I couldn't see the sun, but I guessed we'd been walking for at least five or six hours. Then, just like that, we walked into a clearing where there were at least thirty or more huts made from sticks and leaves sitting in a cleared-out space. From my limited time here in the jungle, I knew it took a lot of work to keep a space clear, because it seemed to grow back almost as fast as you cut it down. You had to constantly be pulling or cutting something, or within a few days you couldn't find where your clearing had been.

Half-naked women stood by the open hole of their huts, staring at me. They too were covered with tattoos from the crown of their heads on down to their waists. Their only clothing was a piece of animal skin wrapped around their loins. Most of the loin cloths looked to be from the skins of the big cats I'd seen, while some were of a more colorful skin – but I had no idea what kind of animal they represented. Naked children stood close behind their mothers, staring at me with curiosity. I guess they'd never seen anyone like me, before.

I was taken to a hut near the far edge of the camp and shoved inside. It was empty except for a gourd filled with water. In the center was a small firepit, and next to it was a pad made from more animal skins. I sat down on the pad and wondered about my fate. Malimar had told me I would die a long, slow, and painful death, but at this moment I wasn't so sure his prediction would come true. From the bones I'd seen strewn around their village, I guessed they may be cannibals and I just might be their next meal.

A little while later, a young woman not much older than me entered with a bowl carved out of wood. It was filled with a broth of some kind and she set it in front of me. She had raven black hair and dark brown eyes. Her skin was the color of a doe, and she would have been quite attractive if not for the tattoos on her face and chest. One of which looked fairly new.

"Thank you," I told her, which got only a curious stare before she turned and left me alone with my bowl of what, I wasn't sure. There was a wooden spoon sitting in the bowl and I stirred it around, looking for meat. I didn't want to be eating the meat of another human being. Fortunately, I found no meat, but did find fragments of what appeared to be vegetables. And after taking a sip, I found it spicy tasting. By now, my stomach was growling and I plunged in and lifted the bowl to my lips and downed the entire contents.

After setting the bowl back down next to the firepit, I could feel myself beginning to relax just a little. I still wasn't convinced I wouldn't be in the next bowl of soup, but for now, I was left alone. The following morning, I was happily dreaming of standing on the bow of my ship, out in the middle of the Atlantic Ocean, the sea breeze blowing my hair out behind me, a cup of tea in my hand and the men of my crew, singing a bawdy song as they went about their work.

Suddenly, I felt a prick against my shoulder and tried swatting away whatever it was, but only got another prick for my efforts. I opened my eyes and instead of standing on the bow of my ship, I was lying on a pile of animal skins and a brown skinned man was poking me with his spear. When I looked at him, he motioned for me to stand up.

I took a large breath of air and climbed to my feet, towering over him by nearly a foot. For just an instant, I was tempted to reach out and take the spear from him, but good sense told me not to because there were a lot of other men outside who all carried spears and knives. If only I had my wizard's powers! Never thought I would miss them.

Outside the hut, the people were squatted around a large fire with a giant caldron hanging above the flames. A woman ladled soup into a bowl and handed it to me. Then, she cut off a piece of meat roasting over the fire and handed it to me with greasy fingers. I shook my head, no, but that only got another stab with a spear. Reluctantly, I took the piece of meat, with no intentions of eating it in case it might be a piece of some poor bloke's leg.

After drinking down the hot vegetable soup, I placed the meat in the bowl and started to set it down, but was stopped by two spears pointed at my chest.

One of the men spoke in a language that sounded like no more than a bunch of grunts strung together, but when he made a motion with his hand, I got the message – I was to eat the meat.

I let my eyes roam the nearby area and allowed myself to sigh. There, just away from the fire, a short distance was what appeared to be the bones and skin of a wild pig. I picked up the piece of meat and took a small bite, chewing it slowly. It took only a little while to determine it was indeed pork, which I like – and in no time I gobbled it down.

Once the meal was over, I was given what looked like a rake and through hand motions, I was directed to clean the area of debris. I began to rake at a slow pace, trying to bide my time and look around for a possible escape route, but my thoughts were interrupted when three of the women began whacking me with long pieces of tree branches, which stung like being whipped.

Apparently, I wasn't working fast enough. I looked around and not only saw, but heard the men snickering. When they began switching me, again, I said, "All right, all right, I'll work faster." Which I did while the women stood close by, waiting to switch me again if I missed something or didn't work fast enough. Within an hour, I had the area clean, and I had to admit, I felt proud of myself. The area was spotless, if I do say so, myself.

However, I got no appreciations from the women. One of them grabbed the rake from my hand and another shoved me toward the fire pit. She then pointed toward a small pile of wood lying close by, and then pointed toward the jungle. Trying to stall for time, I shrugged my shoulders and tried to look as though I didn't understand, but it took only a few times being switched across the back for me to have a clear understanding as to what they wanted me to do.

One woman and two men with spears followed me into the jungle in search of sticks and pieces of wood that could be used in the firepit. If I picked up a piece of wood that didn't suit the woman, I got a flick of the switch across my arm or hands, causing me to drop it.

After the second switching, I learned to point, to see which way her head nodded, yes or no.

When this had been accomplished to the woman's liking, I was sent to help with the days hunt for meat – and by now I was covered with bites and stings from the many tiny creatures who thought to thrive on my blood.

An hour or so into the hunt, a good-sized wild hog was spotted and killed. I was directed to go pick it up and carry it back to the village, but when I bent over to lift it onto my shoulders, I heard a sound that chilled me to the bone, and looked up just in time to see the claws and belly of a large cat coming toward me from the tree limb where he'd jumped from.

I was knocked onto my back and felt his claws dig into my shoulders and his teeth scrape my skull. I had no weapon with which to fight back and could do the only thing I could think of. I reached up and grabbed him by the throat and squeezed as hard as I could. Pain was erupting from his claws as he raked me, trying to make me release my grip, but I gritted my teeth and squeezed even harder.

Finally, one of the men ran over and, from behind the big cat, reached in and cut his throat. When the cat fell to the ground, I climbed to my feet, gasping for breath and bleeding from at least twenty places on my body. When they were sure the cat was dead, I was directed to lift him onto my shoulders and carry him back to the village, while the two men carried the wild pig on a long stick.

By the time we got back to the village, I was so weak from losing so much blood that I could hardly take another step. I dropped the big cat near the firepit, then fell to my knees, gasping for air.

Two of the women stepped up and ripped what was left of my shirt from my body, then poured water over my cuts to wash away the blood. I was then, along with the young woman from the night before, taken back in my hut, where she covered my cuts with a cool, but, soothing salve, then bound my wounds with a piece of cloth. Where they got the cloth, I had no idea, but by the time she'd finished, I still felt weak, but the pain was much easier to live with.

She left for a short period of time, then came back, carrying a small bowl of liquid, which she directed me to drink… when I did, within seconds the world began to spin and before I realized what was happening, I lay back on the pile of skins as everything went black.

The following day I was left mostly alone except for the young lady. Finally, through hand jesters, I told her my name was, Brody - and she pointed to herself and smiled, saying, in a rough translation, Zo'ee. I have no idea what that meant in their language but felt she was meant to be someone special. She brought me broth and cleaned and redressed my wounds, then gave more of the liquid, but I shook it off, saying, "No, thank you. It puts me to sleep and I need to stay awake."

She shook her hands at me, then lifted the bowl to my lips and began to pour it into my mouth. I wrenched my mouth away and spit out what had gone into my mouth, already feeling the effects of the strong drink. Fortunately, I hadn't swallowed enough to knock me out, only make me feel a bit dizzy. She jumped back and stared at me with wondering eyes, shaking her head and again, indicating she wanted me to drink the liquid.

I tried to make her understand that I didn't want to go back to sleep but she must not have understood because she left the hut. Within less than a minute, she was back with four of the men who grabbed me and held me down while she poured the liquid into my mouth. I tried to spit it out, but there was just too much of it in my mouth and I had to swallow. I dreamed of floating on a giant, pillow-like cloud, with lightning bolts striking all around me, then out of nowhere came a humongous hawk. It shrieked and grabbed me in its talons and lifted me from my cloud and carrying me even higher.

I could feel the pain of the hawk's talons digging into my shoulders and grabbed a leg in each hand and jerked myself, loose.

The hawk flew away and I found myself falling and falling. I could see the ground over a thousand feet below. It was barren of life, and as far as I could see, the ground was covered with huge, jagged, boulders. I was headed toward one that looked like a giant cocklebur with spikes sticking out of it.

I began to thrash around, trying to turn my body so I would miss it. My body was about to slam into the spikes of the boulder when I screamed and sat up. I was covered with sweat and my body was trembling. I looked around in the darkness and my eyes came to rest on Zo'ee, who was sitting nearby, staring at me.

Without a word, she stood up and came over and sat next to me, taking me in her arms, holding me close to her. I swallowed and took a deep breath. I had never been this close to a nearly naked woman, before, and I didn't know how to react. When she released me, I sat there, shaking - trying to gulp air into my lungs and calm my nerves.

She left the hut for only a few minutes and when she returned, she bathed my face and neck with warm water, then fed me a small portion of liquid that tasted like beef broth. The next thing I remembered is waking up and seeing light coming through the entryway of my hut. Once again, Zo'ee was sitting nearby, waiting for me to wake up.

Without a word, she cleaned and dressed my wounds and surprisingly there was hardly any pain. The wounds were nearly healed. After rewrapping my wounds, she smiled and pointed toward the opening. When I went through the opening, I was greeted by the same three women who seemed to like beating on me with their switches.

They directed me to the firepit, where once again, I ate soup and a piece of meat, that I later learned was not pork, but what they called puma. Never dreaming I would ever eat cat meat, I found it quite tasty, knowing if I was to survive, I would need to learn to eat a lot of things I had never dreamed of eating, along with living a completely different kind of lifestyle.

My only hope was to try and find a way to communicate with them, if I lived long enough to incorporate some of my ways of life into theirs. My work was the same as it had been before being attacked by the puma, raking the area clean, followed by gathering wood.

I think the Gods must have a grudge against me because as I reached for a piece of downfall wood, I saw something move out of the tall grass. At the same time, I heard one of the women scream. I felt the sting of something being injected into my hand and jerked my hand back, bringing along with it, a snake of nearly six feet long. One of the men swung his knife downward, cutting the snake's head off, then quickly removed the snake's fangs from my hand, and tying a piece of leather thong around my wrist. With an arm over each man's shoulder, I was taken, once again, back to the village, with one of the women carrying the dead snake.

By the time they lay me on the ground next to the firepit, I was delirious – out of my head. My nerves were shaking and my heart was pounding. I was sweating and my mouth felt dry. As I tried to look around me, all the faces were blurry and I knew in my heart that I was about to die. I closed my eyes and everything turned black.

During my unconsciousness as I tossed and turned in my delirium, I found myself in the middle of the river with the man-eating fish all around me, biting me, tearing pieces of flesh from my body. I had only a knife in my hand and I was slashing out at them, but there were too many. I began to swim for the nearby shore, kicking the fish away as they continued to take chunks from my feet. I was close to the shore when one of the fish latched onto my hand. I tried as hard as I could to shake it off. The pain was intense and as I climbed up onto the bank, I grabbed the fish and jerked it from my hand. When I threw it back into the water, its jaws were still snapping back and forth, searching for something to bite onto.

In my dream I lay on the ground, bleeding from head to toe, waiting for the inevitable – a slow, painful death. I found out later, that I thrashed around and cried out in pain, for nine days, and was lucky to have survived. There was never any doubt in my mind that I wouldn't have, if not for, Zo'ee.

I learned that she sat with me day and night, administrating poultices she'd made from various plants, and squeezing the poison from my wound. And because of her, I survived.

Because of my surviving being bitten by one of the deadliest snakes in the jungle, the Bushmaster, along with my episode with the puma, and the many poison thorns I'd been stabbed by that wound up killing most men, they now thought of me as a man who could not die and it scared them. To them, they thought I must have some magical powers of life. Not only did it make them very leery of me, it also made them angry that they did not have the same powers of life that I did, and their anger caused them to beat me even more, trying to see how much pain I could endure.

At first, they were cautious, in case I had the power to fight back, but when they saw I couldn't, they increased their assaults on me. At one point, I was staked out on the ground, spread eagle, then one of the women poured honey on my body. They gathered around, a good distance away and waited for the ants to come.

I was awake and saw them. They were the biggest ants I'd ever seen – as big as my little finger! They swarmed over my body, biting me! The stings were not only very painful, but I felt my body being paralyzed from their poisonous venom.

They must have at some point brushed the ants away and carried my limp body back to my hut and left me there, because when I awoke, Zo'ee was cleaning the honey from my body and putting ointment on the hundred or more ant bites that covered me from head to toe.

Again, I survived, which convinced them even more that I was possessed with a power that kept me from dying. Malimar's curse haunted me – "A long painful death."

How I seemed to keep surviving, I'm not sure. It wasn't because of my wizardly powers because they no longer existed, so it had to have been Malimar's curse.

Using sign language with Zo'ee, I was to learn why my survival seemed so mystical to them. The Bushmaster snake is very deadly because its jaws carries two kinds of poison, instead of one, like other pit viper snakes, and when it bites you, it gives you a double dose of both blood and nerve poison. Most of their people had died in just a few minutes after being bitten. And a Puma could kill a man in just a few seconds. And then there were the many poisonous plants that when pricked by their thorns, caused infections that quickly spread throughout your body, causing you to die, screaming with pain. To them, I was the only one to have survived all of these bringers of death.

Of course, I knew my survival had nothing to do with being a God or a person who could not die, but I lay awake at night, wondering how I had survived? Maybe it was because I wanted to stay alive to learn all I could in the hopes of one day finding my way back down to where the river connected with the ocean, and then, back home.

At one point something extraordinary happened. One of the tribe's council got the bright idea that if Zo'ee and I were mated, maybe our offspring would inherit some of my powers of life and our offspring would be strong, like me. I was brought in front of the council and the head man tried to explain their plan. When I asked Zo'ee if we were to be wed, she became confused. She didn't understand what I meant.

As it turned out, the people of this tribe had never heard of the bonds of marriage. If two people were thought to make strong children that would fortify the tribe, then that's all that was needed. It was as simple as that. The women mated with several men of the tribe for one reason or another, but never in wedlock.

I got out of bonding with Zo'ee by conveying to them I was already committed to a very strong goddess who would be angry if I bonded with Zo'ee – and in her anger, she might smite them all down, or maybe even throw them into the river with the man-eating fish.

I don't think they truly understood, but the mention of me and a goddess who might be powerful enough to throw them to the man-eating fish, was enough to sway them.

After several months, my body was adjusting to living in a devilishly hot and humid, bug infested jungle that was filled with more deadly creatures than one could count. My skin had turned a coppery brown and by drinking a putrid concoction made by Zo'ee, I became somewhat immune to most of the scratches from poisonous thorns.

Zo'ee taught me to make fire by striking two special stones together, creating a spark that caused the dry grass to ignite; along with how to make some of her poultices that helped my skin from becoming sunburnt or bitten by mosquitos. Since I seemed to be exiled to live among these savages, at least for some time to come, I decided to see if I could make things a bit more comfortable.

One of my first feats was to dig a waterway from the spring where they carried water each day into the village. Bamboo shoots were cut in half and lined the ditch, keeping the water clean. Instead of carrying the water from the spring, the water came to them through the ditch and filled a large vat made by hollowing out a tree trunk and lining it with tree sap that hardened and made the vat leak proof. The women especially liked this.

I was learning how to live with them, while still looking for a way to get back to my people. They knew nothing about boats, but the seed of an idea began to grow inside my head. Maybe I could find a way to escape, after all.

One day I cut down a tree and began to hollow it out to make a sort of canoe, I called a dugout. The men were fascinated and watched me work, all the while, wondering what I was building. Of course, I told them nothing for fearing they would try to stop me.

I was getting close to finishing my masterpiece when a new challenge presented itself. I was sleeping soundly when I awoke to screaming and yelling. I climbed to my feet and looked out the opening of my hut and swallowed hard. We were being attacked by another tribe!

By now, I was wearing the same clothing, or lack of, that the other men of the tribe wore, but noticed the invading men work thick pieces of skin across the chest and stomach. And they were not only using spears, but also had metal knives and large sword like weapons, which were also made of metal.

When I saw one of the invaders go down from a spear thrust by one of our men, I rushed out and grabbed the sword and knife from his hands and waded into the fracas. This was something I knew how to do and I parried and thrust, spinning and striking blow after blow against our foe. I was like a whirling dervish and the men of my tribe were in awe.

I ran over to face two of the invading warriors. I was screaming and brandishing my sword in a way none of them had ever seen before and in short order, I left them on the ground as I turned to look for more opponents; but what I saw and heard was the enemy running back into the jungle, screaming some sort of gibberish I couldn't understand.

When it was all over, I turned to see the entire tribe, standing some distance away – staring at me. The men had fear and confusion in their eyes. They knew I was different, but what they'd just witnessed, almost sent them running into the jungle, too.

To my horror, instead of burying the dead on either side, they hauled them down to the river and tossed them into the water.

I stood in awe and watched the water churn with the flailing of the man-eating fish as they attacked each body as it was tossed in the river. When it was over, I moved cautiously back to my hut, hoping their newest fear of me wouldn't cause them to attack me and make fish food of me.

The following day, after my chores had been completed, with less beatings, this time, I resumed my work on the dugout. I worked at a feverish pitch. I needed to get it finished and then plan my escape. By the time darkness came, I was nearly finished and could see myself sneaking away in another day or so. I still needed to line it with tree sap, and make a paddle.

That night, I dreamed of my freedom and uniting with the men of my crew, Cory Anne, and my parents, who were all happy to see me. In my dream, I was no longer covered with bug bites or scars from fighting a puma or being bitten by a giant pit viper; nor was my skin a coppery brown.

I awoke the following morning, filled with hope that was soon to be dashed like a wall of rock falling on me. During the night, they set my dugout afire, and now all that was left was the black, smoldering remains of what once had been my way out of here.

One part of me was very angry, while another part of me understood why they did this. I was new to them, and something of an enigma to them. I don't think they had ever seen the likes of me. I would maybe build a new boat, only this time I would be more careful.

CHAPTER TWENTY-FIVE

Cory Anne, in the accompaniment of the men of my crew, sailed from island to island throughout the many islands of the Caribbean, searching for information about Malimar or me.

Each day, whether out to sea or on one of the many islands, Cory Anne would try to make contact with me. Each time she failed, she would become more and more despondent – so much so that both Mister Logan and Mister O'Callaghan had to take here aside and give her a strong talking to.

"You need to get ahold of yourself, lass. You're becoming intolerable and the crew won't take much more of it. We've all bent over backwards trying to help you. We miss him, too. And finding him is the reason we're out here in the first place," Mister Logan told her.

"I too, along with every man on this ship are filled with anger at not finding him, but we can't take it out on each other. We need to direct our anger on the one who is responsible for all of this – Malimar. We need to concentrate on getting Brody out of his clutches so he can do what needs to be done. And that's where you need to direct your anger, too, lass." Mister O'Callaghan said with a sigh.

She turned and gave Mister O'Callaghan a glare that changed to tears.

Mister O'Callaghan's words must have penetrated Cory Anne's brain because her face became soft once again, and instead of daggers flashing from her eyes, she had tears of hope. She smiled and placed a hand on each one of their shoulders and said, "I'm sorry. I guess I got so caught up in my anger and disappointment that I began taking it out on you and the others. You're right, of course, and I will make my apologies to the crew."

And with that, she turned and blew out a loud whistle, which got everyone's attention. And when they'd gathered in front of her, she said, "You've all been so patient with me while I've been making a fool of myself with my anger and despair. For that, I thank you… and I want to apologize for my rudeness."

At this point, she motioned toward Mister Logan and Mister O'Callaghan and said, "It was these two men who forced me to look at myself and feel ashamed. Again, I'm sorry and I want to thank you for not tossing me overboard."

This got smiles and laughter, since several of them had, at one point or another, thought about doing just that. When the laughter died down, Cory Anne looked at them and said, "From this day on, I promise to try my best to put away my anger and help in the finding of my brother and bringing him safely home." To this, she received cheers and whistles.

Her only hope of finding me was in Jamaica, where Malimar was supposed to have a large plantation that exported, bananas, sugar and coffee beans.

"I think Malimar may be holding him there, and has made a slave of him," Cory Anne told Mister Logan one morning as they stood on the bridge of my ship. "I also think we should go there, now. We've explored almost all the other islands and towns in the whole of the Caribbean. Jamaica is the only place left."

Later, with Mister Logan and Mister O'Callaghan present, she tried to see if she had any powers. "If we're to go up against this, Malimar, I'll feel a lot better if you have at least some powers," Mister Logan said, scratching his neck.

If Malimar could overpower me, how could they think they could go up against him with no powers to fight with? This was the bone of contention with every man on my ship – along with my twin sister.

At first, as hard as she tried, she couldn't even make a cup move across the table. "I can't do this. I don't have Brody's powers," Cory Anne said, shaking her head from side to side.

On the sixth day, Cory Anne was standing on the bridge, next to Mister Collins, feeling frustrated. Suddenly, the wind had dropped to nothing. The ship sat, bobbing up and down on the waves, going nowhere, with the outline of Jamaica visible in the far distance.

She looked out across the deck and saw the men staring at the limp sails, and knew they thought of this as a bad omen. They felt they were being kept from the island by Malimar, proving that is where I was hidden.

Cory Anne overheard one of the men say, "Aye, he's dropped the wind so he can keep us out here where he can observe us with his evil eyes. It's evil wizardry, is what it is, mates."

Cory Anne watched as heads shook in agreement. Filled with outrage because she believed they may be right, she pressed her fingers to her temples and said, 'Wind, I command you to fill our sails and push us toward the island of Jamaica!" And just like that, the sails filled with wind that pushed them toward their destination!

"I did it! I did it!" Cory Anne cried out, jumping up and down with joy and surprise.

Mister Collins had witnessed Cory Anne putting her fingers to her temples and had heard her command – and he pointed and yelled to the crew, "She did it! She brought the wind! Like her brother, she has powers!"

A cheer rose up from the crew as they went about adjusting the sails to get as much speed as they could.

Just below the surface of the ocean, sitting on the back of a large dolphin, King Neptune smiled as he watched Cory Anne jump up and down. "All you had to do is believe in yourself, young lady. Just believe. Soon, we'll be able to talk, for I have a lot to say to you."

The harbor of Kingston, Jamaica was crowded with ships coming and going. Kingston was the center of trade for Jamaica and was bustling with people. Once the anchor had been set, Mister Logan, Mister O'Callaghan and Mister Collins, all surveyed the harbor, searching for a ship that looked like it could be Malimar's, but all the ships in the harbor were traders, flying flags from their home countries.

"He doesn't appear to be here," Mister Collins said with despair in his voice.

"Unless he's changed ships, I think you must be right, Mister Collins," Mister Logan said.

"Well, where is he?" Cory Anne asked, her face filled with confusion. "Is it possible he's anchored on the backside of the island?"

126

Mister O'Callaghan nodded his head. "That's reasonable, lass. Yes, that is definitely a possibility."

Grinning, Mister Logan said, "And I suppose you want us to weigh anchor and hurry out and circle the island, looking for his ship?"

"Yes!" Cory Anne said, excitedly.

Being a little more regimented, Mister Logan smiled and said, "I agree, but only to a certain point. Before we go running off on a wild goose chase, I think someone should go ashore and gather some information – like, does Malimar have a plantation on this island? And if so, where is it located?"

Cory Anne looked up at Mister Logan and said, "As usual, you're right. It's just that sometimes, I get over anxious about finding Brody."

"Aye, lass, you do, but it's all right. And, if he has a plantation on the island, we'll find the location and go there, either by ship or by land."

Mister O'Callaghan was elected to go and when he was ashore, he went to the nearest tavern and ordered a pint of ale, then leaned his elbow on the bar and listened to the many conversations going on.

He was less than half finished with his ale when he heard Malimar's name mentioned.

Sidling up to the men who had spoken Malimar's name, he asked, "Excuse me for butting in, but you mentioned a man named, Malimar. Does he have a plantation near here?"

"And what might your interest be?" a robust man with long, grey hair and a nose that looked to have been broken many times asked as he stepped close to Mister O'Callaghan with his fists doubled.

Mister O'Callaghan, was never one to walk away from a good knuckle buster, but in this case, he was on a fact-finding mission. He raised his hands, palms forward, and said, "Whoa, stranger. I'm not looking to cause trouble. I thought I might be interested in doing business with him, but if it's going to cause trouble, I'll just move on."

The big man with fierce eyes and his fists doubled up was known as Clubber because he loved to beat up on people. His real name was Courtney Stoner. He stared at Mister O'Callaghan for a long time, then relaxed. "Sorry, friend, I thought you might be someone else. Buy me a pint and I might be able to help you. I'm the foreman on that plantation.

After three pints, Clubber told Mister Collins all he wanted to know. Yes, the plantation is on the backside of the island, and yes, it is manned by slaves, mainly brought in by Malimar. And yes, the rumors were true – Malimar is a pirate and a powerful wizard. Finally, "No, he is gone at the present time, but business can still be done through me," he said. Which of course Mister

O'Callaghan didn't believe. He told him he needed some time to consider his options.

Clubber said, "Sure, sure. Take all the time you need. But if you want to do business, bring your ship around to the backside of the island and tie up at the pier. But don't come for a few days because I'll still be doin' business here in town and there ain't nobody can make the sales decisions over there, but me."

"I'll keep that in mind, "Mister O'Callaghan told him, and set him up with another pint to keep him occupied when he left, knowing the man to be a liar and a crook.

When Mister O'Callaghan left the tavern, he didn't go directly back to the ship. Instead, he walked down the wharf in the opposite direction, then circled behind some of the buildings before finding his way back to the pier and easing the longboat toward the ship.

Mister Logan listened to the information Mister O'Callaghan gave him and said, "I agree, the man is a shyster and just wants to bilk us out of some money. I think we should sail on the early morning tide."

Mister O'Callaghan agreed and went topside to tell the bosun to have the men ready come first light.

That night, Cory Anne couldn't sleep. She was too excited, not only about possibly finding me, but she kept trying out her newfound powers. At first, she just moved small things, then moved to bigger things.

Around two o'clock in the morning she left my cabin and went topside where she stood, looking at the star-filled night, then said to herself, "It's time for bigger things."

She moved up to the bow of the ship where she had more open space. She took a deep breath before she turned herself into a dove and flew around the ship a few times. Next, she turned herself into a fire breathing dragon. That one almost caused the night helmsman to have a heart attack.

Satisfied, Cory Anne turned herself back into the young lady she was and went back down to my cabin and climbed onto the bunk. She would be ready tomorrow if she was to be called upon to do battle.

During the night a cold front came through with wind and driving rain, lowering the temperature, which was unusual for this part of the world, as was the fogbank that hid my ship as it eased its way out of the harbor, unseen by anyone.

By the time they'd cleared the harbor by a mile or so, the fog lifted and the sun shone brightly, with the temperature coming back up to normal. The

Caribbean is not known for having cold weather, so it was expected that the people stayed inside until the weather got back to normal.

"The fogbank did us a favor," Mister O'Callaghan said as he came up onto the bridge and looked behind him at the still hidden harbor.

Mister Logan nodded his head and said, "Yes. It allowed us to get out of there without anyone seeing us; especially that Clubber fella."

"I wonder if Cory Anne had anything to do with it?" Mister Collins asked. Both Mister Logan and Mister O'Callaghan grinned and shrugged their shoulders. Before noon, they had rounded the island and were making their way up the west side.

"Landing ahead on the starboard bow!"

The cry came from the man in the crow's nest and everyone looked in that direction. Sure enough, there was a long pier jutting out from the land, but there were no ships tied up to it.

"Guess it's like Clubber said, he's gone," Mister Collins, the helmsman said as he guided the ship up alongside the pier, as three men came running down the pier to tie it off to the pilings jutting out of the water.

When the ship was tied off, an elderly man who walked with a limp came alongside and looked up at Mister Logan. "If you're looking to do business, you'll have to come back next week. The man who does the trading is the owner of this plantation, and he's not here. I don't know when he'll be back. Sorry."

Mister Logan stepped down onto the pier and said, "I presume you're talking about, Mister Clubber as you probably call him."

The man looked surprised, and said, "Who? The owner of this plantation is a man named, Malimar and he's the only one that does the sellin' that I know of."

"Spoke with a man named Clubber, yesterday, in Kingston," Mister Logan told him. "He said to feel free and come over and look around and if we're interested in buying, make note of it and we'll do business when he returns."

The old man looked at the two men who had come down on the pier with him and then back to Mister Logan. "I ain't never heard of nobody named, Clubber, but I guess it won't hurt none if you come up and look around, I suppose."

Once on the plantation, Cory Anne, Mister Logan and Mister O'Callaghan were loaded onto a carriage and toured around the plantation where they saw large fields of tobacco, bananas, sugar cane, and trees filled with coffee beans.

Malimar's house sat on a large rise that overlooked the plantation. People in ragged clothes were working the fields, and the huts where they lived were scattered here and there, but not one sign of any children, which Corry Anne found strange. When the old man was asked, he said, "Children ain't allowed. When one of us passes on, he or she is fed to the sharks and the master brings in a replacement.

When Mister Logan described Brody, the old man said, "Nope. He ain't here. Fact is, there ain't ah body here less than maybe forty years old. Master don't like the young'uns cause they always stir up trouble; them bein' not a-mind ta work the fields. Nope. He may be on the master's ship, but he ain't here at the plantation."

Mister O'Callaghan rubbed the back of his neck and said, "I don't know about the rest of you, but I've seen enough."

Cory Anne and Mister Logan agreed and were taken back to the ship, where they went back aboard, with Mister Logan calling out, "We'll be in touch.". Not wanting to harm any of the slaves, they had come up with a plan to put Malimar out of business – at least for a few years.

The ship was less than half a mile from shore when Cory Anne climbed to the crow's nest so she could see the island, then placed her fingers to her temples and said, "I want a storm to converge on the plantation. First, there will be black clouds and loud thunder, followed by downpour rain that will drive the people into their shelters."

And with that, a cluster of black clouds hovered over the plantation and Cory Anne could see the wind driven rain that pounded down on the people so hard they raced for the shelter of their huts. Next, Cory Anne called for the wind to drive the slaves from Malimar's house – and it did, sending them running for the slave huts. When that had been accomplished, she called for the rain to stop. Next, she made lighting strike the fields and start fires.

Shortly, all the fields and Malimar's mansion were ablaze, but not touching the huts.

Climbing down from the crow's nest, Cory Anne smiled; Malimar's plantation had been destroyed and not one person had been hurt. Once she was down on the deck, she went to the stern of the ship and looked back toward the burning fields with an idea forming in her mind. She wasn't sure she could do it, but it was worth a try.

Just then Mister Logan stepped up next to her and said, "Well done, lass. Well done indeed. But I see a gleam in your eyes that tells me you are thinking about something mischievous. I can tell you're quite enamored with your new powers, so what is that mind of yours thinking about now?"

Cory Anne smiled and said, "Well, if you must know, I was just wondering, now that the plantation has been destroyed and Malimar is off in the Mediterranean somewhere, wouldn't it be a grand time for the people to escape his tyranny?"

Mister Logan needed no long thinking to come to the same conclusion. "Aye, lass, I do, but how do you think you can accomplish that?"

"I'm not sure I can, but before we get too far away, I'd like to give it a try," she told him. And with that, she stared at the long pier jutting out into the water and suddenly, there was a ship tied up to the pier, and both Cory Anne and Mister Logan could see the people running down to the pier and climbing aboard the ship.

Mister Logan looked at her and said, "Lass, I do believe your powers are just as strong as your brothers. And because of that, I think we now have a better chance of finding Brody and getting him back."

Cory Anne nodded her head and asked, "But, where is he? Since he wasn't here on the plantation, he must be aboard Malimar's ship - and as far as we know, he's somewhere in the Mediterranean Sea."

"Then that's where we need to go," Mister Logan said with conviction.

CHAPTER TWNETY-SIX

And indeed, that was where Malimar was, raiding and pillaging along the coast of Italy and enjoying himself. He had gotten rid of me without having to do the dastardly deed himself, believing the natives or poison snakes, or other critters would do the job for him.

And, the natives might have had if it had been a cannibal tribe that had captured me. If you can consider being whipped and tortured each day good fortune, then I was very fortunate.

During my captivity, my skin had grown tough and the whippings were hardly felt any more. As to the rocks and sticks thrown at me, I was now able to shrug them off, since they mainly struck my back and not my head. Although, once in a while, a rock found its way to the back of my neck or the lower part of my head, and when that happened, I endured the pain without comment, which caused them to wonder even more about me.

After they destroyed my only chance of escape by burning my nearly completed dugout, I had to begin all over – only this time, I did it at night, far from the village and put brush over it to hide it before returning for some much-needed rest.

I had just creeped back into my hut to find Zo'ee sitting upright and staring at me. We still had limited communication so she couldn't question me as to where I'd been and I made no attempt to explain. I went straight to my sleeping pad and laid down. I pretended to close my eyes, but in reality, I peeked through the nearly closed eyelids and watched until Zo'ee was certain I was in bed for the night, before she laid down.

I was extremely tired and hoped I would soon fall asleep. But that was not to be the case.

Little did I know that at that very moment, my ship had just sailed between the islands of Cuba and Haiti and my sister, still never giving up a chance to try and contact me, was standing on the bow of the ship, directing her thoughts toward the northeast and the Mediterranean Sea. After some time and no results, she sighed and turned to look at Mister O'Callaghan who had walked up and was standing near her.

"Still no luck?" he asked.

Shaking her head, she said, "No... but I know he's out there, somewhere, waiting for us to find him."

"And we will, lass - sooner or later," Mister O'Callaghan assured her. "It's been a long day and you've been under a lot of strain, so maybe you should go down to your cabin and try to get some rest."

Cory Anne readily agreed and turned to go below, when a thought struck her. She looked at Mister O'Callaghan and said, "I've only been directing my thoughts in one direction. Maybe I should send them out to the other directions, too – in case I may have missed him by sending my signals to the wrong places."

Mister O'Callaghan had no opinion as to whether she was right or wrong, but shrugged his shoulders and said, "I don't suppose it would hurt."

And so, first, Cory Anne tried sending her thought signals to the north, then to the west – both with no response from me. Sighing, she said as she turned to the south, "I don't know why he would be south of us, but I guess I may as well give it a try, too."

I was just about to drift off to dreamland when I heard Cory Anne's voice in my brain, calling out to me! At first, I thought I was dreaming, but when I heard it a second time, I climbed to my feet and hurried out of the hut where I hoped there would be nothing to interfere with the thought signal. "Cory Anne! Is that really you? I'm here!" I sent back.

I couldn't believe it... I thought my powers were gone forever... Then I received her response. "Yes! I'm here! We've been searching for you for so long I had almost given up any hope. Are you ok? Why haven't you answered me in the past? Where are you? And why are you answering me from the south? Are you with Malimar? Why isn't he in the Mediterranean Sea?"

With all her rapid-fire questions, there was no doubt, it was Cory Anne and we could communicate, again!

I felt like someone was watching me and I turned around to see Zo'ee standing in the moonlight, her arms folded across her chest, staring at me. Thinking quickly, I turned and walked away a few steps and turned my back to her, waving for her to go away. She came to the conclusion that I needed privacy and turned and went back inside the hut. As soon as she was gone, I resumed my conversation with Cory Anne, trying as best I could, telling her what had happened.

"He took your powers away and left you in the jungle and you're living as a slave with a bunch of heathen natives?" she asked, finding it hard to believe.

"Yes. And before he cast me ashore, he cursed me with a long, painful death. Until right this minute, I was beginning to believe the curse was coming true."

"If that is true, how am I able, at last, to communicate with you?" Cory Anne asked.

I had to stop and think about that for a moment, and the only conclusion I could come up with is, once Malimar got far enough away, his powers over me kept lessening and after a certain distance, they disappeared completely – and Cory Anne just happened to be trying to contact me when it happened.

After I told her this, I decided to see if my powers had actually returned and willed myself to change into a much larger version of me. And suddenly, I was standing there, ten feet tall. "I'm back!" I shouted to Cory Anne. "I have my powers back!"

Suddenly, becoming the rational one, Cory Anne told me to relax so we could figure out how they could come to me. I smiled and said, "Let me think on this for a bit. I will contact you in the morning. In the meantime, keep sailing south."

Mister Logan, Mister O'Callaghan and Mister Collins were all standing nearby, watching Cory Anne while she was jumping up and down during her communication with me – and when she finished, she yelled, "That was Brody! He's alive and, and… there is so much to tell you!"

Over tea and sweet rolls in the galley, Cory Anne related all that had been said and when she finished, she said, "So, we are to turn and sail south. How far I don't know, but he has promised to contact me in the morning with more directions.

In the meantime, I was too excited to even think about sleep… In fact, I sat up the rest of the night, thinking about what I was going to do to throw a bit of fear into the natives – especially the women who had been switching me at every opportunity they got.   I wasn't going to hurt anyone, but… there would for sure be stories that would be told!

As I sat on my pallet, thinking, Zo'ee sat on the other side of the hut, watching my every move. I believe she knew something had happened, but even in her wildest dreams she could never guess what it was. Apparently, I wasn't the only one who didn't get much sleep that night. Cory Anne and the men of my crew were far too excited by the news, to even go to bed. They all stood around, making plans for when we were together again.

CHAPTER TWENTY-SEVEN

Far away, along the coast of Italy, Malimar awoke in a cold sweat. He was trembling from his head to his feet, but couldn't ascertain exactly why. He stood up and began to pace the floor. Something was amiss. He could feel it. But whatever was causing him to feel so nervous, was, at this point in time, beyond his comprehension.

Suddenly, he stopped his pacing and said to no one in particular, "Brody! Something has happened to the boy! But, if the brat has been killed, why am I trembling and having this feeling of ill will? I should be shouting for joy… yet… I'm not!"

Malimar went up on deck and paced from stern to bow and back again, trying to get a feeling of what had happened? If the natives hadn't done away with me, then what else could it be? Surely, I hadn't been able to break his power over me. He wouldn't even acknowledge that possibility. There was just no way for that to happen – was there?

With that thought in mind, he turned and raced to the bridge and began to ring the bell that would bring every man aboard the ship, on the run. When they were standing before him, he told them, "We are leaving, now! Set a course for, Argentina!"

CHAPTER TWENTY-EIGHT

Morning came with one of the women standing over me, switching me and talking her gibberish, expecting me to jump up to do her bidding. Instead, I turned myself into an angry, growling, tiger. She dropped the switch and ran, screaming from the hut. I then changed back to me and leisurely walked out into the open space and witnessed her ranting and raving and pointing toward my hut.

When the men she was talking to turned and saw me coming toward them, they pointed at me and said something back at her. She whirled and stared at me with fear in her eyes. I'm sure as far as she was concerned, I was a devil of some kind – a demon that could change shapes at will, but how could she make the others believe her?

These are very superstitious people and I was about to give them something to talk about, but waited for the right moment. By now, the entire tribe was standing around, staring from me back to the hysterical woman who continued her rantings, and pointing at me.

The head man of the tribe pushed the woman aside and walked toward me with his spear raised, ready to throw it at me if anything suspicious happened. I raised my hand, fingers forward, and watched as he rose into the air about ten feet. The people gasped and shrank away from me with the women wailing and crying out in fear.

Though they might be afraid, the rest of the men wasted no time thinking about what was happening. Instead, as one, they all threw their spears at me. I laughed and watched as the spears stopped in midair, then turned around and went back toward the ones who had thrown them, falling to the ground before striking them.

I looked at the chief and watched, as did the entire tribe, as he turned upside down in midair and began to beat on himself with the rod of his spear. After a little of this, I turned him right side up, and lowered him back down onto the ground.

Now that I had their attention, I created a giant ball of light and when it dimmed, I stood in front of them, not as myself, but a giant gorilla, growling and showing my huge teeth, while beating myself on the chest.

As one they fell on their knees and began bowing to me and I thought maybe I was taking things a bit far, so I created a mist around me, then changed back to me and stepped from the misty cloud just as it began to dissolve.

The head man stood up and slowly approached me with his spear laying on the palms of his outstretched arms, then bent down and laid it at my feet. Because I had my powers back, I could now speak and understand his language – and I told him not to be afraid; that I would not hurt them, unless they tried to hurt me first. I also told them they were to never again beat me or treat me mean.

Of course, they were all surprised that I could speak their language and vowed to do as I said. They thought of me as a God, which I never acknowledged or denied. As I said before, they aren't bad people, just uneducated to the ways of the outside world. So, I sat about, creating huts that sit up on stilts so that snakes and wild animals couldn't enter them at night and cause harm. We named them *boheas* which meant in their language, house on poles.

Over the next two days, I helped them make several changes that would lead to living a longer and better life.

But on the third day, I was anxious to be on my way. With my powers back, I no longer needed to be rescued, although I had given Cory Anne directions on how to find me.

It was my thought to turn myself into a bird and fly down the river until I met them, then land on my ship and turn myself back into me, again. As luck would have it, things didn't go exactly as planned.

I was standing on the bank of the river, trying to teach them how to fish, when I looked downriver and saw my ship coming toward us. I smiled and was about to wave to them, when out of the jungle came a tribe of screaming natives. They had bones sticking out of each side of their noses, and tattoos on their faces and upper torsos. Their hair was long and black as night, and flew out behind them as they rushed into the clearing.

One of the newest items I had given my now adopted tribe, were regular hand knives and larger knives called machetes, which they used to defend themselves. By now, my ship was pulling close to the bank and I could see my men were ready to jump onto the bank and join the fracas. While I was pleased that they would come to my rescue, I couldn't allow them to join in when they didn't know which ones were the enemy.

I raised my hand and yelled, "No. I will handle this!"

I turned myself into a giant troll and waded into the fight, grabbing the raiders and tossing them into the upper parts of the trees. Several of the invaders threw spears at me, which bounced off me like hitting a stone.

Within minutes, they turned and fled back into the jungle. The ones I had thrown into the trees climbed back down onto the ground and when I roared at them, they too, ran into the jungle, screaming at the top of their lungs. I laughed. They wouldn't be coming back here again. When I changed myself back into me, again, the men of the tribe gathered around me and patted me on the shoulders, thanking me.

Once I was able to get them to stop thanking me, I waved to my sister and my crew to come and meet these strange people. After telling the people of the tribe who my sister and my crew were, I explained they had come to take me back to where I came from.

Then, before I left them, I created a ten-foot wall all around the living area that would prevent raiders attacking them without warning. They were amazed and again began thanking me. The last I saw of them, they were standing on the bank of the river, waving as we sailed away.

As we made our way down the mighty Amazon River, I stood on the bridge and told the story to my sister and the entire crew, getting oohs and aahs, and a shaking of heads. When I'd finished, Mister Logan said, "And so, lad, that's why you now have copper skin, covered with welts."

Cory Anne held my arm, tightly and said, "I can't imagine what it must have been like to go through what you did. How did you survive without your powers? Was there no way for you to fight back? Were you really bitten by a poisonous snake and attacked by a huge cat? Oh, I feel so dreadful for you!"

I laughed out loud for the first time in many moons. I was truly back. My sister was firing questions and statements at me and instead of dreading them, I was happy. Even the men of my crew had asked at least a thousand questions.

We had been sailing with the current, down the river at a good speed for four days, and there was a never-ending complaint about the heat and many kinds of bugs that attach themselves to you and try in earnest to relieve you of all your blood. Also in this part of the world there were giant mosquitoes, huge horseflies, black flies and a horde of others – all parasites that can and do infect a person with various diseases, which for the most part, can be deadly. Of course, because of the medicine Zo'ee had given me, I was immune, but my sister and my crew weren't. We'd laughed about the color of my skin and not being bitten by the bugs but because of what happened next, I realized I needed to do something.

First, it was Cory Anne, whose face and arms began to swell and she became gravely ill. Within an hour, three of my men, including Mister Collins, our helmsman, were also, swollen up and very ill. I was on the bow of the ship when it happened and wasn't aware of anything until Mister O'Callaghan approached me and said, "Captain, we have a problem."

By him calling me Captain, I knew it had to be something serious. "What is it?"

When I heard, I went immediately to my sister and then to the galley where the three men lay stretched out on tables. I cursed myself for not realizing what might happen to them by coming into such a disease infested area. I had no medicine like what Zo'ee gave me, but I hoped my powers might work instead. I knew I couldn't magically make them well, but maybe I could create some medicine. I went to the stern of the ship and sent out my powers and in just a few moments, Zo'ee was standing next to me, with a bowl filled with her medicine.

She looked around with terror in her eyes until they rested on me. "What am I doing here?" she asked. "And why have I so much medicine? Are you sick? You don't look sick." I quickly explained about my sister and the three men and asked if she would help. Within an hour, my sister and the three men were all feeling better and the swelling was going down.

Next, I asked her if giving some of the medicine to the rest of the men would prevent them from the illness. She smiled and informed me that in their village, they began taking the brew, shortly after being born. I lined the men up, explaining that by taking the medicine, they would not end up like my sister or the three men.

"How does it taste?" Miles Longjohn, asked.

I locked my fingers together against my stomach and banged my thumbs together, as I looked at him and asked, "Tell me, Mister Longjohn, which would you prefer, drinking a cup of something putrid, and being safe from the illness, or not take the medicine and in all probability, come down with the sickness and die?"

He grinned and reached out for the cup. And yes, it tasted terrible, but it was that or suffer the alternative. When everyone had taken the medicine, I was ready to send Zo'ee back to her people, but she pleaded to see the ship before she left. She had seen a few ships coming and going in the river, but had never been aboard one and was quite curious – asking at least a thousand questions.

Finally, after checking on Cory Anne and the three crewmen, and finding them well and able to resume life as normal, I invited Zo'ee to eat with us.

Our cook, Jack Cook, made up a stew with vegetables Zo'ee had never heard of which also included some dried meat he'd been keeping, along with some Irish bread that Zo'ee thought was wonderful. In fact, she ate three large bowls of stew and a whole loaf of bread. For dessert, he made a bread pudding that caused Zo'ee's eyes to go wide with delight.

Before I told her to close her eyes so I could send her home, each man came by and thanked her for giving them the medicine. When I sent her home, I wondered what stories she would tell when she magically reappeared. Would they believe her or would she be thought of as touched in the head? Knowing of my powers, they would probably believe her, and she would repeat the story around the campfire for years to come.

CHAPTER TWENTY-NINE

On the sixth day of my departure from the native tribe, the river widened considerably and we began to see atolls and small islands, with some of the islands being inhabited. We could see houses and huts scattered here and there amid the jungle-like forestry. Plus, there were what looked to be fishing boats tied up to rickety piers. The water here was muddy brown and it made me wonder what kind of fish were caught here and what would they taste like. I didn't think I would like a muddy tasting fish.

The crew lined the sides of the ship and marveled at the width of the river. At this point, we couldn't see either bank, the river was that wide. None of us could venture a guess as to how wide it really was.

As we passed natives in fishing boats, who were casting nets into the water, the natives smiled and waved at us, and the men waved back, shouting hellos that the natives didn't understand, nor did my men understand their replies, but we didn't need to. It was the jester that counted.

Finally, on the eight day we pulled anchored in the deep water next to Belem, a city sitting at the mouth of the Atlantic. It really wasn't much of a city – more like a trading village, but it was the only place anywhere near where we could replenish our supplies. There were six other ships anchored there – all from different countries, with two of them flying flags I couldn't identify.

Cory Anne and I wandered through the muddy streets and stopped here and there as Cory Anne looked for presents to take back to mother and father. For father, she found a unique bone handled knife that had the picture of a man with a spear, facing an attacking puma carved on the handle. And for mother, she found a red shawl with a beautiful pattern of flowers on it. Of course, I didn't know the names of the flowers, but Cory Anne did and that's all that really counted.

I found father a cap and ball pistol that had a curved handle like those depicted to be a pirate's pistol. And yes, it was shootable, but I suspect father will hang it on the wall as a show piece. I had a difficult time finding anything for mother until we entered a small store on the far outskirts of town. The old man who owned the store was sitting, hunch-backed, over a table with only a candle and window sunlight to see by, but I was astounded by the craftmanship. Where he got the ivory, I don't know, but the pictures he was carving in the pieces was incredible! I chose a curved piece that sat on a piece of red and black wood as a base. The picture was of a very tall waterfall and a river that had fish jumping out of the water. Cory Anne agreed that she believed mother would love it.

We were about to leave the shop when another piece of ivory art caught my eye. It was of a group of people and in the middle of them was a young woman holding a baby lifted in the air. At the top of the piece of ivory was an angel smiling down at her. It would make a perfect gift for Kathleen. When we went back aboard the ship, we found the men had also purchased gifts for people back in Boston – mostly, girlfriends, but some for friends they'd made.

We'd weighed anchor and was in the throes of maneuvering the ship around so we could leave, when I heard a loud shout and saw one of the men jump back. Coming from under a bunch of bananas stacked on the deck, was the biggest spider I had ever seen. It must have been at least six or seven inches across the back and stood eight or nine inches off the deck. It was an ugly brute, for sure. It looked to be about ready to jump toward the screaming deck hand when I raised my hand and lifted it off the deck and tossed it far out into the bay.

The last we saw of it; it was swimming toward one of the ships whose flags I couldn't identify. As we neared the place where the river met the ocean, I couldn't believe the force of the river. It virtually shoved my ship out into the Atlantic. I looked behind us and marveled. There was a distinct line where the river met the ocean. I'd never seen anything like it.

During my time with the natives, I hadn't had a haircut, and I had grown whiskers on my face. The natives used to approach me and tug on them. I don't know why, but none of them had facial hair. Down in my cabin, I looked in the mirror and decided I would keep my hair long, but the facial hair had to go. It itched something awful. I didn't mind the suntanned look, which to me gave me a bit of a roguish – more manly, look.

After shaving and tying my hair in a ponytail with a piece of leather string, and donning my regular clothes, I stepped in front of the mirror and admired the change. I was me, again. When I went topside, the men noticed and hooted and whistled. Cory Anne came up to me and said, "Now, you look like my brother, again! A little older and more mature looking but, still as handsome as ever. I do believe Kathleen will approve."

"Am I to presume we'll be setting a course for Boston, Captain?" our helmsman, Mister Collins asked.

"Aye. Boston it is and as fast as the winds will take us!" I told him.

It was going to be a long and arduous trip, what with having to sail against the current and waves the entire way, but no one was complaining. In fact, as they set the sails, they were singing a lively tune, but not a bawdy one, since Cory Anne was aboard. I stood on the stern of the ship and watched the village of Belem and the mouth of the river disappear in the coming of darkness.

A new custom, Mister O'Callaghan and Mister Logan came up with, was now being implemented. Lanterns were lit and hung from the bow and stern of the ship, with six more hanging on both the port and starboard sides of the ship. Mister Logan explained that it would allow other ships to see us in the darkness and hopefully, prevent a collision – which on occasion happened.

To test his theory, I turned myself into a sea gull and lifted into the air and flew off a good way, then looked down at my ship. And sure enough, I couldn't actually see the ship, but the lanterns gave enough light to show the image of a ship. I landed back on my ship and when I was me, again, I congratulated both men on their ingenuity.

"We're hoping this will catch on and make sailing at night, much safer," Mister Logan said.

I had to agree, at least for the most part. The only question I had were pirates. I knew they wouldn't do this because they didn't want to be seen. If a pirate ship was in the vicinity at night, and a ship had lanterns hanging on the outside of it, that ship would be easy prey. When I mentioned this, both men agreed, but still thought it was a good idea.

We had been at sea for more than two weeks and the men were getting lackadaisical in their duties. It was much the same - day in and day out - when sailing on a beat in a straight line. We were abreast the Caribbean Islands when the monotony turned into a nightmare!

Suddenly, a wind strong enough to blow the stripes off a zebra hit us from the starboard side and we heeled over to the point where we were taking on water over the port rail – and would have capsized had I not used my power to bring us upright again.

Without my having to say anything, Mister Collins turned our bow into the wind on a quarterly tack, as the crew slipped the sails and adjusted them to a storm mode.

Waves, at least thirty feet high, crashed over the bow of the ship and sent water all across the deck, making the scuppers work hard to send the water back into the ocean. The bow rose and fell, driving into the now full-blown storm. All hands secured themselves by tying lines around their waists and the other end to something secure.

When the storm suddenly hit us, I was standing on the bridge, admiring the warm sunshine and light wind, and I was as baffled as the crew. There had been no warning. No black clouds approaching, no picking up of the wind, as normally there would be. Nothing. One moment, the sky was a beautiful blue and pleasant, the next we were in a hurricane!

This was not Mother Nature at work and I felt sure my uncle, King Neptune had nothing to do with it, either – which left only one other person powerful enough to create a storm this strong – Malimar!

Braced against the bridge railing, I stared into the storm, trying to see if another ship was close by, but I could see nothing but the heavy rain that was being driven against my face.

Next, I tried to force the wind to die down and the storm-clouds to disappear, but my power wasn't strong enough. On her hands and knees, Cory Anne crawled up next to me and tied herself off to the same railing I was tied to. And when she could, she yelled, "What can I do to help?"

And just as I was about to suggest we put our powers together to quiet the storm, it was over. The wind dropped to a gentle fifteen knots and just like that, the dark clouds and rain disappeared behind us.

Cory Anne and I stood, transfixed as the storm continued on across the ocean, and both of us spoke at the same time. "Malimar!" That was the only logical explanation for the moving storm.

How he'd missed seeing us or feeling our presence, I didn't know, but I was glad for whatever distracted him.

Malimar was so anxious to get back down to where he'd left me in the jungle, he was standing on the bridge of his ship, blowing wind into his sails to make his ship go faster. It was his anger and frustration that created the storm. He was so bent on making time he failed to notice any ships near him, and for sure, hadn't felt our presence.

As Cory Anne and I stood there, watching the storm disappear, my uncle's voice came to me. "Brody, are you all right, lad?"

"Yes," I told him, then asked, "That was him, Malimar, wasn't it?"

I heard my uncle, sigh, then he said, "He knows something is up and he's terrified you have broken the spell he cast on you and he's rushing to where he put you ashore. He's so upset and distracted that he sees nothing but his final destination. As a matter of fact, I'm a little bit curious as to how you broke his spell, and how you wound up back on your own ship?"

I grinned and said, "It's a long story, but I will say this; It was a combination of a couple of things. First, I believe once Malimar got far enough away, his power over me was no longer strong enough to sustain itself. And second, my twin sister, Cory Anne, you remember her; well, she and my crew were searching the ocean, looking for me. And apparently, they got close enough for us to mind speak. I gave her directions and now we're on our way back to Boston. I truly do need some rest and recuperation before I try and go against Malimar, again."

There was a momentary silence before my uncle spoke, again. "I understand, lad, and whole-hardily concur. You've proven yourself by your survival and now you need to go home and rest up. I'm afraid your next encounter will be even tougher than this last one. He is very upset and will not hesitate again to do away with you. Stay safe and we will talk again, soon."

And with that, he was gone. I looked at Cory Anne who had stood patiently by while my uncle and I spoke.

"He talks to you like I do, doesn't he?" she asked.

"Yes," I told her. "He confirmed that the storm was caused by Malimar." I then went on and repeated all he had told me. And when I'd finished, Cory Anne ground her teeth for a moment, then said, "The next time, he will have to fight both of us! And I won't take no for an answer. You'll need my strength tied to yours if we are to defeat him."

I could see the determination in her eyes and just nodded my head. This was no time to argue with her about the dangers of going face to face in a battle with Malimar. But... now that she had found her powers, I could see her side of the argument. But, still and all, she is my sister and I don't want to see any harm come to her.

Once we get back to Boston, I hoped I could distract her in some way to take her mind off becoming a female wizard-warrior.

As I went down to the galley to see if I could steal a snack, it came to me. Cory Anne needed a boyfriend! The perfect distraction! Of course! The solution had been right there in front of me all this time. It was like I couldn't see the forest for the trees. She would be enamored with her new boyfriend and I would be free to do what needed to be done.

Luckily, the cook wasn't in the galley and I flinched a big piece of cake and a cup of tea, then slipped away to my cabin, while Cory Anne wasn't using it.

I sat, munching on the cake and sipping my tea, reveling in the fact that Malimar had passed right by us, never knowing we were so close. I guess sometimes the Gods do smile down on us.

After thanking the powers that be, I went again up topside and surveyed the situation. Other than the bow of the ship pushing its way through the oncoming waves, causing the ship to rise and fall over and over, things looked fine. The light-blue sky held a few puffer clouds that were drifting lazily above us, and a steady wind from the west that pushed us along.

My sister joined me on the bow and asked what I was thinking about, and rather than bring up how close we'd come to facing Malimar in battle, I said, "I was just thinking how good it will be to be back home, again – helping father with the horses and all. Eating too much of mothers good cooking and gaining weight – and of course, seeing Kathleen again."

Cory Anne admitted this had been an adventure she would never forget, but told me it would, indeed be good to get home again. As daylight faded into darkness, Cory Anne stood on the bow of the ship and played her violin, sending the sweet sounds of her music into the hearts of each one of us.

CHAPTER THIRTY

Malimar sailed his ship into the entryway of the Amazon River and created a wind that would push them up the river, crashing into several small fishing boats along the way, that was noticed by only the crew, who could only hope the fishermen would be able to swim to safety.

Malimar had only one thought in mind, which kept him from sleeping or eating – and that was to find my body and prove I was dead.

Five days later, the ship came to rest just off the shore where Malimar had left me and instead of taking a longboat to the riverbank, he turned himself into a bird and flew the short distance. When he landed, and turned himself back into a man, he could see the shelter had been taken back by the jungle growth, which caused him to wonder where I had gone?

Needing to be able to travel through the jungle at a faster pace than he could do in his present configuration, he changed himself into a puma and ran into the thick growth.

A short time later, his nose caught the scent of people and he climbed a huge tree whose limbs grew out from the trunk at least a hundred feet. From there he could see a village and its people.

He was concentrating so hard, trying to locate me somewhere among them that he didn't see the native boy who had seen him and had creeped up within throwing distance. Malimar's first knowledge that someone had seen him, was the sharp pain in his side where the spear had driven itself between his ribs.

He let out a scream from the pain and turned to see several more natives running up and stopping next to the boy – all with spears in their hands, ready to impale him.

Malimar turned his head and with his teeth, jerked the spear from his side, then leaped down onto the ground, turning himself back into a man. Since the natives had seen me turn myself into a creature and back to myself, they weren't afraid, and just stood there, glaring at Malimar.

Malimar looked at them and, at first, was surprised at their lack of fear, then it came to him, I had somehow gotten my powers back and they had witnessed this type of wizardry. Wizards have the powers to understand and speak any language they choose and he asked about me.

Their chief had arrived and went into a long orientation about how good I had been and how I had saved them from other attacking tribes. Of course, Malimar cared not a whit about my kindness or my helping them fight off other tribes. His only concern was me and where I was now.

In a long-winded tale about being attacked on the riverbank just when a big boat, just like the one Malimar had come on, came along, I talked about turning myself into a huge monster and chasing the invaders away, then leaving on the big boat. After all of that, as the head man stood, grinning and shaking his head, Malimar came to the conclusion that I had, somehow, gotten my powers back. He was also confused about the ship that had picked me up and taken me away. Who could have known where I was and how to find me?

"The boy's power must be much stronger than I gave him credit for. He must have contacted someone through his mind and given them directions. That had to be the answer. But, how did he know where he was? Could my brother somehow be involved? I think not, but I can't rule him out," Malimar said to himself.

Without another word, Malimar turned himself back into a bird and flew out to his ship, as the natives yelled and danced around. They had seen another miracle! There would be more stories to tell around the campfire.

Giving the natives no more of his attention, Malimar sailed his ship back down to where the river met the ocean and anchored off the village of Belem. It took hardly any time to confirm that I had been there, buying supplies and trinkets, but giving no information about where I might be going.

Back on his ship, Malimar set sail for Jamaica and his plantation. He needed some time to rest and think. Racing across the ocean from the Mediterranean to the Amazon River, then up the river had taken a lot out of him. After all, he wasn't getting any younger.

On his way back north and the island of Jamaica, Malimar spent long days in his cabin, resting. He would bide his time, figuring I would surface again, soon.

Malimar was lying on his bunk, staring at the ceiling when his first mate tapped on his door and called out, "Captain, you need to come up on deck and see this."

"See what?" he asked as he climbed the stairs up to the deck – and when he stepped out onto the deck, his knees almost buckled and his heart began to pound. His entire plantation had been burned to the ground, along with his mansion! And there was not one slave to be seen!

"What has happened to my plantation? When I find who did this, they will suffer my wrath!" Malimar screamed.

Turning to his first mate, he yelled, "Lower a longboat and take me ashore!"

Not only had the plantation been destroyed, but the pier as well. It was now, nothing but a few black stumps sticking out of the water.

Malimar walked the road leading up to where his mansion had once sat – his anger growing with each step. With his power, he could rebuild his mansion and his crops, but that wasn't the issue. Either, this had been the work of his slaves before somehow escaping, or someone had come here and destroyed his holdings. No one he knew, who was in their right mind, would do this for they would have to know how angry he would be and what he would do to them when they were found.

He turned and walked back down to where the man sat in the longboat, waiting for him to return. Without a word, Malimar climbed in the longboat and sat down, and when they reached the ship, he went straight to his cabin and slammed the door. He would deal with all of this in the morning – for now, he needed to rest, and think…

But morning brought no relief. His mind was still swirling and his anger was still at the boiling point. During the night, it came to him. The only one who would dare to do something like this was, me. The way he saw it, I was angry for what he'd done to me and wanted revenge.

He paced the floor of his cabin, trying to decide how to deal with this. His biggest problem was that he didn't know where I was. And his first priority had to be - find me. He raced up onto the deck, then lifted himself up, into the crow's nest, which would allow him the best chance of locating me if I was anywhere within a thousand miles or so.

After half an hour of mind searching, with no results, he came down onto the deck and in a fit of anger, lifted three of his crew into the air and tossed them over the side of the ship, screaming insults at them, before storming back down to his cabin.

Malimar brooded and paced the floor of his cabin throughout the rest of the day, and all through the night. His crewmen could hear his angry screaming, and stayed as far away as they could.

The three men he'd thrown overboard had been safely pulled out of the water by their crew mates, and felt lucky that's all he'd done to them. When he was in a fit of anger, like he was now, there was no telling what he might do.

The following morning, Malimar came up topside and his men stood in silence, waiting to see what he would do, and gave a sigh of relief when he seemed calm and told them to set sail east. No exact location, just east.

Only Malimar knew once they were beyond the Caribbean Islands, they would turn the ship north and sail along the coast of the new world, sending out mind probes to see if that is where I had escaped to.

CHAPTER THIRTY-ONE

We arrived in Boston Harbor close to dusk and it was raining. No thunder or lightning, just a gentle rain. Cory Anne and I were naturally, anxious to get ashore and go home.

The only light we could see coming from the stores and offices along the wharf came from the window of O'Shea and Son, Freight Company.

"Look!" Cory Anne exclaimed. "I think father is still at his office! We must hurry!"

I looked around and saw the men were busy setting the anchor, since all the available places to tie up to the pier, were already taken.

"As soon as you can, lower a longboat over the side. It seems my sister is most anxious to go ashore!" I called out to the bosun.

Even as the ship was being secured in place, a longboat was lowered over the side and when it was floating next to the ship, I escorted Cory Anne to the rail, saying, "We can come back tomorrow for our belongings."

I didn't need to say it twice for Cory Anne was already climbing down the rope ladder into the waiting longboat. I turned to Mister Logan and said, "I'm leaving you in charge. Secure the ship, then do as you feel best."

"Get your sister ashore before she busts a gut," Mister Logan said. "We'll be fine, here and I can expect to see you on the morrow?"

"That you will, Mister Logan. And thank you again for coming to find me," I told him in all earnest.

"We did no more than you would have done for us," Mister Logan said, then added, "Now be gone with ya. Your family awaits."

When we opened the door to father's office and stepped inside, he was just reaching for his coat and hat – and when he saw us, he turned pale and rushed over and took Cory Anne in his arms and said, "You're home, lass. Where have you been? One day you just disappeared. Your mother and I have been worried sick."

He looked over and noticed me, then back at Cory Anne. "You went with them in search of your brother, didn't you? We suspected as much."

Father released Cory Anne and stepped over in front of me and took me by the shoulders and asked, "Are you all right, son?"

I told him, thanks to Cory Anne and the men of my ship, I was fine – and that I would explain everything when we were all together, because I knew mother would want to know each and every little detail, and I didn't feel like telling it twice.

When father pulled the carriage into the barn, he suggested he go in and prepare mother for he didn't want us to just walk in and give her a heart attack, because as he reminded us, they weren't getting any younger.

So, when we heard her yell, we started for the entryway of the barn, but didn't get there before mother came running into the barn like a racehorse headed for the finish line.

She pulled us both into an embrace, and as you would suspect, there were plenty of tears all around, and at least a hundred questions, which I fended off until we could get into the house and be all together.

Over lambchops, potatoes, green beans, fresh bread and Yorkshire pudding, Cory and I told our stories, leaving out, only the part about having a near run-in with Malimar on the way home. I would deal with that situation later, after conferring in private with Uncle Neptune.

Of course, all during the orientation, mother dabbed the tears from her eyes and shook her head at some of the things I told her about living with the natives. While Cory Anne and mother cleaned up the kitchen, father and I went out on the porch and sat in the rockers – father enjoying his evening pipe, while he brought me up to date with the business.

To my surprise, we now owned a racetrack where horseracing events were held each Sunday afternoon.

"You won't believe it, lad," my father said, "the arena is filled to capacity every Sunday and horses come from everywhere to race here. And to be fair, I only race our horses on challenge runs. So far, I have challenge races lined up every week for the next four months! And we have another cross-country steeple race coming up the first weekend of next month. So, I'm glad you'll be here for that because we've had several requests for their horses to run against ours and I'll be needing you up on Hurricane. Oh, we've been exercising him, but I'm sure he'll be excited to see you."

"And I'll be excited to see him," I told my father. The truth was I'd been thinking of how it would be to race him across the fields, feeling the wind against my face and the thrill of sailing over the fences. I loved being at sea and feeling the pitch and roll of the ship under my feet, but I loved riding Hurricane, too, as well as being with Kathleen.

During the next few weeks, things got back to normal, reuniting with Kathleen and helping with the horses and the stables, and seeing to the cleanup of my ship.

Father sent them out on a delivery that went down the coast to Georgetown where they were to deliver medicine and blankets and other dry goods, and load tobacco, cotton and corn for the return trip. The men seemed to enjoy these short runs that brought them back in just a couple of weeks.

At mother's encouragement, my crew attended church on Sunday, when they were in port. To our surprise, one Sunday morning, both Mister Logan and Mister O'Callaghan arrived at church with two ladies who were identical twins and informed us there was to be a double wedding soon, and it was to be held right there in the church. Of course, mother insisted the reception was to be held at O'Shea Stables, and she wouldn't take no for an answer.

So, added to the horseracing each Sunday afternoon, and coming very soon after the cross-country steeple chase, was a wedding reception to plan. I hadn't seen mother so excited since Cory Anne's and my arrival back home. With Cory Anne standing nearby, she asked at least a hundred questions and we found out all the information about the ladies we needed to know.

As I said, the brides to be were identical twins. Their names were Annabel and Adair Spencer. Annabel was to be the bride of Mister Logan and of course, Adair was to wed Mister O'Callaghan.

They were from Scotland - Westray, an island just north of the mainland. It was the largest of the small group of islands there – with a population of just over five hundred people. Their father, Westmorland Spencer, owned the largest sheep ranch on the island. They loved growing up there but when they became adults, they wanted to have some adventure in their lives, so, they came to the Americas.

As it turned out, they arrived in Boston shortly before Cory Anne and my crew set out in search for me – and had met Mister Logan and Mister O'Callaghan in church when they were asked to join choir, where both Mister Logan and Mister O'Callaghan were already members.

Being both good on the eyes and with lovely singing voices, Mister Logan and Mister O'Callaghan, being somewhat gentlemen, asked the ladies out to tea. And as they say, "The rest is history."

Always the curious one, Cory Anne asked how they came to both be such good singers?

Adair, being the older by six minutes, said their parents were both grand singers and both sang with the choir in their church. When they were seven years old, they became members of the junior choir – and had been singing ever since. Mother then invited them to dine with us after the horseraces.

When the service was over and we were leaving, I frowned at the two husbands to be and asked, "And just when were you planning on telling me about this new adventure you'll be taking? When you are old and ready to retire, would be my guess?"

Both men seemed embarrassed and it was Mister Logan who spoke up. "We weren't exactly hiding anything… It's just that… Well, it was like this…"

"Yes?" I asked, cocking one eyebrow.

"We didn't know ourselves until the girls brought it up this morning," Mister O'Callaghan said, shaking his head from side to side. "Adair brought up the subject and well… we thought it was a grand idea and said, yes. So, ya see, there really wasn't any time before we got here, now was there?"

I conceded there had been no time, and congratulated both of them, just as their brides to be walked up.

Annabel said, "My ears were ringing. Does that mean you were talking about us?"

"Aye, we were," Mister Logan said. "We were just explaining how our plans to wed the two of you came about?"

"And?" Annabel asked.

"And what?" Mister Logan asked her back.

"And are you still planning on making honest women of us?" Annabel asked with a gleam in her eyes.

"Of course," both men said at the same time.

"How could you think any different?" Mister O'Callaghan asked with a confused look on his face.

Both ladies broke out in hysterical laughter as their husbands to be, blushed – their faces turning beet red.

The afternoon races were a big hit with both Annabel and Adair. This was their first time at an actual track. Their father owned a racehorse, but he only raced him in steeple races down on the mainland, and they had never gone with him.

At this, I asked them if they would, in their next communication with their father, invite him to bring his horse and participate in one of our cross country, steeple races. And as family, they could stay with us and stable the horse in our barn. Both ladies thought that to be a grand idea and thanked me profusely.

Supper was served outside on the patio, where Cory Anne played for us, and then we were treated to not one, but three lively Scottish songs, sung by none other than Adair and Annabel, accompanied on the violin by Cory Anne.

Mother and father even got up and danced, as did Kathleen and I. And as we danced, I looked around, thinking it was good to be home. Any thoughts of Malimar were far, far away, instead of wondering what he was up to which is what I should have been doing.

CHAPTER THIRTY-TWO

Six cargo ships had wandered into Malimar's path as he sailed north along the coast pf the New World, and they all suffered the same fate – their wares taken and the ships sunk with all hands still on board.

Day in and day out, Malimar searched the skies for any feeling of me using my powers and each night, he went to bed angry and frustrated. "Where are you?" he would shout.

Weeks turned into months, but he wouldn't relent his vow to find me and make me pay for flaunting my power in his face by regaining my power and destroying his plantation. How could I have overpowered his curse and regained my powers? This shouldn't have happened. He needed to see me face to face – to challenge me to a wizard to wizard fight to the end, with only one survivor – which he never doubted would be him.

He spent several weeks sailing the waters of the Atlantic Ocean, sending out thought waves, probing and searching for me – desperately hoping to get even a faint signal, but again, he got nothing. During all this time, the men of his crew cringed anytime he came near them and hid whenever possible in case he loosened his anger on them.

Next, he left the Americas and searched along the western coast of Portugal, the northern part of Spain, through the English Channel between England and the Netherlands and on up into the North Sea – past Denmark and Norway. Finally, he turned west and came down the west side of England and then all-around Ireland.

With each country, and not finding me, Malimar was becoming more frustrated. With each day, his desire for revenge grew stronger – which also was taking a toll on his health. All this pent-up anger was causing his heart to beat faster and his breathing more labored. He'd lost weight from having no appetite, and his lack of sleep or rest was making him weak.

But he was so wound up with hatred of me, he noticed none of this and continued on; his crew watching and waiting... wondering what was going to happen to him. At one point, Malimar wondered if I had run away and hidden somewhere on one of the many islands of the Pacific Ocean. Then, after some thought, decided I hadn't. Then changed his mind and decided maybe I had. Because of his long attempt at finding me, with no results, he guessed anything was possible.

Feeling weak and tired, Malimar decided to go back down to Jamaica and get some much-needed rest, and maybe restore his plantation. He would need slaves to run it, but that shouldn't be too difficult. He would raid some ships and this time, take captives. They were maybe forty miles off the coast of the Americas when he felt the vibrations in his brain. "Hove to!" he shouted!

CHAPTER THIRTY-THREE

The minister had just finished with his blessing the marriages and the two men were kissing their new wives when my uncle interrupted my thoughts. "Brody! We need to speak! There is great danger!"

As quickly and as quietly as I could I left the church and hurried out under a tree where I wouldn't be seen. "I'm here, uncle. What danger are you talking about?"

Things had been going along so well, I had almost forgotten about Malimar. Mister Spencer and his wife, Claudine, along with their racehorse, Swift Fortune, had arrived for the wedding of their two daughters and a look-over of their future sons-in-law.

At first, he wasn't all that pleased when he found out they were seafaring men, but when I took him aside and explained the money that had been put away for each man, his whole demeanor toward them changed.

Coming from behind in the cross-country steeple chase race Mister Spencer's horse, Swift Fortune, ran hard in the final stretch and edged just in front of Beauty and just behind my horse, Hurricane, to take second place.

"Another fifty feet and I may have won," Mister Spencer told the reporters that gathered around him. And agreed that O'Shea Stables had two of the finest cross-country racers he'd ever had the privilege to race against.

"To me, he said, "We shall race again, lad. Only this time, on my turf."

Feeling a bit cocky, I said, "It will be my honor to beat you on your own turf, Sir."

The following Sunday was the wedding and the day I got the bad news.

Standing under the shade of the large elm tree, my uncle wasted no time telling me why he had pulled me from the wedding. "Malimar is near and he feels your power."

"But... but how? I haven't been using it?" I asked.

"I'm not sure. But I do know he found out about you escaping from where he left you in the jungle and he found what was left of his plantation in Jamaica. And, Brody... he is very angry and wants revenge. He has been traveling far and wide looking for you and now, he is less than fifty miles off the coast of Boston!"

I was stunned and for a moment or two, I didn't know what to say or what to expect. But finally, I came to my senses and asked, "Do you think he knows where I am?"

My uncle was silent for a few seconds, then said, "He knows you are nearby, but I don't think he can pinpoint your location, especially if you're not using your powers."

I was about to ask another question when the worst thing that could happen, happened.

People had lined up outside the front of the church to greet the newlyweds and just as they were coming down the steps to cheers and people throwing rice at them, the sky turned black, with lightning striking all around.

Everyone stopped and looked up at the menacing clouds, just as a strong wind began to blow through the churchyard, taking with it hats and scarfs. As people scrambled to grab their belongings, Malimar's face appeared like a giant picture – his eyes blazing and fire shooting from his mouth like a dragon. When he spoke, his voice sounded like it was coming from deep down in the bowels of the earth.

"Brody O'Shea! I know you are somewhere within the sound of my voice. Hear me, whelp, I have come for you, boy! You slipped through my fingers once, but no more. Come and face me if you dare! I'm waiting. And if you don't want to see your city and its people, destroyed, you will not delay!"

And just like that, he was gone. The sky was once again, a beautiful blue, with a gentle wind and small clouds floating around. Kathleen was suddenly by my side and I could see all the people from the church, staring at me.

"Who was that? And what did he mean, you slipped through his fingers once? Have you been out fighting against wizards? Tell me it's not so! Oh Brody, what is going on?"

Before I could answer her, Mister Logan, Mister O'Callaghan and Cory Anne came running up and stopped just in front of me.

"We'll have the ship ready to leave within the hour," Mister Logan said, as Cory Anne added in her two cents worth – "I'm going with you. We can leave now, with Mister Logan and Mister O'Callaghan."

I looked beyond her at the people and my mother and father who were all staring at me.

I looked at Cory Anne and said, "No, this is between him and me."

Kathleen grabbed ahold of my arm and asked, "What does that mean? Why would you want to face a wizard in mortal combat? That doesn't make any sense!"

I looked at Kathleen and said, "You need to stay with Cory Anne. She can explain it to you, but for now, I have to go."

"No! You can't go. This is insane! Please, Brody!" Kathleen said as I pulled away.

I looked at Cory Anne and said, "Watch over her. I hope I won't be gone long. And please, if you will, explain it to Kathleen."

I then turned to Mister Logan and Mister O'Callaghan and said, "Go back to your brides, I won't be needing the ship, this time."

Mister Logan got a stunned look on his face and said, "You can't be serious. You can't face him, alone!"

"Like I said, this is between him and me. You're all staying here, and that's an order!"

Just then, the sky turned black again and Malimar's face appeared once more...

"Where are you, brat? I'm waiting but my patience is wearing thin and I won't wait much longer!"

"I'm coming!" I yelled at the sky, then ran over and leaped on my horse and rode toward the wharf, leaving a stunned bunch of people behind.

Things would never be the same again once Cory Anne and maybe even my father, told the story. Would they shun me, I wondered? I knew they would not ever again treat me the same. But what choice did I have?

When I reached the pier, I leaped from Hurricane's back and into the air, changing myself into a sea eagle. As I flew over my ship, I could see my men looking up at me – pointing and talking, but I didn't have time to stop and explain.

Malimar would be true to his word and destroy Boston and all the people who live there if I didn't do something to stop him. As I flew out to sea, I had no idea what to expect, but decided worrying about it would do me no good. I would face things as they came. In the far distance, with my sharp, eagle eyes, I could see a small dot on the far horizon and flew toward it.

I was still some distance away from Malimar's ship when my uncle's voice filled my head. "You can do this, lad. You just have to believe. He will tell you, you don't stand a chance against him, but you do! You are more powerful than he is, if you will only believe."

"This time, I am not afraid. I am determined. I will not think about the fact that he is my blood father, any more than he will consider me his son. No, he is an evil wizard who is out to destroy me and everything I believe in. I will not fail."

As my uncle's voice faded, the last words I heard were, "Believe in yourself, lad, believe in yourself."

Malimar was standing on the bow of his ship and felt my presence coming toward him. He looked into the sky and saw a giant sea eagle coming, and grinned.

Malimar immediately turned himself into a *Tropeognathus Mesembrinus*, a huge prehistoric man-eating bird with a wingspan of twenty-seven feet and a four-foot bill, filled with two rows of sharp, pointed teeth for ripping and tearing its prey. Its feet had long, razor sharp talons that could carry away a large animal with hardly any trouble. I saw him lift off the bow of the ship and swallowed. He was at least a hundred times bigger than me, and far more vicious.

I knew I stood no chance of winning the fight at the size I was, so, I turned myself into a bird that had a chance of defending itself against; a *Pelagornis Sandersi*, and soared into the sky. I now had a wingspan of twenty-four feet and also a long beak with a mouthful of sharp teeth and razor-sharp talons.

We came at each other with talons stretched out, ready to drive them into the chest of the other – which indeed we did, then turned off to come from a different direction. I felt severe pain in my chest and hoped Malimar felt the same.

We fought like this for nearly an hour, each one from time to time gaining the advantage and I knew I needed to do something. I was not only in pain, but I was getting tired and knew Malimar had to be tired, too.

We circled each other and when I thought I had the advantage, I dove at him and at the last minute, lifted my wing and rolled sideways. Then, turning back, I was now just inches above his back. I didn't hesitate. I dug my talons into his back and reached out and bit down on his neck.

His squawking scream of pain filled the air as he tried to twist away, but my talons held him in a firm grip. I had him and I was about to end the fight, but as I bit down, my teeth grabbed nothing but air. Malimar had changed himself into a small hawk and flew away.

Immediately, I changed myself into a falcon and flew after him, but before I could reach him, he landed on the deck of his ship and turned himself back into a man.

I lowered my left wing and veered off to the side, circling around the ship, wondering what he was going to do. I could see that he was breathing hard and had blood streaming from a great many places on his body.

I was thinking of landing on his ship and challenging him to a duel, but before I could, his ship disappeared and I was left flying around over the ocean, alone. I guessed Malimar was wounded enough that it had taken all his strength and he decided to run away; where he could mend his wounds and recuperate. Since I too was bleeding from several places, I turned and flew toward land and home.

When I flew into Boston Harbor, instead of landing on the wharf, I landed on the deck of my ship and turned myself back into me. As luck would have it, the doctor was sitting on a keg, on the deck, enjoying his evening pipe. He took one look at me and without a word, led me down to the infirmary.

Why I didn't just use my powers to take care of my wounds, I don't really know. Maybe I wanted to remember who and what I was up against. In short order, the upper part of my body was covered with stitches where the doctor had sewn up all the wounds from Malimar's talons.

When he'd finished and I stood in front of the full-length mirror in the infirmary, I could only hope Malimar had suffered as much as I had - although I was confident that he had used his powers to heal himself and had not gone through what I had.

CHAPTER THIRTY-FOUR

After making his ship vanish, he used the last of his strength to move the ship several miles away – far from my sight, then went down to his quarters and breathing heavily and bleeding from his head to his waist. He sat down on a chair, exhausted, and tried to regain his composure.

After a few moments, he felt strong enough to heal his wounds, but that was about all the strength he had left. As he sat at the table in his cabin, he realized all the months of trying to find me, along with lack of food and sleep, had drained him of his powers, and he had paid the price for it.

He now knew my power was strong – even stronger than he'd imagined. He would need rest and recuperation before facing me again. Once his wounds were healed and he'd changed clothes, he went to the galley and yelled, "Bring me food! Lots of food!

During the trip back down to Jamaica, Malimar lounged on the deck of his ship, soaking up the sunshine and fresh air, and tried very hard not to let me back into his thoughts. Once he reached Jamaica and his burned-out plantation, he set about rebuilding it using his powers, a little at a time, allowing himself to gain strength.

While the plantation was being rebuilt, with a few improvements, Malimar kept his crew busy cleaning and repairing his ship – with also a few improvements.

With his house rebuilt and his crops growing once more, Malimar sat on the patio and looked out across his vast holdings and sighed. He had to admit, this was what he'd always liked about the place – peace and quiet. The only thing he did miss was the slaves going about their work, and sometimes the songs they would sing.

But it never seemed to last very long. After a few weeks, he would get the urge to raid and pillage, again, and off he would go.

Standing up, he stretched. Today was one of those days. He needed slaves to grow his crops so he could continue to pretend to be a rich farmer. Oh, everyone on the island of Jamaica knew of the evil wizard who terrorized the seas, but only a few of them associated him with Malimar. They only knew of him as Abdul Salazar, the richest farmer on the island. Smiling, Malimar sauntered down to his ship and went aboard.

A week later, Malimar and his men sneaked the ship into a small harbor on the west side of the island of Cuba, and after making it invisible, he created a second ship and made it also invisible before he went ashore.

The place he'd chosen was a large plantation, owned by an Englishman who went by the name Squire Belvidere Seamus Pierce. Whether the man really was a squire or not meant little to Malimar. His only concern were the six hundred slaves the man owned that he wanted for his plantation.

First, he went up to the main house, where the supposed squire lived and entered the house, walking through the kitchen, then into the dining room where, the squire, his wife and several guests sat, eating.

At Malimar's sudden appearance, they all looked up and Malimar smiled, and looked directly at the squire and said, "Good evening, Squire, or whatever your real title is. I am Malimar, the great wizard, and I have come to inform you that I am relieving you of your slaves."

"What? Relieving me of my slaves, you say? That's preposterous! Now, begone before I have my manservant throttle you to within an inch of your life."

At that, Malimar leaned his head back and gave out a hearty laugh.

"Now see here," Squire Pierce said, standing up. "You have invaded my home and now you shall pay the price!"

The squire was a man of medium height, with a good twenty extra pounds around his middle, and his hair was almost white, while his wife was rail thin and twenty years younger than the squire.

"And just what do you plan to do, Squire? Physical abuse?" Malimar asked as he made himself disappear, then reappear on the opposite side of the room.

"God's tarnation!" the squire shouted as he jumped back, knocking over his chair. "How in creation did you do that? While I will admit, was a nifty parlor trick, it will not lessen the punishment I'm about to give you," he said as he stepped to the wall and took down a whip that was hanging there.

Malimar looked at the people sitting around the table with their eyes wide and their mouths hanging open. He was about to do something evil to this pompous would-be squire, then got an idea that he thought would be amusing.

Malimar stared at the squire's wife and watched as she stood up and walked over to her husband and took the whip from him and said, "Here, let me do it."

And then she stepped back a few paces and began lashing the squire…

The squire jumped back and yelled, "Here now! There'll be none of that! Stop it and give my whip back to me!"

But she didn't. Instead, she stepped back even farther and began to flick the whip back and forth like she'd been doing it for years – and each flick cut the skin of her husband, causing him to run for safety, screaming and yelling.

Suddenly, the people at the table burst into laughter as they watched the squire's wife chase after him.

The squire circled the dining room table and when he came abreast of Malimar, he yelled, "For the love of God, stop her before she kills me!"

Having had his fun, Malimar raised his hands in the air and watched as the squire's wife stopped flicking the whip at her husband and stood there, looking at the whip, with a puzzled look on her face.

Malimar decided he'd had enough fun and decided to get down to the business he'd come to do. After ordering the squire and his wife to sit back down at the table, he instructed everyone to reach out and hold hands with the person next to them. And when they'd done his bidding, he smiled and left the room.

To the people's dismay, they couldn't release their grip on the person next to them, nor could they speak in protest – and lastly, they seemed to be glued to their seat. All they could do is sit there and squirm and make mumbling sounds.

Malimar walked outside and raised his hands in the air and watched as the slaves left the main house and the huts they lived in and walked, zombielike down the path to where the ships sat at anchor. When they got close, Malimar materialized the ships and the men of his crew came in boats to take the slaves aboard.

As the two vessels sailed away into the night, Malimar stood on the bridge of his ship and grinned his wicked smile. He wasn't sure why he had just toyed with the squire and the rest of them. It wasn't his normal way of doing things. But, for some reason, he'd felt playful and he had to admit, he'd enjoyed himself. It had been a good day. He'd gotten new slaves to work his plantation, along with new houseslaves, as well, and he'd not actually harmed anyone, which was rare for him.

They would be joined together until sunrise the following morning, then they would be released from his spell. They would not remember anything of the night before, only flashes of memory from time to time that would cause them to pause and wonder why they had been holding hands. Of course, the squire would wonder where his slaves disappeared to?

The story and the unexplained disappearance would be hashed over for years to come. And the pompous windbag squire would have to open his tightly closed purse to shell out money for new slaves. Once they were back at his plantation, the slaves were unloaded, and the second ship made to vanish. The slaves went straight to work as though they'd always been there – with no recollection of ever working for the squire.

Malimar stood on the front porch of his home and looked out across his holdings, listening to the slaves sing their slave songs, and all was right with the world again – except for the brat who still got under his skin, and who was still alive. But he would bide his time, and when the time was right…

CHAPTER THIRTY-FIVE

Except for the scars left by the talons where they tore at my body, I was fine. I had healed the rest of me, and felt it was time to go home and face all their questions. I rowed a longboat to the wharf and climbed up the ladder. It would be a long walk to O'Shea Stables, but the fresh air would do me good.

I hadn't gone far when my uncle's voice came to me in my head. "Brody, this is your Uncle Neptune. Are you all right?" Grinning, I answered him, "If you mean my now having a multitude of scars on my upper torso to be considered all right, then yes, I'm fine. I'm back in Boston and I'm heading home to be bombarded with a million questions, including as to my health."

There was a moment of silence before my uncle spoke again, and when he did, he said, "I sense my brother is back at his plantation in Jamaica, but he is being too quiet for my thinking. You got the best of him and he won't like it. I believe he's gone back there to rebuild and think about how he will destroy you the next time you meet."

"I'm not so sure I defeated him. It was more like a draw. We were both injured, and the only thing in my favor was the fact that I'm younger and have more stamina. I could tell by the time he escaped, his energy and power seemed to be waning," I told my uncle with a great deal of surety.

"Yes, that could be the reason he left, but rest assured he won't be caught off guard the next time you meet. If he has anything to say about it, it will be on his terms," my uncle said with a bit of sadness in his voice.

"Yes, I'm sure that's the way he'd like it to be, but I have a few plans of my own. Yes, he's your brother, and my blood father, but he tried to kill me. He has no more feelings for me than he does a snake trying to bite him. From now on, he is just another evil wizard who needs to be brought to justice," I said with more confidence than I felt.

When we parted, he reminded me to stay alert and always believe in myself, and that what I was doing in the name of right and wrong was the right thing to do.

As I approached O'Shea Stables, the sun was low in the western sky and shining directly into my eyes, so I didn't see Cory Anne when she came galloping her horse down the road to greet me.

The first I knew of it was the sound of hooves pounding the road and a cloud of dust filling the air all around me – then her excited squeal as she leaped from the horse's back and slammed into me – her arms crushing me tightly.

"Oh, Brody, you're home!" she sang out, then stepped back and looked at me from head to toe. "And you're still in one piece," she said with a grin, then hugged me, again.

"Oh, I have a million questions," she said, "beginning with, is he alive or gone to Davey's Locker? Did you have to face him, man to man to get the job done? Did you fight him man to man, like regular men do, or was it a match of powers?"

She stepped back and looked at me. "Well, what have you to say for yourself?"

As I started on down the road toward the gate to O'Shea Stables, I called over my shoulder, "You'll just have to wait until we're all together so I don't have to tell it over and over."

Her reaction was exactly as I expected it to be – she stamped her foot, raising a cloud of dust, then said, "Oh Brody! Sometimes you…. Oh, you just…"

At that point I saw father coming out of the barn and when he saw me, he broke into a grin and began running toward me – and I toward him. We met in the middle of the road and he embraced me so hard I thought the stitches on my cuts would pop out.

Next, he stepped back and looked me in the eyes and said, "Is it finally over, lad?"

I took a deep breath and let it out, slowly, then said, "No, father. Not yet, but it will be, soon. I promise."

Throwing his arm over my shoulder, he pulled me toward the house. "We need to let your mother know you're home."

Of course, the first thing mother did when she saw me was to hug me and I could hear and feel her sobbing tears of joy – then after a long while, she leaned her head back and kissed every inch of my face. Next, she stepped back and looked at me and said, "Let me fix you something to eat. You've lost weight."

I grinned as she led me into the kitchen. I'd only been gone a short while – and not enough time to have lost much weight… had I?

The evening was spent with me telling them a softer version of the story about what had happened than the way it really was. I wouldn't intentionally lie to them, but on the other hand, I didn't want Cory Anne or mother to grieve – which I knew they would if I told all the gory details. Not to say they wouldn't bother father, because they would. Only in a different way.

Finally, it was father who asked, "Will you be going back out to try to find him?"

Now, here was something I for sure couldn't lie about or even soften the answer. "Yes, at some point I will have to. But not right away. I will give it some time."

Cory Anne smacked me on the back of my head and said, "And you won't be leaving me behind this time! So, don't even try!"

And with that, she turned and walked away before I could come up with a rebuttal.

Mother just looked sad.

The following morning, life's routine began again – cleaning out the barn stalls, feeding and exercising the racehorses, then brushing them down to cool them off. Then there was mending the corral fence where a horse had kicked it and broke several of the boards in the fence. On a daily basis, the racetrack had to be smoothed out after exercising the horses. On Mondays, after the Sunday afternoon races, the stadium was full of trash of one sort or another and had to be cleaned up for next week's event.

When I wasn't busy at O'Shea Stables, I worked alongside father at our freight business, which was thriving nicely – and kept my crew busy. With all of this going on, Malimar and our ultimate face-off, completely slipped away.

What little free time Kathleen or I had, we spent it together. I especially remember one Sunday when I wasn't involved with the races. We slipped off and I borrowed a small sailing craft from a man about my age, who had built the boat himself. We'd met one day when he was standing on the wharf, admiring the big ships in the harbor and when I saw him, I approached him and introduced myself. "Good morning. My name is Brody O'Shea, and you are?"

He stood about my height and weight, and looked to be healthy, but his clothes spoke of poverty. He turned and looked at me and grinned. "Yes, I know who you are. You're famous," he said. "You've sailed the oceans far and wide, with you still a lad like me, except a mite richer, I'd guess. And, because you asked me, I'll tell ya. My name is Bryan O'Toole, not long from Dublin."

"Not long, you say? And what is it that brought you to Boston?"

With that, his head dropped and he stared at his shoes, that needed the soles repaired. "I'm indentured," he said.

Well, about now, I felt embarrassed, for being indentured was only slightly higher than being a slave. "To whom, if you don't mind my asking?"

"I guess I don't mind," he said, raising his head and looking at me. "My father had what ya might call, ah love for gambling". He'd bet on anything, and with every farthing he had, thinkin' each time that he would win, big. But it wasn't ah two-way love affair. Gamblin' didn't seem ta care for him, too much, and he got himself deep inta debt to Master Kane."

"And your father indentured you to Mister Kane to pay off his debt?" I asked.

"Aye. That's exactly what happened." Bryan said with a sigh.

We stood there for a moment, neither of us saying anything, then I asked, "Are you a sailing man?"

"Aye, that I am, but I'll admit, I have no time on the big ships. My sailing has all been on small craft, back home – owned by a lad I met down on the wharf in Dublin; Teddy O'Rourke, was his name. His folks owned ah business there in town and doin' well, I'm guessin'. Anyway, he had a twenty-two-foot sloop and taught me ta sail. And, I fell in love with sailin' and the sea. So, when I can get away, I come down here and look at the big ships, hopin' one day when I become a free-man, I can get a job on one of them."

I knew of this Austin Kane and didn't like much about what I knew. It was said he was a harsh taskmaster and had no respect for any of those who worked for him. And that all of those that did were all indentured to him from the old country.

Just then, an idea struck me and I asked, "How long is your indebtment?"

Again, Bryan looked down at his feet… "Seven years."

I was stunned for a moment. His father's debt must have been substantial to have gotten him such a long indenture.

"Have you had breakfast, yet?" I asked him, my mind mulling over a plan.

"What?" he asked. "Breakfast? No, I can't say that I have. He feeds us gruel every mornin' with stale bread, and this mornin', well, I just couldn't abide it."

"Then, come with me," I told him. "Breakfast is on me. And while you eat, I have a proposition to speak to you about."

I could tell by the way he was shoving food into his mouth that it had been a long while since he'd had a decent meal – so I sat there, sipping on my tea and waited until he was finished.

He looked up at me as he shoved his plate back on the table and said, "Thank you. I'm indebted to you. That was the best meal I've had since I was just a young'un and still fed by my dear, sweet, mum."

"No, you're not indebted to me. I brought you here to speak to you about something that is mulling around in my head."

My father and I had opened our business with funds from the bounty I had acquired and there was still plenty left. I sat my cup on the table and came straight to the point. "Do you happen to know the amount your father owed Mister Kane?"

"Aye, I do. It was eighty pounds. Why do you ask?"

After a moment, I said, "I have a good feeling about you, and I want to help. How would you like to come to work for me?"

"For you? Doin' what?" he asked.

I thought for a moment, then said, "Probably working in the warehouse at first – then when an opening comes about, going aboard one of our ships as a member of the crew. What say you?"

His eyes were as big as his plate and his mouth was hanging open. When he finally composed himself, he said, "If only that could be true. But you did understand that I'm indentured to Master Kane for seven long years?"

"But if you weren't indentured, would you be wanting the job I just described?"

"Oh, that I would. Yes, that I would, if only it was possible."

Two days later, I walked into the barn where Bryan was mucking stalls and told him to put down the shovel he was using.

"Your debt has been paid and you now work for me, not as an indentured man, but as a free man, with wages."

He couldn't believe his good fortune and broke down and cried.

And that was how we met and became friends, two years ago, next week.

And along with my surprise that he had been promoted to lead man in the warehouse and would soon be going aboard one of our ships, I found out he'd built his own twenty-eight-foot sloop, which I was borrowing from him to take Kathleen sailing.

She had packed a basket and we sailed out of the harbor and up the coast a few miles to a small cove I knew about. I anchored and we took the small rowboat that was towed behind the sailboat and went ashore to the white, sandy beach, surrounded by high cliffs and forest. It was like we were the only two people on the earth.

I helped her spread the blanket on the sand and she set the food basket off to the side, then joined me where I lay stretched out on the blanket, watching her. She smiled and laid her head on my shoulder, and the next thing we knew, we were opening our eyes to the sound of a bunch of seagulls. There were at least ten of them trying to get to the fried chicken inside the picnic basket.

I jumped up and shouted at them and they flew away, squawking at me for interrupting their chance at our meal. We laughed at falling asleep and then she kissed me, and quickly turned away and opened the basket.

The moon was just starting to rise when we sailed back into Boston Harbor and eased up to the pier on the far side. As I tied off to the pier, Bryan came running toward us, and when he reached me, he said, "You need to come, quick. There is a man at the freight office accusing your father of cheating him and is threatening to kill him!"

We raced up the pier to where it connected to the wharf then I sprinted down the wharf toward our freight office, leaving Kathleen and Bryan in my wake. And as I got closer, I could see a large crowd of people standing in front of the office.

When I got to the back edge, I called out, "Step aside and let me through!"

When the crowd realized I was there, they parted and left a path for me to walk through, and as I walked down the opening they'd made, I could hear whispers…

"It's him, the wizard son."

"Do you think he'll use his magic to save his father?"

"Reckon he really has powers, like they say?"

And so on, as I made my way to where I saw my father standing with his back against the wall of our office. In front of him stood a giant of a man, pointing a pistol at my father's head, and yelling, "You killed my son, and now I'm going to kill you!"

"Hold on there," I yelled as I approached them.

The man turned slightly in my direction and pointed his pistol at me, asking, "Who are you and what's your interest in this?"

I could see my father giving a slight shake of his head and a look on his face that meant for me to say nothing. But I wasn't about to let this man, shoot my father. "Who am I, you ask? Well, I'll ask you the same question – who are you and why are you pointing a pistol at my father's head?"

I could see my father's face drop. He gave a sigh. The cat was out to the bag, now, so to speak, that is. So... this man is your father, is he? Well now, that makes everything perfect."

As I stood there, sizing this man up, it was hard to believe a man could grow to the size he was. He stood a good six foot seven or eight inches, and had to weigh at least three hundred pounds. The pistol in his huge, beefy hand looked small. "He is," I said, "but you still haven't told me who you are."

He stared at me and I could see the anger in his eyes that were shaded somewhat by his long shaggy hair that covered his forehead and part of his eyes. He didn't have a beard, yet, but I could see that he hadn't shaved in more than a week.

After glancing over toward my father, then back to me, he said, "My name is Ezzor Banks. Ring ah bell with you?"

I scratched my cheek with my forefinger, then shook my head, no. "Sorry, but no-sir, it doesn't. Should it?"

All the while I kept him talking, I was trying to figure a way to disarm him, but as big as he was, I couldn't think of any way to do it without using my powers. I could feel the tension coming from the crowd like a heavy fog falling over me.

"Then, what about, Amos Banks? Ever hear that name?" the big man asked.

Shaking my head, again, I said, "Sorry, but no."

I could see a snarl form on the man's face and he shouted, "Well I'll tell ya who he is, or was. He was my son and your father killed him! That's who he was!"

By now, the man was so angry that the fist holding the pistol was shaking and he was spitting as he talked. "And I come here ta kill your father, but you showin' up is even better because now, I'm gonna kill you so's he'll know how I feel."

My father started to say something, but the big man swung his pistol and pointed it at him and said, "You! Shut up! I don't want ta hear no more of your lies!"

At this point, I truly was in the dark about all of this. There was no way under the sun that anyone could convince me that my father had purposely killed anyone, let alone a young boy."

"Maybe you don't want to hear it, but I'd like to hear my father's side of the story."

I looked at my father and asked, "What's this all about, father?"

My father took a deep breath, then said, "It was tragic, but actually, quite simple. Mister Banks booked passage from England to here on one of our ships. Somewhere in the middle of the Atlantic Ocean, they ran into what I was told was a terrible storm – heavy wind, rain, and giant waves crashing over the rail. All the passengers, nine of them I believe, were told to go below and out of harm's way. According to the captain, they all went below, except young Amos, who defied the captain and stayed topside, arguing that as a paying customer, he had a right to be wherever he wanted to be, and he wanted to stay on the deck to see the storm."

My father shook his head and said, "The captain ordered two of the crew to take the boy down below for his safety, but he fought them and during the struggle, all three were washed over the side by a huge wave. All three were drowned. And because of this man's son and his arrogance, we lost two good men."

I could hear the oohs, and aahs from the crowd, as I turned and looked at Mister Banks.

"Don't make no difference what he said. My son was killed while aboard his ship and, in my books, that makes him responsible, and I'm gonna have my due," Ezzor Banks said, pointing the pistol at me.

I saw the look of panic in my father's eyes and before I had a chance to stop him, he launched himself at Ezzor, shoving the man's arm upward, just as he squeezed the trigger. There was a loud explosion as Ezzor swung his arm, sending my father, back against the wall of our office. At the same time, I lowered my head and drove my shoulder into Ezzor's stomach and heard a loud gush of air.

He staggered backward, but didn't fall down. Instead, he grabbed me by the hair on my head and lifted me off the ground with one hand and with the other, he drove his fist into my jaw. For just a moment, I saw bright lights flickering on and off and knew I was about to lose consciousness. Willing my brain to keep me awake, I grabbed the hand he hit me with and hung onto it, while I used his leverage to lift my legs and kicked him in the stomach. This time, he went down – and me with him.

But quick as a cat, I landed on my feet and jerked myself clear, leaving some of my hair in his clutched fist. As my father came off the wall, someone from the crowd handed him a long chunk of oak – and my father wasted no time slamming it against Ezzor Bank's head. About then the police showed up, but my father refused to press charges. Instead, he asked them to lock him up until morning, allowing him time to cool off.

"Kathleen came over to me and asked, "How can you be so calm? I was scared half to death."

"He is just a grieving father," I told her. "He'll be alright when he calms down and can think straight… Enough of this," I said, "Let's talk about more pleasant things while I take you to supper."

Before we left, I spoke to my father, asking if he was all right, to which he replied, "Why shouldn't I be? I had my son here to help stop a man from doing something out of grief."

Kathleen and I were enjoying our evening meal at a seafood restaurant that sat along the wharf. She was telling me about a patient she'd recently had who thought she looked just like his daughter and kept calling her, Cora May - when Cory Anne came storming in and stopped next to our table. Her face was flushed and her eyes were blazing daggers.

"Why didn't you call out to me and tell me you and father were in danger? Didn't you think I would want to be there to help? What were you thinking? Brody! Answer me!"

I smiled and winked at Kathleen, then stood up and put my hand over my heart and said, "From this day forward, if anyone is trying to shoot me for being my father's son, I promise to contact you, and inform whoever it is that he'd better turn and run away, for my sister is on her way, and she will talk him to death."

Cory Anne reached out and punched me in the chest. "Sometimes, Brody O'Shea!" she said as she turned and stormed out of the restaurant. I sat down, grinning, but when I looked across the table at Kathleen, she was standing up and glaring at me.

"What?" I asked. "I was just having a little fun with her," I said, raising my hands in the air.

"Well, I think it was very rude of you. She was very worried about you. Goodnight, Mister O'Shea. And please, don't contact me again until you've learned some manners." And with that, she too stormed out of the restaurant.

As I sat there, watching her leave, the older woman who had been attending us, came up to the table and asked, "Will that be all sir, or would you like some crow to eat for your dessert?"

"I was only having some fun with her," I said to myself as I laid money on the table and left.

CHAPTER THIRTY-SIX

By the time I got home, father was sitting on the front porch, waiting for me. When I got near, he stood up and walked out to meet me. "We need to have a little talk," he said and turned and headed for the barn.

Once we were on the inside of the barn, he stopped and looked me in the eye and said, "Ever since you and Cory Anne were small children, you've been wisecracking about how she says things, and you've been able to get away with it."

I started to protest. "but…"

That's as far as I got before father raised his hand and said, "I'm not finished."

"Yes-sir," I replied and waited for what I knew was coming.

"Maybe it's our fault. Maybe we should have put a stop to it a long time ago, but she seemed to enjoy the bickering as much as you did, so… we looked at it like a brother and sister teasing each other. And, well, I guess it was alright back then, but today it's a completely different matter."

My father took a moment to form what he would say next, then he asked, "Do you realize that your sister came home yesterday and broke down and cried? She thinks you don't give a whit about her and I know that's not true, son – but you have to realize, the time has come to stop teasing her. When women get a certain age, well... they... they look at things different and their feelings get hurt much easier, and we have to understand that and do our best to not do or say anything to hurt their feelings."

We stood there, staring at each other for some time before he asked, "Do you get my meaning, lad?"

I nodded my head and said, "Yes father, I think I understand, now. Cory Anne isn't the only one mad at me. Kathleen said I was being rude and told me not to call on her until I learn some manners. But I guess I didn't understand. I thought she was still all right with my teasing her."

"Oh, I'm sure the bantering will continue, but you need to be mindful of when you do it, and how harsh your words are. You need to remember, son, she's your twin sister and she loves you very much... and right along with your mother, she worries about you when you're out galivanting about on the ocean, chasing down rogues and rascals, and putting your life in danger. And as far as that goes, so do I."

I nodded my head and said, "I'm sorry and I will apologize to her. I'll set things straight."

"Good lad," he said, patting me on the shoulder.

Her bedroom door was slightly ajar and I found Cory Anne in her room, staring out of her window.

I tapped lightly and stepped inside, saying, "I'll understand if you never speak to me again, but I just want you to know, I'm sorry. I didn't set out to hurt you, I just didn't understand about you worrying about me and I guess I've been so used to teasing you I fell into the old habit, not realizing I might have hurt your feelings. I really am sorry and I hope you can find it in your heart to forgive me."

I guess she was very upset and I wasn't sure what she would say or do. Maybe she would tell me to leave and never wanted to speak to me again. Instead of saying anything, Cory Anne turned around, then ran across the room and threw her arms around my neck and hugged me. I could feel the wetness of her tears on my cheek.

"I forgive you, and it's all right if you tease me once in a while, just not in front of people and not after I've been worried sick about you."

"All right," I said, "I promise. And if you must know, Kathleen isn't speaking to me for how I acted."

Cory Anne stepped back and looked at me, then slapped me on the chest and said, "Oh get out of here and go make up with Kathleen. You can tell her I have forgiven you."

I found Kathleen in her small office at the medical center, going over some papers, and when I stepped inside her office, she looked up and stared at me without saying anything.

I pulled off my cap and held it in both hands, staring at my feet, trying to find the right words to say. Finally, I took a deep breath and said, "I'm sorry for being insensitive to you and Cory Anne. It won't happen again. Cory Anne has forgiven me and now, I'm here to ask your forgiveness."

Kathleen stood up and walked around to the front of her desk and looked at me for what I thought was hours, but in truth, it was less than a minute.

"Do you truly understand what you did?" She asked.

"I do. My father and I had a long talk. More correctly, he talked and I listened, but what he said made sense and I've seen the error of my ways... I truly have. I guess I didn't understand that you girls think differently about things. Oh, I know we think different, but not about the being so sensitive. We've been bantering at each other our whole lives, and, and..."

Kathleen stepped away from the desk and put her fingers against my mouth, and said, "Hush. I accept your apology." And then she kissed me full on the lips and I felt my knees go weak.

She stepped back and said, "Now get out of here. I have work to do."

And with that, she walked back around her desk and sat down.

"You may take me out to eat tomorrow evening. I get off at seven," she told me as I turned to leave.

"Seven it is then," I said, grinning from ear to ear. I wasn't sure I would ever completely understand women, but trying was much better than the alternative.

CHAPTER THIRTY-SEVEN

The following morning, I was mucking out one of the horse stalls when I heard the voice of my uncle, filling my head. "Brody, lad, can we talk?"

I looked around and saw that I was the only one in the barn and said, "Yes. I'm alone – working in the barn. Is something wrong?"

"That's the thing, I don't know," Uncle Neptune said. "Malimar is being too quiet. He's rebuilt the plantation and has slaves working the crops. His ship sits tied up to the pier while his crew idles away the hours, doing small things on the ship, but otherwise they seem to be free of staying battle ready. As far as my brother himself, he rides around on his horse, like… like some gentleman farmer! As we both know, that isn't like him. I don't like it when I can't figure him out. He's up to something, I just know it, but what? Have you had any contact with him since you got back?"

"No," I said. "In fact, I've been so busy, I've almost forgotten about him, completely. Do you think, maybe, he's changed? I know that sounds preposterous, but do you think it could be true?" I asked, grabbing at the straw of hopefulness.

"One can only hope," Uncle Neptune said. "But, no… I don't think it's that, but I can't seem to put my finger on what exactly he's up to. I have been able to almost predict his next move for years and years, then he goes and does something like this, that is so out of character that I'm baffled."

I scooped up another shovel of horse dung and dumped it on the cart with the rest of the dung from other stalls, and said, "We can only hope that something has happened to make him change his ways, but while we do, I believe we need to keep a watch on him and see what he does next. As you said, this could just be a ploy to throw us off track, hoping he can make a surprise attack when we least expect it."

"Yes, you could be right," Uncle Neptune said. "Yes, that's what I'll do. I'll keep a close watch on him and when he tries something, I'll let you know, right away."

Uncle Neptune and I had just finished talking when my father came into the barn with a big grin on his face. Communication between me and my uncle was terminated and I turned to my father and asked, "What are you up to, father? You don't grin like that unless you're up to something."

He walked up and laid his hand on my shoulder and asked, "How's Hurricane? He feeling well? In shape to make a little run, is he?"

"He's fine. I just rode him yesterday and as always; he was eager to run. Why do you ask?"

"I was at my desk at the freight office, going over some papers when the door opened and in walked this short, balding man who by his appearance, looked to be quite prosperous, meaning that the man was wearing an expensive suit, and the walking stick he carried looked to be made of some exotic wood."

"So, did he want to do business with us?" I asked.

My father grinned even wider and said, "In a way, lad. In a way."

I was confused. Why would he come into the freight office if not to do business, being a stranger and all? "And, what does, in a way, mean? Either he wants to do business with us or he doesn't."

"That's what I'm getting at, lad. Yes, he wants to do business with us, but it has nothing to do with hauling freight. It has everything to do with horseracing."

"I… I still don't quite understand. Are you saying he wants to race his horse on one of our horseracing days? If so, all he has to do is register the horse and put up his fee."

My father shook his finger at me and said, "Not at all, lad. No, he wasn't interested in racing on Sunday at the track. No, lad, it was something far more exciting. He's seen you race Hurricane in more than one cross country steeple race and he's here with a horse of his own and wants a challenge race against

Hurricane… And here's the interesting part, he wants to bet a thousand pounds and winner take all – meaning, if he wins, he gets Hurricane, and if he loses, you'll get his horse, plus the thousand pounds. What say ya, lad?"

I just stood there. My head was spinning. It wasn't that we needed the money, for sure, but a thousand pounds was a lot of money. After a moment, I asked, "Have you seen his horse?"

"Not yet," father told me, "But, he wants us to meet at the stable in town and have a look, then discuss his challenge.

I was always up for a race, but this one was interesting in a way I wasn't sure I wanted to deal with. "I'll need to wash up and change clothes," I told my father.

When our buggy came to a stop at the stable, the man was standing just in front of the door, puffing on a large cigar, looking a might too smug for my liking. When we stepped down, he walked up to us with his hand outstretched, Cranston Wallingsworth at your service, young Brody O'Shea. Has your father explained my proposal?"

"He has," I said, shaking his hand, which was like grabbing onto a piece of raw liver. The man had no grip at all, and I wasn't sure I liked his shifty eyes. Something didn't seem quite right, but I would see things through. "And I've come to see this horse of yours that you seem to be so proud of."

As he led us into the stable, I said, "You do know that Hurricane has never been beaten. And I doubt he ever will be."

Mister Wallingsworth just kept walking like he hadn't heard a word I'd said, blowing out a cloud of cigar smoke. Halfway down the run, he stopped at a stall and pointed. "Cyclone," he said.

Cyclone? Interesting, I thought. I could see the newspaper headlines, Cyclone against Hurricane, who will be the strongest?"

I turned and looked into the stall, and at first, I wasn't impressed at all. His mane was unkept and his head was hanging down like he was tired. But then, I studied him more closely and saw the muscled legs and chest. There was more to this horse than met the eyes. He was buckskin in color and stood maybe fifteen hands. I approached him and lifted his head by the chin, and looked deep into his eyes.

There was spirit in those eyes and like Hurricane, he didn't flaunt his abilities.

Turning back to Mister Wallingsworth, I asked, "Where are you from and what races has he won to merit running against my horse?"

"He's never won a race," Mister Wallingsworth stated mater-of-factly. In fact, he's never been in a race, before. As to where I'm from, it matters not at all. But I will tell you, we come from far south of here. I have a plantation on the island of Cuba, and I have spent a good deal of money to come here to race against you, young man. So, you've seen my horse, and of course, I've seen you race, and now I ask you, are we to race, or not?"

I had a knot in the middle of my stomach, telling me he hadn't told the entire story, but if I said, no, what would my reason be? I really didn't have one. "When do you propose we race, and where?" I asked.

He smiled and said, "The very track you always race on is fine with me, and how about, next Saturday? That should give you enough time to raise a crowd. I want the world to see my horse beat the mighty Hurricane."

I looked at my father who had stood by all this time without saying a word. He looked at me and said, "Your call, lad."

Still not able to put my finger on why my stomach was doing flip-flops, I stuck out my hand and heard myself saying, "Saturday it is. Two o'clock start time, if that's all right with you?"

He took my hand in another limp handshake and said, "We shall see you on Saturday, then."

On the way home, I told my father of my feelings and asked if he had an opinion.

"Well, he is sort of an oddball, making a bet like he has, to race against a horse who has never lost a race with a horse that has never even been in a race before. You're right, it does seem strange. But the horse is real and the money he's already put up is real."

"That is all well and good, but what does he know that we don't know?" I asked.

To that, my father had no answer, and when we got home, he went into the house and I went to the barn to check on Hurricane. Over the next several days, father put out word of the race, and I worked with Hurricane on a daily basis, riding the course at an easy lope. He had the course down so well that I had to do very little urging.

Basically, all I did was hold him down. To him, this was his racetrack and he wanted to run. After supper one evening, I asked my father if Mister Wallingsworth had asked to practice on the course, and he said he hadn't spoken to him since that day we made our deal.

"Don't you find that at least a little bit strange?" I asked.

"Indeed, I do," father said. "But the owner of the stable told me there was a man who came to the stable every day and rode off on him and didn't return until evening-time."

"Was the man the jockey who will be riding him in the race?" I asked.

Father shrugged his shoulders. "The only thing I know is the owner of the stable said a man came each day and rode the horse. He didn't say whether the man was large or small, just that a man came. That's all he said."

Saturday morning came with a beautiful blue sky and plenty of sunshine. The high was in the mid-sixties, which was good running weather for the horses, even if it did make swimming the rivers a mite chilly on the riders.

Hurricane seemed to know what was going on because he was as nervous as a turkey at thanksgiving time. He pranced around the corral with his tail arched in the air as if to say, "I'm ready, why are we waiting?"

As I walked out the back door and started for the corral, Hurricane circled the corral once, then easily leaped over the fence and ran up to me and stopped. I put my arms around his neck and whispered, "It won't be long now." And to that, he raised his head up and down and whinnied.

As we walked back toward the barn where I would give him a rubdown, I said, "I don't know anything about this horse or the rider we'll be facing, so we'll just play it by ear and see how it goes. But in the end, I know you'll come through."

Hurricane raised his head and let out another whinny. I laughed as he led the way into the barn and into the stall as I gathered my brushes. The word must have gotten around because there were more than five hundred people in the bleachers and more at the betting tents.

Not that I couldn't afford to lose it, but because I had absolutely no knowledge of what kind of runner he was, I abstained from placing a bet – although, I was pretty sure father had wagered a good sum on me and Hurricane. In reality, it didn't matter anyway because all our winnings went to providing medicines for the hospital we'd built.

Once again, mother was on the podium to start the race and as I rode up, I could see a small man in his thirties sitting astride Cyclone. Both of them looked like they were just out for an afternoon ride – nothing exciting, just a trot around the pasture.

That alone made me suspicious.

CHAPTER THIRTY-EIGHT

Cranston Wallingsworth was sitting on the podium with the mayor and several other men who ruled Boston. He was sitting in the back row, trimming his fingernails with a small knife, acting as though he had nothing on his mind.

Which, he didn't. He'd been instructed to set up this race and that was exactly what he'd done. His part in this was basically over. He couldn't give a whit whether the horse won or lost. He had been given enough money to pay off the bet in case the horse lost, so it was no skin off his nose, one way or another.

He jumped when the gun sounded and watched as the two horses and their riders headed off toward a fence on the far side of the pasture. And then, went back to trimming his fingernails. He hated it when his fingernails got too long. Cyclone leaped off the starting line at a much faster speed than I'd thought he might, but Hurricane was running just off his right hindquarters without a problem.

When we came to the first fence, which in my opinion was the worst of the fences the horses had to jump, Cyclone sailed over it like it was nothing – as did Hurricane, but he had jumped this fence many times before. To the best of my knowledge, this was Cyclone's first try at this fence and I was surprised. Yes, there was more here than met the eye.

For the first mile and a half, both Cyclone and Hurricane ran the same race, but after coming out of one of the rivers the horses had to swim, Cyclone seemed to be filled with new energy and began to put some distance between us. Of course, Hurricane didn't care for that too much and began to pick up the pace as well. Just as he did, a bolt of lightning struck the ground in front of us and Hurricane went headfirst into the hole created by the lightning. I went off to one side and Hurricane lost his balance and landed on top of me. I felt the wind knocked out of me but I didn't think any bones were broken.

He rolled back over and we climbed out of the ditch. Then, just as I mounted him, I heard laughter coming from the heavens. And it was not a fun-filled laughter. It had an evil tint to it, that caused chills to run down my spine. I knew that laughter and now it all made sense. Malimar was behind all of this. He had staged this horserace, and it was his way of trying to get rid of me by making it look like an accident created by Mother Nature!

As soon as I was on Hurricane's back, again, he took off like he'd been shot out of a cannon, trying desperately to eat up the space between him and Cyclone. I could see the next fence coming up and watched as Cyclone sailed over that one as easy as he had the first one. Hurricane was pushing off with his hind legs to go over the fence, when all of a sudden, the fence rose to ten feet high. I didn't want to use my powers, but I had no choice or we would go headlong into a rock wall. I closed my eyes and wished for the wall to be only two feet high, which he sailed over, easily.

Next, a tree fell and knocked us to the ground, with both of us having the wind knocked out of us and I wound up with a cut on my head and right shoulder. Without using my powers, we would have never gotten out from under all those branches that were pinning us to the ground. I was also afraid the tree might get struck with lightning if I didn't do something, very quick. Fortunately, no one was around to see me lift the tree off us, which allowed us to continue on with the race. I was now angry and wasn't about to lose this race because of a few setbacks.

By now, Cyclone was clearly a good quarter of a mile ahead of us, but I could feel the energy between my legs and I let Hurricane have his head and run, he did. In no time we were within a few feet of Cyclone and gaining fast. At this rate, Hurricane would pass him within the next minute or so. But just then, a strong wind hit us in the face and did its best to push us backward. Along with the wind, there was a cold, hard driving rain that drenched us and made running treacherous.

"Stop this!" I yelled as I sent my power against the heavy wind and rain, diverting it away from us, then I tapped Hurricane in the sides, lightly, with the sides of my feet.

He acknowledged my urging by stretching out his legs in an all-out effort to catch and pass Cyclone. By now, there was a little over four miles of the race behind us with less than a mile to go.

Malimar's answer to my demand was another bolt of lightning that created another hole in front of us. Only this time, I was prepared for it and leaped Hurricane into the air and easily landed on the far side. This was no longer just a horserace, it was a challenge to overcome Malimar's powers and not only stay alive, but to win the race!

Again, I looked at the sky and yelled, "When this is over, I'm coming for you! And this time, you will not get away!"

The voice of Malimar filled the air. "I seriously doubt there will be another meeting, but should you survive this race, I shall await your coming, which will be your last, brat!"

Leaning over Hurricane's neck, I said, "Come on, boy. You can do this."

There was less than a quarter of a mile left. I could see the finish line and Cyclone was still a good distance ahead. I leaned close to Hurricane's neck and patted him. "Now!" I called out. And suddenly, I felt his muscles ripple as he drew energy from deep within and I felt the wind against my face as his speed increased. We had gone only a short distance when the ground ahead of us was filled with at least forty man-eating tigers, which I turned into sheep who went running off to the side.

The sky rumbled with Malimar's anger.

Suddenly we were running neck to neck with Cyclone and I could see the anger in the jockey's eyes and I felt the sting of his riding crop as he slapped it against my shoulder. I urged Hurricane on, but he did the same with Cyclone and when we were side by side, again, he began flaying me again with his riding crop.

By then, I'd had enough and I stared at him and he pulled his arm back and began to slap himself in the face with the riding crop. We crossed the finish-line a full body length ahead of Cyclone, to loud cheers and boos to Cyclone and his rider. At the winner's circle, my father came up to me and said, "I saw lightning several times, along with that jockey slashing at you with his riding crop. What happened out there?"

I briefly told him what had happened and my encounter with Malimar, and had just finished when Mister Wallingsworth walked up, leading Cyclone, and handed me the thousand dollars, and then turned the horse over to me, and walked away as though nothing had happened. He seemed to just disappear into thin air.

Later that same afternoon, while I was grooming Hurricane and congratulating him on a fine performance, my uncle, King Neptune, came to me with his apologies for not giving me warning of what Malimar had been up to.

"I'm truly sorry, Brody, but I was distracted by an incident created by a whaling ship and a pod of angry whales over in the other ocean they call the Pacific. It seems the whalers were trying to harpoon one of the whales and of course, the whales didn't like it, and were attacking the ship by ramming it with their noses."

Uncle Neptune gave a chuckle, and said, "I do have to confess, I waited until the ship had been destroyed to the point the only thing the whalers could do was to slink away and hope they could make it back to wherever they came from, before calling off, the pod of whales. Anyway, while I was busy with the whales, Malimar came up with that race in the hopes of doing away with you."

"Yes, I realized that, a little too late, but I was able to deal with it," I told him.

"Yes, you did, and I'm proud of you. But now that he has come out in the open, again, I'm afraid we can't wait much longer before doing something, ourselves.

And..." Uncle Neptune said, taking a moment to think. "Whatever we do, it needs to be on our terms, not his – thus, keeping him off balance. And, Brody... I'm sorry to have to say this, but I'm afraid, this time, it has to be the end of his reign of terror."

I nodded my head. "I understand. And to be honest, I've known for some time that it was inevitable. Do you have any ideas as to how we should go about it?"

"Not at the moment," he said, "but if we put our heads together, I'm sure we'll come up with something."

Three days later, just after breakfast, my Uncle Neptune came to me, again. I was about to leave to help my father at our freight office.

"Brody, I'm afraid I have bad news, my brother has left his plantation and is sailing north toward you. I don't know for sure what he's up to, but you can bet it isn't good. I'm afraid he's coming to you for a showdown. Knowing him like I do, he won't rest until you are no longer a threat to him."

"Well," I said, "I can't have him coming here to Boston to raid and pillage. I will sail on the next tide and meet him somewhere at sea."

"I guess you have no choice," Uncle Neptune said. "Know that I'll be with you as best I can."

I wheeled around and went back to my room and packed a few essentials, then told my mother I had to leave on another mission. She was surprised and upset, but nodded her head, then hugged me and told me to come back safe and sound – and soon.

I promised to do my best, then saddled Hurricane and rode into town, leaving my horse at the stable.

Walking down the wharf toward our office, I saw Mister Logan and called out to him. "I need the crew ready as soon as possible. I would like to leave on the next tide."

"Malimar?" he asked.

I nodded my head and said, "One last showdown."

Mister Logan gave a sigh and said, "We'll be ready. The next tide is around two this afternoon."

He left to hunt down the crew and I turned back and went to the medical center to inform Kathleen about my leaving.

She begged me not to go. "He's very powerful and he wants only one thing, and that is to destroy you! Please, don't do this, I beg you!"

I held her close and whispered, "I'll be fine. This has been coming for a long time, and I'm prepared."

"But I don't understand why it has to be you?" she cried.

Kathleen still didn't know about my someday becoming King Neptune when my uncle decided to step down, and I didn't think now was the time to bring it up – so, I said, "Try not to worry. Just believe that I will return, safe and sound."

As I put my foot in the stirrup and stepped aboard Hurricane, Kathleen called out to me, "You'd better return or I'll never forgive you, Mister Brody O'Shea!"

I smiled, and blew her a kiss, then touched my feet to Hurricane's sides and he took off at a high lope.

My father stared at me and I could see he was holding back his tears. He placed a hand on my shoulder and said, "Let's hope you can end it this time, lad."

I smiled and said, "That is my hope, too, sir."

Father looked at Mister Logan, who was standing nearby and said, "Take care of him for me, if you will…"

"I'll do my best," Mister Logan said.

Just as he finished speaking, Cory Anne came in from the warehouse and asked, "At what will you be doing your best, Mister Logan?"

I swallowed, trying to figure out what to say. I hadn't wanted to let her know about the showdown between me and our blood father, because she would insist on going and if things went wrong, I didn't want her to die, too.

Before I could say anything, father blurted out the whole story and I watched as fire blazed in Cory Anne's eyes. When he finished, she looked at me and said, "And you were going to sneak off, again, without me. Well, not this time, little brother. You're going to need help and I'm the only one who can give it to you!"

All I could do was stand there and stare at her because she was probably, right. If this was to be my last time to test my powers against Malimar, I was concerned about my ability to do what needed to be done. And when it came right down to it, if I didn't have the tenacity to do it, would Cory Anne have the courage to step up and do it?

This was the challenge I'd been trained for, going against all those lesser wizards, gaining my confidence as an agent for King Neptune – and now as the time grew near, I was as nervous as a young boy about to be paddled by the school principal... And to be honest, I was scared. This was my blood father that I was being asked to fight in mortal combat.

Cory Anne must have been able to read my thoughts because she laid her hand on my shoulder and said, "It will be all right. Trust me."

CHAPTER THIRTY-NINE

As we sailed out of Boston Harbor and into the wide Atlantic Ocean, with Cory Anne standing next to me, I steeled myself against what would soon be, the hardest challenge of my life.

I turned and looked into the faces of my crew and I knew I could not let them down. Not a one of them was a wizard, nor did any of them have any powers, but there they stood, ready to fight against the mightiest, and most evil of all the wizards, Malimar…

Oh, I knew if it came down to it, his men had no powers, either, and it would be the skills of my men against the skills of his men – and felt my men held the upper hand.

What it would actually come down to was, Malimar and me – each of us trying, through the use of our powers, to find out which of us was the most powerful. When this fight was over, only one of us would be left standing.

As my ship turned south and headed for our destination, the sky was clear and blue. The wind, warm against my face and the current helping us along the way – pushing us to face the evilest man on the face of the earth.

Cory Anne lifted my hand and laid my arm over her shoulder, standing close to me - brother and sister facing our greatest challenge, together.

"You can do this," she said. "And if you need me, I'll be there for you."

Earlier, we had had a serious talk about her coming along, and I stood firm, telling her that when it came down to the showdown between me and Malimar, she was to stay in hiding, where she could observe, but not come out unless it was absolutely necessary.

I could see no need for the both of us showing up at the same time, which might put her life in danger, or cause Malimar to run and wait for a more opportune time.

As Uncle Neptune said, it needed to end, now, once and for all.

As I stood on the deck, breathing in the salt air, Malimar was already sailing north with the intention of creating such a disaster in my hometown of Boston, that I would be forced to fight him. There was no doubt in his mind that he would be victorious. He was Malimar, the most powerful wizard in the world! And he was now reinvigorated!

Black clouds filled the sky. Lightning struck the ocean. And the wind created a great cyclone that sent water spiraling into the sky hundreds of feet above his ship. His evil laughter could be heard above the roar of the great storm.

Nine days we had been at sea with a man in the crow's nest both day and night, looking for Malimar's ship, but so far, all they'd seen was a few trading ships. I thought the men were becoming restless until Mister Logan informed me it was just me – pacing the deck, not being able to sleep, and sometimes a bit short tempered.

"We can all see how worked up you are, and believe me, we too are a little nervous, but you need to calm down, lad. All this worrying is not good for you. In fact, I'd say it was doing you more harm than good. If it's a final showdown that is to be, then we'll find him and do what needs to be done. It's as simple as that, doncha see…"

"He's right, you know," Cory Anne said as she came up to us and stood next to me.

"I know," I said. "It's just that…, well… it is Malimar and I don't know if I'm strong enough to defeat him?"

Mister O'Callaghan had just come to join us and he leaned his head back and laughed. Then, after catching his breath, he looked at me and said, "Do you know how many times we've heard you say those same words? More times than I have fingers and toes. And what happens when it comes right down to it? You step up and do what needs to be done, you do…"

"And we're all thankful you don't use those powers for evil, for if you did, there would be no force that could stand against you," Mister Logan piped in.

"I know, I know, I just have to believe in myself," I said.

"That's the spirit, lad," Mister O'Callaghan said with a wide grin.

Even though I'd been told this a hundred times before, I still became very nervous each time before doing battle against this or that wizard. And yes, I'd always been victorious, but this time... this time, it was somehow, different. Later, when I climbed onto the bunk I was sleeping on because Cory Anne was using my cabin, my uncle came to me.

"Brody, lad, I have news."

I sat upright and swung my legs over the side and leaped to my feet, ready to go to battle, but my uncle calmed me down.

"Easy lad, he's not out there, yet. You need to edge your ship a few miles more out to sea. That's where you'll find him before the sun is at its highest point. There is where you will defeat him."

I wished I had my uncle's confidence, but I replied, "I'll do my best, uncle."

"Oh, you'll do much more than that, lad. You will at last, rid the world of an evil force that has dominated the seas, far, far, too long."

Suddenly, his face filled the ceiling of the small, sleeping quarters I was using. "Look at me, Brody," he commanded.

We stared at each other for a long time before he said, "I may only be your uncle, but you are like a son to me, and I would never send you into this battle if I didn't believe with all my being that you will win. You have the power, Brody. And as I've said many times, just believe in yourself. You are the next in line to take my place and nothing can stand in the way. Not even Malimar."

Again, we stared at each other for several minutes before his image began to fade away.

CHAPTER FORTY

After the encounter with my uncle, I went topside and gave the order to change course to the night helmsman, who said, "Aye, Aye, Sir," and eased the bow of the ship to port, calling out to the night bosun, who, after receiving his orders, called to his men and they began adjusting the sails.

I knew I should go below and get some rest, but I was too keyed up. The thing I'd been fearing for such a long time, would be taking place tomorrow.

When the sun tried to break through the dark, cloudy sky, Cory Anne found me standing in the basket of the crow's nest, looking toward the horizon, and called up to me, "What are you doing up there? What do you see? Is it him? Is he nearby? Brody! Answer me!"

I climbed down and instructed one of the men to go up to the nest and keep a watchful eye on the horizon. I wanted to know the moment he saw another ship and not a moment later."

"What's wrong?" Cory Anne asked. "You're as nervous as a rabbit facing a hungry wolf."

"We'll meet him this morning," I told her.

Cory Anne had a confused look on her face. "How do you know that?" She looked all around and then said, "I don't see another ship."

I told her about my discussion with Uncle Neptune and watched as her face grew pale. "It truly is going to happen, then, isn't it?"

"Yes. According to Uncle Neptune, we'll see his ship before noontime. Here's what I want you to do."

She started to say something but I raised my hand. This time, she would do as I told her and there would be no argument. "You will stay in hiding. He doesn't know of your existence and I want it kept that way, if at all possible. If I get to a place where I have no choice and I need your assistance, I will shout out, if possible. If I can't then use your own judgement. But do not sacrifice yourself trying to help me. One of us has to stay alive. Do you understand what I'm saying?"

Cory Anne nodded her head and said, "Yes, I understand. I can't say I like it much, but I do understand, and I will do as you say."

The rest of the morning was spent with me pacing the deck and every few minutes, lifting the long glass to my eye and staring out over the water – or calling up to the man in the crow's nest to ask if he could see anything.

As I stood on the bow of my ship, staring at the horizon, my uncle's voice came to me, again. "He is but two hours away and coming on fast. Try, if you can, to relax and compose yourself. You can do this. Remember, he's angry and wants to end this, so he will be acting wild and not thinking straight. But you, on the other hand, will be calm and rational. And that is what will see you through. So, now, be a good lad and get this final challenge, over with."

And with that, he was gone. Two hours seemed both a long time and a very short time.

I called a meeting with my crew and explained to them what I knew, and told them, "No matter what happens, I do not want you to engage in battle with his crew unless they try to come aboard. Remember, they're not on that ship of their own free will. They are captive slaves who don't really want to fight you – and will only do so if commanded by Malimar because they are afraid not to. But if they do…"

I didn't have to say more because they knew what I meant. I could tell by the, "Ayes," and, "You can count on us," phrases that came from them.

I looked down at them and said, "Good. Now, Mister Logan and Mister O'Callaghan, prepare the men for a battle I hope they never have to fight."

About then, the man in the crow's nest called out, "Captain! Have a look, sir!"

Along with my sister and every man on the ship we turned and looked to where the man was pointing, and suddenly, the men grew very quiet, for they knew what was coming. And there it was, close to two hours away, a black cloud with lighting flashing through it, was coming our way. And in the far distance, among the black clouds, we could hear the heavy rumble of thunder.

I looked at Cory Anne and said, "It will soon be time for you to disappear. I fear, if he gets too close and you're still here, he'll feel your presence and any surprise we might have had, will be gone.

Cory Anne looked at me and smiled. "You can do this. I have faith in you. Now, relax and prepare yourself, mentally – for as our uncle said, that is where you will win the game."

All this encouragement was great, but when it came right down to it, I was the one who had to put all my fears away and do what must be done. I walked to the bow of the ship and looked at the oncoming black cloud and said to myself, "Brody, lad, it's time to allow all your power to come to you. The world is depending on you."

CHAPTER FORTY-ONE

The tension felt like a heavy blanket falling down on me. The cannoneers stood next to the big guns and the rest of the crew stood holding swords, pistols and rifles, ready for whatever may happen.

By the time the two ships were close enough to fire on each other, the wind was rocking our ship up and down – stinging rain pelted down on us like hail and lighting struck the water all around us, creating great geysers going high into the air.

I looked around to see where Cory Anne was, but she was nowhere in sight. Little did I know, she had changed herself into a crate, sitting on the deck, where she could come to my aid, should I need her. I made my way to the bridge and told Mister Collins to maneuver the ship around so that our starboard side guns could be put to use if necessary.

I had barely made it back to the bow when a bright light appeared in the sky, and within the light was Malimar. He was at least ten feet tall and looking vicious with his blazing red eyes and evil snarl on his mouth.

"Well, Brat, are you ready to finally meet your Lord and Master in mortal combat?" he yelled.

"As ready as I'll ever be," I said to myself, as I willed myself into the air, facing him and just as tall as he was.

He leaned his head back and laughed, causing a rumbling in my stomach, as my uncle's voice filled my head. "Stay calm, Brody. You can do this."

I too, leaned my head back and laughed, which caused him to stop his laughter and stare at me. When I stopped my laughing, I looked at him and said, "Oh you pompous windbag. You think you can scare me with this bit of bravado?"

And then, without warning, I sent a ball of energy into his chest that knocked him backward. Recoiling, he came back toward me with two bolts of lightning flashing from his hands. I rolled sideways as the lightning bolts passed by me, but the electricity radiating from it caused me to shudder.

Gathering my strength again, we came at each other, both of us throwing power balls that met in the middle and exploded, causing both of us to be knocked backward. As soon as each of us recovered, we came at each other, again, and again, until nearly an hour had passed. We were both covered with burn marks, cuts and bruises. Our clothes were in tatters. The men on both ships could only stand and watch.

I could see his strength was beginning to drain and I was about to send a powerful bolt of power at him, when he turned himself into an even bigger warrior with armor and a giant shield in his left hand, and a great broadsword in his right. He leaped toward me and swung the giant blade down at me that would have cut me in half if I hadn't been lucky enough to move quickly. The blade swished past me so close that it tore the buttons off my shirt.

With another sweep from the side the blade came toward my head and I ducked, but felt hair being ripped from my head. After barely being cut in two, five different times, I was able to move far enough away to turn myself into a warrior that carried a shield and a three balled mace.

We stood there in the sky, two giant warriors, lightning striking the ocean all around us, and each trying to bring our weapons to bear on the other. Parry and strike. Parry and strike. Neither of us giving an inch. But after nearly another hour, I could feel his blows beginning to soften.

Next, he turned himself into a giant, fire breathing dragon, and I barely had time to do the same before we spat fire at each other and clouted each other with our wings. This time it was me who felt my powers beginning to dwindle, and I was knocked about by his wings, and got a scorching burn on my chest, and my left wing would not function like it was supposed to.

I felt myself falling and saw him diving toward me, ready for the kill. In my mind, I called out, "Cory Anne!"

And, with a flash of light, she was there by my side, only it was not Cory Anne, it was a huge female dragon slayer. She had a spear in one hand and a slingshot in the other., and before Malimar could dodge her thrust, she threw the spear at him! It struck him in the side – and he screamed in pain.

By then, I had regained my strength and turned myself back into me and began sending bolts of lightning at him, while Cory Anne whirled her slingshot over her head and then let loose a burred stone that struck him on the shoulder and exploded.

Before falling into the ocean, Malimar turned back into himself and we could see that his left shoulder was injured and bleeding. He looked at Cory Anne and asked, "Who are you and where did you come from? This fight is of no concern to you!"

Cory Anne changed into herself and grinned at him and said, "Oh, but it is, father… I am Brody's twin sister and your daughter. So, it very much concerns me."

"No! This can't be!" Malimar cried out. Just then, out of the water came a huge blue whale with Uncle Neptune standing on his back. He looked at Malimar and grinned, then said, "Oh, but it is true, dear brother. Your tomfoolery created twins. And either of them is more powerful than you. So… here are your choices, surrender and pay for your inequities by whatever means the courts come up with, or, yield your powers to me, here and now, and live as a regular human.

Malimar looked at his brother and said, "Surrender, indeed. You know what they will do to me. As for relinquishing my powers and living as a human, that can never happen. I have lived as a wizard far too long. They would attack me like a swarm of hornets. I wouldn't last a day."

"I suppose you're right," Uncle Neptune said. "So… what do you propose we do with you?"

"Turn me loose. I promise to go and never be seen or heard of again. You have my word as your brother," Malimar said with an evil sneer.

I could see in Uncle Neptune's eyes that he was tempted, but the set of his jaw told me he couldn't trust his brother any further than I could throw a whale. I could see he was wrestling with his conscience, when out of the blue, Malimar sent bolts of lightning in the direction of both his brother with one hand, and Cory Anne and me, with the other.

Cory Anne and I dodged the lightning bolt and leaped back on my ship, preparing to send lightning bolts back at Malimar, when the most astounding thing happened.

A giant whirlpool of water rose up, engulfing Malimar in its swirling funnel and pulled him inside, then swallowed him in less than the blink of an eye before he could react and free himself.

All the while, King Neptune stood on the whale's back, watching his brother disappear, and when Malimar was gone, our uncle said, "I've been hoping to find a way to do this for many years, but the opportunity had never arisen until now."

I looked at Cory Anne, then back to Uncle Neptune and when I had my senses back, I asked, "Is he…?"

Uncle Neptune smiled and said, "Dead? No lad. I could never kill my own brother. No, he will be locked in Davey Jones' Locker, where he will spend the rest of his days and never be able to bother anyone, ever again. One of Malimar's crew stepped up onto the bridge and shouted at us, "Does this mean we're free men, then?"

Uncle Neptune called out to me, "This decision is up to you, lad. Do what you will. We will speak again, soon," and with a loud splash, my uncle and the whale disappeared beneath the ocean. I looked over at the man standing on Malimar's ship and asked, "What will you be doing if you were to be freed?"

He looked at the men on his ship, then back at me. "With your permission, we'll set sail for Jamaica and go back to the plantation and run it like it should be, with equal shares for all, including the slaves, who we'll set free."

"And no more pirating?" I asked.

"Never again, Sir. None of us ever wanted to be pirates in the first place. We were all shanghaied and put under his power. And now that he's gone, we can go back to being honest men just trying to make a living, if you know what I mean."

I looked at Mister Logan and Mister O'Callaghan, who both nodded their heads.

I turned and looked toward the man standing on the bridge and called out, "Go then and with God's blessing. And don't make me come looking for you!"

We watched them leave and when they were a good distance away, Cory Anne looked at me and asked, "What now?"

I put my arm around her shoulder and hugged her close and said, "And now, we go home, little sister, we go home."

Cory Anne smiled up at me and nodded her head in agreement.

As the ship turned back to the north, I felt myself relax. Unless my uncle called upon me, again, I hoped to live a long, normal life with Kathleen by my side.

Somewhere, deep beneath the surface of the ocean, a chuckle rippled through the water.

THE END

MEET THE AUTHOR

Jared McVay lives in Oregon where he writes his books, does storytelling, book signings, speaking engagements, and gets in a little fishing from time to time. Before becoming a novelist, Jared was a professional actor – stage, film and television, and a ghostwriter for screenplays.

As a young man he worked as a cowboy, a rodeo clown, a lumberjack, barker for a carnival and a truck driver. During the 1950's he rode the rails as a hobo and during the 80's, a blue water sailor. He spent his military time in the US Navy Sea Bees, where he learned his electrical trade as a power lineman, then spent ten years as a lineman for Kansas Gas & Electric. But it was his love of entertaining people that led him into acting and writing.

Jared has five children, eleven grandchildren, fifteen great grandchildren and four great, great grandchildren.

When not writing or talking about writing, or answering e-mails from his fans, you can find him enjoying life with his girlfriend, Jerri.

ALSO BY JARED McVAY

Other works by Jared McVay

Jared McVay is an award-winning author who writes, Westerns: A western series: Historical Fiction: Action/Adventure: YA: Children's books: screenplays: teleplays: Short stories, and also does storytelling.

NOVELS:

Clay Brentwood western series:

Book 1 – Stranger on A Black Stallion

Book 2 – Unjust Punishment

Book 3 – Hammershield

Book 4 – Cinch Mountain

Book 5 – The Storm

Book 6 – The Chameleon

Book 7 – Ol' Son

Book 8 – Loralie

Book 9 – Comanche Justice

Book 10 –Double Revenge

Kathleen McClusky mystery Series:

Book 1 – Retribution

Book 2 – Murphy's Law

Historical Fiction: The Legend of Joe, Willy & Red – award winner

Historical Fiction: Silent Runner, Guardian Warrior

Western: Hacker's Raid – award winner

Action/Contemporary - Not on My Mountain – double award winner

JUVENILE FICTION

Brody O' Shea: Book 1: The Wizard of Morador Island

Brody O' Shea: Book 2: Abigor: Wizard of Evil

Brody O' Shea: Book 3: Malimar: The Final Challenge

CHILDREN'S BOOKS

Bears, Bicycles & Broomsticks – 11 short stories

Randal Gets A Hit

Santa's Magic Ring

SCREENPLAYS

The Hobos, Jared & the Warden, Talltree,

TELEVISION PILOT SCRIPTS

McClusky [6 episodes] - Drama/Comedy, ACT Acute Care Transport - Drama/Comedy, Melinda: Award winning short story

THANK YOU
FOR READING!

If you enjoyed this book, we would appreciate your customer
review on your book seller's website or on Goodreads.

Also, we would like for you to know that you can
find more great books like this one at
www.CreativeTexts.com

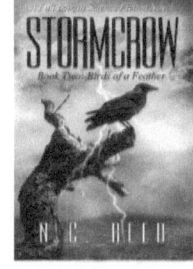